Out of the Darkness

Katy Hogan

Out of the Darkness

A tale of love, loss and life after death

ILLUMINE

First published in Great Britain in 2015 by Illumine Publishing

'Trust Your Heart' music and words by Dave Davies © 1978 Dabe Music, Carlin Music Corporation.

OUT OF THE DARKNESS

ISBN 978-0-9933139-0-5

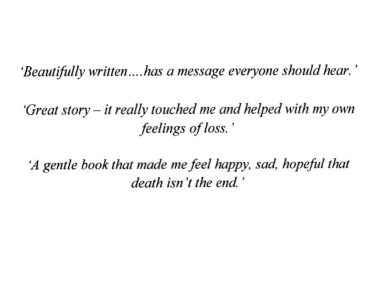

'*Beautifully written....has a message everyone should hear.*'

'*Great story – it really touched me and helped with my own feelings of loss.*'

'*A gentle book that made me feel happy, sad, hopeful that death isn't the end.*'

www.outofthedarknessnovel.com

Dedicated to

Margaret Giles

and

Rosina Vincent

'Love will always light the way,
Until we meet again some day.'

One

A church bell echoed across the deserted graveyard, its monotone voice slicing through the hovering mist. It was a cold, still morning, the very last day of the year, as the reluctant light of winter crept slowly across the vast cemetery. As reluctant as Jessica herself.

Her legs carried her in dogged rhythm along the path, past countless rows of headstones. They looked so orderly, so upright, like lines of unquestioning soldiers standing to attention, blindly awaiting instructions that may send them to oblivion. How Jessica now yearned for oblivion, to be cocooned within the familiar cloak of denial. The one she had worn continuously since that fateful day back in February.

But today the brutal truth was impossible to deny. Clutching tightly to a small spray of white roses, Jessica walked between the weathered graves for the first time in all those desolate months, searching for an escape from the stark reality that was on the brink of engulfing her. And there it was: Anger, her ever-loyal friend; the friend she could call on whenever pain confronted her head-on. Her only friend. She swore out loud, hurling curses against the blameless wind for pricking at her eyes and making them smart and water. For she had vowed to herself that she would never cry, never feel, never succumb.

She couldn't remember much about the funeral; it had been a day of disbelief and diazepam. But the tree. She remembered the ancient oak tree, the landmark that stood as dark and bare and barren as her soul. Today it confirmed that she had reached her destination, her mother's final resting place. And there, from a slab of cold, grey granite, the words 'Linda Victoria Gibson', shone out in gold italics. So terse and so final, momentarily taking Jessica's breath away. The reality was there now, right in front of her, literally written in stone. Her mother's name and below it, the date of her birth; the date of her death. No sentimental verse, no words of enduring love. Jessica's face darkened with regret, for she knew she should have allowed her mother the tender epitaph that she so deserved. But what difference did it make? Her mother wasn't there to read it. Her mother wasn't anywhere, was she? She was gone forever.

Staring down at the neglected, leaf-strewn grave, adorned only with a white splash of pigeon excrement, Jessica wondered how many people must have looked at it and shaken their heads in pity. With a flush of guilt, she hastily spat onto a tissue and attempted to wipe the headstone clean, before placing the roses into the flower holder, empty, save for a solitary worm wriggling in the brown rain water that had collected there.

Standing back, she took in the ghastly picture. How could this, from now on, be her only point of contact with her mother?

The sharp coastal breeze pricked at her cheeks and Jessica pushed her hands deep into her coat pockets with a sigh. 'Happy birthday, Mum,' she said quietly, brushing away a single stubborn tear. Then, turning abruptly, she retreated back into her protective cocoon.

The heavy hospital doors swung open violently and Jessica attracted more than a few wary glances as she marched along the corridor later that morning on her way to the Geriatric wing, where she had been a nurse for the past five years. She had worked her way through various departments at the

Brighton hospital since qualifying eight years ago, but after a stint in what the nurses wryly called "the departure lounge", Jessica believed she had finally found her niche. She'd discovered she had a natural affinity with older people and although the job's rewards were bittersweet, her patients' often erratic, sometimes cantankerous, but mostly endearing behaviour, appealed to her. It was refreshing to be with people who were genuine and who didn't care what other people thought. Just like her.

She pressed the button and waited for the lift to arrive to take her to the Geriatric department on Level 3. A cheerful voice called out, 'All right, sweetheart?' But as usual, Jessica didn't respond to Dave, the hospital porter, as he wheeled a trolley by, and instead she entered the lift without giving him so much as a glance. She was relieved to find it was empty, and was thus spared the agony of small-talk. However, there was one thing Jessica couldn't avoid: her own reflection there in the shiny, metallic doors as they slowly closed before her. Shoulder-length auburn hair matted and windswept; wide copper-coloured eyes, lifeless and empty; winter coat fitting just a little too tightly. The person Jessica saw staring back at her was the only person she had in the whole world.

The nurses milling around the central desk looked up as Jessica arrived.

'Morning!' chirruped Bernie, the cuddly senior staff nurse.

Jessica managed to raise an eyebrow in acknowledgement, but a scowl soon flashed across her face when she saw Dr. Ladbroke standing there. He glanced up at the clock on the wall and sucked in air between his teeth.

'Right then, now that Jessica has deigned to grace us with her presence, we can continue,' he frowned.

Dr. Ladbroke was a vertically-challenged 58-year-old Registrar who hadn't quite made it up the ladder to Consultant, and clearly felt the need to exert his position of authority in any way that he could. Peering over the rim of his glasses, he glared at the late arrival, waiting for some kind of response. But Jessica simply stared ahead. She'd never liked Ladbroke, but had always managed to tolerate his petty small-minded ways. Until fate dealt her a body-blow, and she'd lost patience with him, and everyone else in the universe.

'So…who's taking Mrs. Jacobs down for her MRI scan?' Ladbroke's question was met with silence. 'Well, whose patient is she?' the doctor asked, flicking through his notes impatiently.

Bernie alerted Jessica with a sharp nudge in the ribs.

'Mine,' Jessica muttered.

Dr. Ladbroke shook his head disdainfully. 'Surprise, surprise…for goodness' sake girl, wake up!' he shouted, his words puncturing the thick haze that enveloped her. 'Another hangover, I suppose, is it? Well, enough is enough young lady…'

He was clearly beginning to enjoy this opportunity to belittle the nurse who he'd never quite been able to dominate.

'…You haven't had your mind on the job for months. You're always late, you're rude, you're unapproachable, and you think with a few wisecracks you can…'

Jessica felt more like a spectator than the object of Ladbroke's diatribe, as his malicious words simply washed over her. She didn't care what he said. She didn't care what he thought. She didn't care about anything. She just wanted to run away from all of them, from life. 'I don't need this shit,' she muttered, and spun on her heels to leave.

Bernie grabbed her by the arm. 'Jess, calm down darlin', calm down. It's okay, we know how tough it's been for you without your mother, especially over Christmas. We know you're still grieving. Well, most of us do,' she added, throwing the doctor an icy glare.

'Ah, yes, yes, of course,' Ladbroke stuttered. 'Look, Jessica, don't you think you should make an appointment to see your GP or something? This really is becoming a bit of a problem now, isn't it?'

Ladbroke had never been much of a people person, unfortunate for a man in the medical profession, and his attempt at empathy was as clumsy as it was patronising. 'I believe we have some very good leaflets on bereavement somewhere. Find one for her, will you, Bernie?' And with that, he scuttled away, burying his head in his notes, as the group of nurses quietly dispersed.

Bernie's face softened and she wrapped a sympathetic arm around Jessica's shoulders. 'Listen Jess, darlin', he might be an idiot, but he's right about one thing. You do need some help. How long has it been? Ten, eleven months?'

Jessica shrugged, almost nonchalantly. But, of course, she could have told Bernie exactly how long it had been since her mother had died, practically down to the minute.

'You might feel better if you had someone to talk to.'

'I don't need to talk to anyone, Bernie, but thanks, anyway.'

'I'm just worried about you, Jess, that's all.'

'Honestly, there's no need,' Jessica said unconvincingly and walked off down the ward.

It was a day of firsts for Jessica. But then, nearly every day had been a day of firsts since Linda Gibson's death back in February. The first Mother's Day without her; the first Christmas without her; the first lonely cup of coffee in a café without her. And today was no exception: the first visit to her mother's grave; the first visit to her mother's house. In her world of denial, Jessica had managed to avoid both hurdles for all this time. But an overdue sense of decency, and the fact that it was her mother's birthday, meant Jessica could avoid these tasks no longer. And while she might be able to make a start on sorting through Linda's belongings today, it was far too soon to make any decisions about what to do with the house itself.

Standing at the bus stop outside the hospital that afternoon, Jessica waited for the bus that would take her on the short journey from work to her mother's house, the journey that she once took so frequently. In theory, she'd 'left home' a couple of years ago, when she and Linda had both reluctantly agreed that Jessica should lead a more independent life. But in practice, she'd spent almost as much time there as she ever had. And shivering now with trepidation, Jessica remembered the rather too long lunch hours spent sitting in Linda's kitchen drinking tea, and their film nights together, when she'd stay over and take the bus to work the following morning. But there had been times when her mother's job with the university had taken Linda abroad for weeks at a time, and Jessica recalled how difficult she'd found those days without her. And, as the bus approached, her mood grew darker still with the painful realisation that she hadn't appreciated just how perfect her life had been back then, and how she now really, truly knew what it meant to be without someone when they went away.

Sitting on the crowded bus, Jessica gazed blankly out of the window. She didn't hear the cries of scavenging seagulls circling above the empty beach, nor the spirited busker singing by the pier. She didn't see the now-weary Christmas lights and decorations that still adorned Brighton's streets and shop fronts. She was a forlorn figure, oblivious to the world outside. But her bubble of isolation was soon burst by a piercing shriek of laughter when two women, overloaded with carrier bags and exuberance, took their seats across the aisle from her.

'You're going to look so gorgeous in that little black dress, darling. It's absolutely perfect for the party tonight,' gushed the older one.

'I know, I know! I can't wait to wear it,' the other squealed. 'I love it when we go shopping together. You always manage to find the perfect outfit for me. Mummy, what would I do without you?'

Jessica looked over at the two giggling women, her face flashing with resentment.

The palpable bond, the warmth between them…every single self-satisfied word was like a kick in the guts. She turned to look out of the window again.

The mother gave a sigh: 'Oh…just think, next time we come shopping, we'll be looking for a wedding dress. Now, that'll be fun, won't it, darling? I don't know where all the time's gone, I really don't…it only seems like yesterday you were my little girl.'

Jessica was relieved to see she was nearing her destination, and she stood quickly to make her escape, but the women's shopping bags were blocking the aisle. Once again, she felt the heat of her anger rise.

'Excuse me,' she growled.

'Oh, I'm so sorry, dear,' the older one replied, scrambling to gather her purchases.

Jessica reciprocated with an unforgiving glare, then stepped off the bus and out into the sobering winter air. Taking a deep, steady breath she walked, almost robotically, the few hundred yards towards Linda's house, the women's voices still buzzing like bluebottles inside her head. *Mummy, what would I do without you?*

As Jessica approached the humble semi-detached house, with its white front door and sunny-coloured stained glass, it appeared as welcoming as ever. But today, as she walked closer, it seemed to be jeering at her as though it were concealing a dark secret, a nasty surprise, just like the gingerbread house in the story of Hansel and Gretel. Hands trembling, she fumbled with a huge bunch of keys, searching for the one that would, again, force her to confront the truth. It was silver, like the others, but with a piece of purple ribbon her mother had tied to the end, to distinguish it from the rest. Slowly she turned the key in the lock, but was suddenly startled by a voice behind her in the dusk.

'Hello! Miss Gibson, hello!'

Jessica turned to see her mother's neighbour, Mr. Singh, rushing along the path eagerly.

'I'm very pleased to catch you at last,' he said with an awkward grin. 'It's been such a long time. I haven't seen you since your mother's funeral.' And without pausing for breath, he continued: 'Now, I'm so sorry to have to bring this matter up, Miss Gibson, but it's the fence, in the back garden. I'm afraid it really must be replaced, it's falling apart, you know.'

'Oh, right...okay,' Jessica replied, somehow managing to control her irritation. 'Just leave it with me. If you'll just give me a couple more weeks...things have been very difficult...'

'No, no, no, of course, I understand,' he said sympathetically. 'I remember, when I first heard the dreadful news, that your mother had suffered a stroke and died so suddenly, I couldn't believe it. She was so fit, so strong. And so young...it must have been such a shock for you.' Mr. Singh swallowed hard and blinked rapidly, his lip tensing over his sparkling dentures. 'When my dear wife Nita passed away, I didn't think that life would ever be worth living again. But, you know, Miss Gibson, it does get better. Believe me, life does get better.'

He nodded earnestly to himself, as he turned and walked back up the path.

Jessica found herself feeling strangely sorry for the sprightly little man, who didn't really seem convinced of his own prophetic words.

The hallway, although in reality only small, seemed to stretch ahead like a dark, gaping chasm, as Jessica stood on the threshold, paralysed and pale with dread. With a deep breath she stepped over a mountain of newspapers and letters, and launched herself into the cold, musty front room. The heavy curtains had been left open on that morning back in February, but the room was now veiled in semi-darkness, lit only by the soft glow of the streetlamp outside. Looking around her, in the strange, eerie half-light, nothing was recognisable – everything seemed to merge into one grey, molten silhouette. At first, Jessica was disorientated, but when she switched on the light, there it was, like a slap in the face, everything just as it had always been. Except for the dust. The fossil collection proudly displayed on the shelves; the bookcase crammed with encyclopaedias; the treasured souvenirs from around the world. There was the big comfy sofa, with its richly-coloured, ethnic pattern, scattered with an array of mismatching cushions, and there was the jewelled throw from Nepal. In front of it stood the little wicker coffee table her mother had always meant to replace, still with the folded piece of cardboard tucked under one leg to keep it from wobbling. It almost made Jessica smile, until she caught sight of the empty mug, stamped with a smudge of her mother's burgundy lipstick on the rim. And there next to it, the newspaper lay open at the crossword, half-finished in her mother's familiar hand. Jessica's heart raced as she fought against the images building in her mind, the images of Linda's routine that morning. Fists tightened, she drove her fingernails deep into the flesh of her palms; desperately struggling to substitute her mental pain for physical pain.

Where to begin? Where to rip out the heart of her mother's world? Where to start the dismemberment of her very existence?

The bedroom. Dare she confront the ghosts that lay in wait behind that door? The fragrant, jasmine-scented perfume, the hairbrush, the soft cotton nightie – all so evocative of her mother, all so full of foreboding. She had to do it. Get the worst over with first. Get it over and done with.

She climbed the stairs, slowly, deliberately, delaying the inevitable even if only by a few seconds. Her mouth was dry and her stomach hollow, as she tentatively pushed open the door and switched on the light. The room before her seemed to glow with its warm, deep pinks and its soft, soothing femininity. An unexpected sense of calm enveloped her, and Jessica found herself being drawn into the safe, womb-like haven. She sank onto the thick, downy bed and breathed in the familiar, sweet scent of her mother, cherishing the precious closeness that she hadn't felt in such a very long time. Somehow she felt recharged by this unexpected sense of comfort. She felt brave again. But it wasn't enough: she wanted more; she needed more. Craving another fix, yet another connection with the woman who'd been her world, she instinctively reached over to the bedside cabinet and opened the small cupboard door. She knew what she would find there, and pulling out an old photo album, she eased back into the pillows.

The pages fell open at a photograph of Jessica aged eight, with her classmates and schoolteacher. Her eyes were immediately drawn to the chubby little girl in the third row, with the ginger hair and crooked fringe. She'd always been such a shy, self-conscious child. She remembered how readily she would blush whenever anybody spoke to her: a teacher, a kindly neighbour, the man in the sweet shop. And looking at that photograph now, she felt once again the chest-tightening sense of panic she would experience every morning when she was taken to school and left among the noisy, boisterous throng. She'd pretend to be ill frequently, and her trusting, doting mother would have to abandon her work commitments to keep her safe at home, comforted by beans on toast and daytime TV.

'Separation anxiety' someone had once called it, but Jessica's mother had always heroically jumped to the defence of her sensitive little girl. And now they were separated forever.

Suddenly she tossed the album across the bed. What the fuck was she supposed to do with all this useless junk, anyway? How could she be expected to sort everything out on her own? Why the hell had this happened to her?

Jessica's self-induced bitterness was, as always, her salvation. Mentally, she began to count to ten. One, two... At ten, the butchery would begin. Three, four...There would be no mercy, no reprieve for any object no matter how special the memory imprinted upon it. Five, six... Everything would be placed in boxes and bin liners to delay making a decision as to its fate. Seven, eight, nine...ten! She sprang from the bed and hastily swept every ornament, scent bottle, lipstick and trinket box from the surface of the dressing table into black bags, along with the three dressing-table drawers crammed with underwear, socks, tights and nightdresses. Jessica barely even glimpsed at these, her mother's most personal items, and rapidly turned her attention to the ottoman beneath the window. For just a minute she allowed herself to recall how every evening, as a small child, she would perch on its worn velvet upholstery and watch, fascinated, as her mother smoothed cold cream over her face and brushed her chestnut hair. Jessica stared ahead as the memories played out before her eyes, like a grainy home movie. But the images were suddenly too vivid, too crushing to bear. She blinked hard to force them to the furthest reaches of her mind. The pictures blurred and the vision of her mother gradually faded into a mist, until it was gone.

And there it was again, that familiar body-blow, punching deep at her aching solar-plexus; acid scorching the back of her throat. She wiped a stray tear from her cheek, lifted the ottoman's heavy lid and urgently unpacked the blankets, tablecloths and batiks.

Everything went into the boxes and black bags, including the piles of National Geographic magazines and long-forgotten copies of The Guardian, all dog-eared and dusty under the bed. And reaching further still beneath the iron bedstead Jessica retrieved several cardboard shoeboxes, though she couldn't steel herself to look inside. Yet another memory: she and Linda had always shared a weakness for quirky footwear and had often borrowed one another's shoes. But Jessica knew she would never have the heart to walk in her mother's shoes again, for every step would be a reminder, and so they too went into the sacks, to be given up for charity. One day.

All that remained now was the wardrobe, the warm honey-coloured antique that had belonged to Jessica's grandparents. Back in those days, it had towered so high and strong, Jessica had thought it must touch the ceiling, but today it looked so small. She unhooked the little black catch and pulled open the walnut door, averting her eyes from the row of outfits hanging inside – many from second-hand stores but all with Linda's distinctive ethnic, earthy style. Then feverishly she grabbed handfuls at random, and thrust them into a bag.

Within seconds the wardrobe had been emptied of its humble contents. Tying a knot in the top of the plastic sack, Jessica breathed a sigh of relief. Then, as she spun around to push the wooden door shut once and for all, she froze.

There it was hiding in the darkness, at the back of the wardrobe, so unlike anything else ever worn by her mother. Sleek and black and velvet, almost feline. It lurked expectantly, waiting to be held. Jessica's eyes fixed on the coat's luxuriant sheen and she was immediately transported back to Linda's 45th birthday. Four years ago, to the day. On that unforgettable afternoon in London, as Jessica and her mother had ambled arm in arm around Covent Garden, they'd been struck by the brilliant lustre of the coat as it adorned a solitary mannequin in a boutique window.

It wasn't meant to be a shopping trip – they'd planned to go to London for a culture fix, to visit museums and art galleries. To celebrate Linda's birthday, just the two of them. But after a spot of lunch in a cosy little trattoria and a particularly robust bottle of Chianti, Linda had been persuaded to try on the elegant coat, with its neatly nipped-in waist and soft faux fur collar and cuffs. And there it was, the perfect present from daughter to mother; to hell with the cost, for once.

They had both known it was an extravagance, and that Linda would rarely have the opportunity to wear anything quite so smart and sophisticated. Which was why Jessica was so thrilled when, a week later, she'd found her mother waiting for her outside the hospital – resplendent in the sensational coat. With a girlish twirl, she'd whisked Jessica off to The Grand hotel for afternoon tea. And as they'd sat in the opulent lounge, Jessica had never felt so proud of her beautiful mother, radiant in her new coat, and she remembered thinking there and then just how lucky she was to have her. They'd spent the next two glorious hours nibbling on tiny cucumber sandwiches, piling mountains of whipped cream onto crumbly, fruity scones and giggling into their cups of Earl Grey.

Back in the bedroom, her head was filled with the sound of giggling. But now it wasn't Jessica and her mother laughing. It was the two women she'd seen on the bus earlier that day. She could hear their smug, self-indulgent chit-chat; their vulgar high-pitched voices. 'Mummy, what would I do without you?'

Mummy, what will I do without you?

Two

It was about eight o'clock that evening when Jessica finally left her mother's house. She'd only managed to make a start on the bedroom. She simply hadn't been able to face the rest of the house and, anyway, it was getting late and she was exhausted. She'd just have to come back and carry on another day.

Remembering it was a public holiday, Jessica decided to pop into the supermarket to pick up a few provisions on the way home. It had been some time since she'd cooked herself a proper meal, succumbing instead to the lure of comfort-eating, so her shopping list was a short, unhealthy one.

New Year's Eve. While the rest of the world would be partying, celebrating the birth of a new year, Jessica rather dreaded saying goodbye to the old one. Traumatic as it had been, she ached to cling on to it, as if moving into another year would mean moving even further away from her mother.

She drifted from aisle to aisle, in slow motion, picking up just enough to see her through the next couple of days. Coffee. Bread. Vodka. And as she dropped a carton of milk into her basket, she was jolted back into the land of the living by a sudden, shrill voice.

'Hi, there! Did you have a great Christmas?'

Jessica was confronted by the Cheshire-cat grin of a young bottle-blonde salesgirl, dressed in a bright red suit, holding a clipboard. Before the question had even registered with Jessica, the girl continued brazenly: 'Well, I'm about to make your new year even better. Did you know that if you switch your mobile network provider to Tel-Plan today, you'll be entitled to unlimited free calls and text messages to one designated number for a whole year?'

Not another bloody sales pitch. Jessica sighed and shook her head. She didn't have the energy to respond in her usual belligerent way.

'Just think, you could speak to your mum for as long as you like, whenever you like,' the young woman went on. 'I mean, they do go on a bit, don't they?'

Jessica recoiled. Stupid, skinny little girl, with her over-plucked eyebrows and stiletto heels. And her mum and dad waiting for her at home in front of the TV, no doubt.

'Tell you what, sign up today and not only will you be able to take advantage of this promotional offer, but I'll throw in three months free on a designated mobile number for your mum, too!'

Jessica could only utter: 'I'll take a leaflet.'

But the salesgirl was on a roll. 'Oh, come on! Wouldn't it be great to phone your mum to wish her a Happy New Year, knowing it's not going to cost you a penny?'

Now this was becoming a joke. A very bad joke. Like some perverse reality TV game show, where an unsuspecting member of the public is put through an emotional endurance test. How many rounds before she slashes her wrists?

'Well? You know your mum would be delighted! All you have to do is give me your full name and address, and we can get this form off today.'

'No thanks,' Jessica replied, walking away.

'Why not? Think how much you could be saving. I mean, how often do you speak to your mum? I bet it's every day. Every other day?'

Jessica could hold her tongue no longer. 'Look, my mother's dead, right? She's *dead*!' And with that, she made her escape, trembling, eyes stinging, leaving her shopping basket abandoned on the floor.

She trudged home, empty and alone, through the streets of

grand Victorian terraced houses, her misery tinged with anger. Anger at allowing herself to feel. Why hadn't she just walked away? And why hadn't she just walked away from Ladbroke earlier that day? Her legs ached and her head pounded as her thoughts turned to the deep, hot bath she would run once back at her flat in Hove. How she longed to cleanse herself of the painful events of the day, to see them disappear down the plughole. Then, with a couple of pills, she would withdraw into the sanctuary of sleep, escape into the world where she was safe from reality.

Jessica could hear the thumping bass of loud music in the distance. And as she turned the corner, she could see a group of noisy revellers smoking and drinking outside a house where a party was obviously in full swing. She quickened her pace and, head down, stepped off the pavement to avoid the crowd. As she passed, she caught a sweet, heady, familiar aroma in the air and fleetingly envied the smokers in their illicit cloud of anaesthesia.

A high-pitched voice suddenly called out her name: 'Jess? Jess Gibson?'

Jessica stopped to see a young woman scrambling through the crowd towards her.

'Oh, my God, it *is* you! How are you?' the woman squealed, only to be met with a blank expression. She persevered: 'It's me, Sarah. You remember? Sarah Crawford. From school?'

Jessica then recognised the once-pretty face that, she observed wryly, had clearly seen too many sun-beds.

'Oh, yeah, hi,' she replied, making absolutely no effort to feign enthusiasm.

'I don't believe it! You haven't changed a bit! What are you up to? Do you live round here? Do you still see anyone from school?'

Jessica tried to fend her off: 'Er, yes...no...sorry, Sarah. Actually I'm just on my way...'

But Sarah persisted: 'Oh don't go! Come in, we're having a party. Come in and have a drink!'

'I won't. Thanks. I'm absolutely shattered. I'm on my way home from work, and...'

'Oh, come on!'

'No, really,' Jessica insisted. 'I'm not feeling brilliant, to be honest, and I'm certainly not going to a party in my uniform...'

'Oh, you look fine, don't be so boring!' Sarah continued relentlessly. 'I won't take no for an answer.' And with that, she grabbed Jessica by the hand and dragged her up the steps and into the large, rundown house.

Entering the second floor flat was like encountering a dark, hedonistic underworld. Demonic faces, flashing red, then green in the disco lights, leered at her; laughter shrieked above the music; the walls reverberated with the pulsing beat.

Sarah thrust an icy bottle of beer into Jessica's hand, and pushed her through the writhing sea of bodies, stopping in a corner by two young men who were deep in agitated conversation.

'Now, now, boys, stop talking shop!' Sarah intervened excitedly, grabbing one of them by the elbow. 'Mark, Mark, I want you to meet an old friend of mine. Mark, this is Jess.'

His glazed eyes hardly flickered in response. The gangly, hollow-cheeked man almost lost his balance, but steadied himself by grabbing the back of a chair as Sarah continued, struggling to be heard against the loud music.

'Jess and I were at school together, just like you two! Can you believe it?' Sarah giggled unnecessarily. 'Jess, this is my gorgeous boyfriend Mark, and this is Finn,' she said, turning to the other man. 'These two clever boys are on their way to becoming squillionaires, aren't you, darling?'

'Something like that,' Mark slurred disdainfully.

Finn seemed embarrassed, and ran his fingers through his shoulder-length hair. Dressed casually in jeans and a grey t-shirt, he was obviously sporty but probably as dim as he was handsome, Jessica thought. For a moment, a very brief moment, she felt sorry for Sarah, who obviously hadn't noticed her drunken boyfriend's indifference. True, Jessica had known her at secondary school, but they certainly hadn't shared the kind of relationship that had warranted her slightly hysterical reaction. In fact, Jessica hadn't had many friends as a teenager. Having had such a close, loving, exclusive friendship at home, meant she hadn't needed any one else. She'd had the only real friend she needed. Her mother.

Sarah was still blinking at her expectantly, like a puppy waiting for its owner to tear open a packet of treats.

Oh, God, say something, say something, Jessica thought to herself.

'Squillionaires, eh? What do you do, then?'

The sullen one answered: 'What do we do? Oh, it's very technical, you wouldn't understand,' he sneered.

'We're in web design,' interjected Finn with an apologetic smile.

'Finn's the arty one,' Sarah said. 'Mark's the business brains, aren't you darling?'

Mark slowly looked Jessica up and down, a mischievous smirk bringing a curl to his lips.

'And you? You must be the stripper-gram,' he scoffed, clocking her nurse's uniform.

For the first time, Jessica felt painfully self-conscious, and pulled her coat closer about her, despite the party's stifling heat.

Mark continued, his voice getting louder, playing to the crowd now, as heads started to turn. 'I think you've come to the wrong party, love,' he laughed. 'But I'll tell you what, give us your number and next time I'm going to a stag do, I'll give you a call.'

Jessica felt the hot, sharp prickle of anger sting her neck, but before she could compose a retort, Sarah took her hand again and trilled: 'Oh, take no notice of him, Jess. He's smashed, as usual. Come and dance, come on!'

'No, I'm off now,' Jessica replied firmly. She had already allowed herself to be dragged into that wretched party; she wasn't going to be dragged about anymore. But Sarah didn't hear, and Jessica watched her sashay through the crowded room to where other people were dancing. Jessica felt the music pounding around her, the people closing in. Suffocating, she looked around for the door, desperate to make her escape.

'That was a bit out of order.' Finn glared at his friend.

'Look, mate,' Mark slurred. 'I know you're pissed off with me for letting you down at the meeting and everything, but, for God's sake, man, just chill.' He sniggered to himself and stumbled into Jessica, spilling beer over her uniform. 'Look where you're going, Matron!' he jeered.

'I know exactly where I'm going,' she snapped, turning to leave.

'Oh, come on, I thought you lot were meant to be right goers. Or maybe you've got some doctor waiting for you at home with an enormous stethoscope!'

This was the last straw. Jessica swung round, grabbed Mark by the belt and plunged the neck of her beer bottle into the top of his jeans. Mark froze as ice-cold beer trickled down his thigh, stinging his skin.

'Repeat at regular intervals!' she spat, as the beer dripped down around his ankles, forming a puddle on the floor. Jessica quickly found the door and, with trembling hands, put a cigarette to her lips. Fumbling in her bag for her matches, she marched down the stairs, leaving the sound of laughter far behind her.

'Idiot!' Finn hissed at Mark, back inside the party, and then ran after Jessica as fast as he could. He caught up with her in the hallway, where she was feverishly tipping the contents of her handbag onto the floor.

'Can't find my fucking matches!'

'Here,' Finn said, igniting a silver lighter. And without a word, Jessica lit her cigarette and inhaled deeply. Finn smiled. 'Well, you certainly put Mark in his place!'

Jessica looked at him in silence then, gathering her belongings, she stormed out through the front door. As she strode ahead, her legs quivered beneath her. She knew she should never have set foot in that hell-hole of a party, least of all on a day like today.

She could hear Finn's eager footsteps pacing close behind her.

'Hey, slow down!' he called out. 'I know he was asking for it, but he's just had too much to drink. He's not a bad guy, really.'

'You could have fooled me!' Jessica retorted, still staring ahead as she marched on.

'Just wait, come on, talk to me.'

Suddenly Jessica felt Finn's hand on her shoulder and she stopped. Turning her head slowly, she met him with an unmistakable look of hostility.

'Look, please don't take it personally,' Finn sighed, removing his hand from her shoulder. 'Mark's just not himself at the moment. He was totally ripped apart at a board meeting today, and I'm afraid he took it out on you. He didn't mean it, he's having a rough time, that's all.'

Jessica almost laughed: 'Oh that's okay then, is it?' she snapped sarcastically. 'Well maybe he's not the only one having a rough time? Look, I'm not the slightest bit interested in your vile friend, or in you for that matter - I've got far more important things to think about!'

It was uncharacteristic, but she instantly felt a little ashamed of herself for being so off-hand. After all, he was only being kind. She took a deep drag on her cigarette. 'Listen, I know you're just trying to help, but it doesn't matter. Really, forget it'.

'Are you sure?'

'Absolutely. You just go back to the party and your friend, and let's forget we ever met.'

'Well I'm not sure about that…' Finn said, his green eyes twinkling. 'Hey, listen, let me take you for a drink – just by way of an apology.'

Jessica didn't have the energy to protest anymore. And, if she were honest, she could certainly do with a drink after the dreadful day she'd had.

'…But only on one condition,' Finn added solemnly. 'You promise not to tip it down my trousers!'

The small wine bar was crowded, full with groups of friends there to celebrate the passing of the old; the arrival of the new. People who had considered one another special enough to spend this special night with. And then, at a small table in the corner, there was Jessica and Finn. Strangers, yet Jessica had quickly found herself letting down her guard and answering Finn's gently probing questions about herself, about her life. She'd confessed she'd never known her father, the man who'd abandoned her mother before Jessica was even born. She'd admitted that these days, her life was void of any sort of relationships, save for those with the elderly patients who came into her care at the hospital and then went, some more unexpectedly than others.

And for his part, Finn also seemed relaxed in Jessica's company. 'But you've lived round here all your life,' he continued. 'You must have had friends? What about Sarah?'

'Oh, she and I never really hung around together…and at work I'd say they're more like acquaintances than friends. Everyone's got lives of their own outside the hospital.'

'And boyfriends?' he asked bravely.

Jessica knocked back her drink and shrugged. 'Well, I have had relationships of course, but I can honestly say at the ripe old age of twenty nine, that there's never really been anyone special. Anyway,' she added, 'my mother managed perfectly well without a man, and so can I...'

Finn looked across at Jessica. 'Maybe you just haven't found the right one yet, that's all,' he said.

'...You know, my mum was very young when she had me,' Jessica continued, oblivious to Finn's suggestion. 'We were more like friends than mother and daughter,' she said wistfully. 'I'd even spend every school holiday on digs and climbs with her, hunting for rocks and fossils...'

'Fossils?'

Jessica laughed. 'Oh, she was a geology lecturer. When I look back, I really don't know how she did it. She was brilliant at her job and put so much into it, but, at the same time, she was always there for me, no matter what.'

'Sounds like she was pretty amazing,' Finn smiled.

'Yeah, she was...you know, it was only this time last year that we went to the States together, to Yosemite. Mum was collecting geological data...we had the most incredible time, climbing and exploring...' Jessica's eyes glazed over with nostalgia. 'I remember so clearly standing on the top of a mountain, just the two of us. It was fantastic, all we could see for miles and miles were mountains and valleys – it felt like we were the only two people in the whole world.' She stopped, her face suddenly crumpling with emotion. 'And now she's gone...well... it's not easy.'

Jessica was shocked by her own words, for this was the first time she had ever divulged the extent of her suffering to anyone. Yet with this admission, from months of suppressed anxiety, came an extraordinary sense of release, an extraordinary sense of liberation. 'Actually, it's bloody hard,' she added.

Finn reached across the table and cupped her hand in his. 'Maybe you're not – on your own, I mean,' he said gently.

Jessica stared back at him blankly.

'Well, don't you think your mum might still be around you, looking after you?'

A sweet and comforting notion this may have been to many people, but not to Jessica. To her it was a provocative, ludicrous suggestion, and the perfect opportunity to distract herself from her pain.

'What? You're not one of those religious freaks, are you? Don't bother trying to convert me...I'm with Karl Marx on this one,' she quipped. 'Religion's just the opium of the people.'

'Er, no, I just meant...' Finn stuttered, clearly embarrassed by the reaction his well-intentioned remark had provoked.

'It's all a load of bullshit!' Jessica continued, then nodded towards the aquarium by the bar. 'Next you'll be telling me that goldfish over there is the reincarnation of Elvis!'

'Okay, okay, I get the message!' Finn said, knocking back his beer.

Jessica realised her outspokenness might have been a little too much for him. 'Sorry, I didn't mean to bite your head off,' she said. 'I know I've got a big mouth, maybe I should learn to keep it shut sometimes.'

'No, not at all,' Finn smiled. 'There's nothing wrong with speaking your mind. I really like your honesty...Funny, isn't it? I wasn't going to go to that party tonight...Mark and I were going to work right through the night to salvage what's left of the business, but he insisted on dragging me along...' Finn looked across at Jessica more intently. 'But now I'm really glad I went,' he said.

'I'm kind of glad you did, too.' Her eyes were still haunted, but Jessica seemed lighter somehow, as if their encounter had made a difference.

'You know, you really do intrigue me,' Finn said softly. 'I'd really like...' Just then his mobile phone rang, its piercing tone shattering the moment. 'Shit!' he said, glancing at the screen. 'Sorry, I'll have to take this.'

Jessica watched him walk out onto the street, where he paced up and down, speaking into his mobile. From her seat near the window, she had her first opportunity to take a really good look at him. Tall. Nice broad shoulders. Sensitive. Single? Unlikely.

Moments later Finn returned to the table. 'I'm really sorry…'

'That's okay,' Jessica replied coolly. 'But I hope your girlfriend doesn't mind you being such a good Samaritan.'

'What girlfriend?' Finn frowned.

A waitress appeared and asked if they wanted any more drinks. Finn looked at his watch.

'Well, seeing as it's nearly midnight, I think we should celebrate! We'll have a bottle of Moet, please,' he said.

The waitress cleared away the empty bottles and glasses from their table and the two of them sat in silence as she returned with the champagne.

'Are you okay, Jess?' Finn asked. 'You've gone all quiet on me.'

'No, not really,' she said, without making eye contact. 'To be honest with you, I just don't feel like celebrating. I'm sorry. D'you mind? It's been a bad day. I really ought to go.'

Then, without warning, Jessica stood up and bolted from the wine bar, leaving Finn at the table, looking bewildered. Throwing some cash onto the table, he grabbed the champagne and hurried after her.

Outside in the street, Jessica gulped the cold night air. The deep undercurrent of nausea that had been there in the pit of her stomach ever since her mother had died was surging over her again like a tidal wave.

'What's the matter?' Finn asked, appearing at her side.

'I'm sorry,' she gasped.

'No, I'm sorry. Of course you don't feel like celebrating. I always think New Year's Eve is bloody awful at the best of times…'

'No, it's not just that,' interrupted Jessica.

She looked up enviously at the stars, so far away in the clear winter sky. If only she could float, weightless, carefree, empty in that huge expanse that stretched above her.

'It's just, it would've been…it was my mum's birthday today.' Her voice sounded so small. Suddenly she felt like a lost child, panic-stricken and alone again. Giving in to her pain at last, her body shook with sobbing and Finn's arms surrounded her and drew her close.

'Oh Jess, I'm so, so sorry.'

A cheer rang out from inside the wine bar and as raucous voices called their greetings of 'Happy New Year!' Jessica pulled away. In control again, she wiped away her tears self-consciously.

'I think I'd better go.'

'Why?'

'Because I'm working tomorrow and because I've had much too much to drink.'

Finn looked at her in disbelief. 'What? You're working on New Year's Day?'

'Yeah, well, it's a tough job but somebody's gotta do it,' she sniffed acerbically. 'Actually I had nothing else to do and, anyway, the day will pass more quickly if I'm at the hospital. How about you?' she asked.

'I'm going to call in at my parents' place,' he answered. 'They always have a full house on New Year's Day. But I've got to get back to the office by the evening. There's a business matter I need to sort out urgently.'

There was an awkward silence.

'Right, well, I'll be off then,' Jessica said at last.

Finn looked up and down the high street, busy with late-night party-goers. 'I don't reckon we'll have much luck finding you a cab, do you?'

'Oh, it's not that far to Hove, I'll walk.'

'Not on your own, you won't. The very least I can do is see you safely home.' Finn smiled in that easy way he had and lit them both a cigarette. 'C'mon, let's go.'

The walk from the wine bar to the flat should only have

taken half an hour, but it took them twice as long, with all the stopping and laughing and swigging champagne. With his boyish jokes and amusing sailing anecdotes, Finn had managed to lift Jessica's spirits once again and reawaken her sense of fun. Arm in arm, the two of them were completely unaware of the other diverse groups of revellers they passed on their way – gangs of rowdy teenagers relishing the excuse for a particularly late night out; intoxicated middle-aged couples staggering out of restaurants; and an assembly of unruly Hells' Angels congregated on the beach. They were only aware of one another.

Finn was the funniest, most gentle and considerate man Jessica had ever met. It didn't matter that her mascara was smudged or that her feet ached. She just knew that she felt safe – safe from the hostile world devoid of her mother. Safe for the first time in months.

At last they approached her modest home: a small basement flat in a large Victorian property.

'This is me,' she chirruped between hiccups, and then proceeded to trip on the steps that went down to the door. They both chuckled as Finn helped her up onto her feet.

'Are you sure you live here? Because she doesn't seem to think so!' he laughed, pointing to a neighbour peering disapprovingly from a window up above.

'Hello Mrs. Campbell!' Jessica called out mischievously, as the scowling old lady retreated back behind her curtain, tutting at the high spirits outside. And as if they hadn't already caused enough disturbance, there was a sudden crash as Finn stepped backwards into a couple of empty milk bottles on the doorstep. They rolled and scattered like skittles, the noise of breaking glass prompting more than just Mrs. Campbell's curtains to twitch in the quiet street.

Jessica tried hard to contain her laughter. 'Sssh!' she hissed, with her finger to her lips. Then quickly she opened her front door and bundled the offender inside, where they both collapsed in hysterical laughter onto the sofa.

Finn could barely speak. 'Oh my God...how am I going to get out of here? How am I going to get home without being stoned by your angry neighbours?'

This flippant comment suddenly quietened their mood. Jessica hadn't thought beyond the present. She'd been so elevated by Finn's company, she hadn't contemplated the evening actually coming to an end.

And Finn seemed to realise the implication of his words, too. 'It's getting late. I'd better go and face the enemy,' he laughed weakly, his eyes capturing Jessica's like magnets.

'Well,' Jessica grinned mischievously. 'I've heard Mrs. Campbell has a black belt in karate...And, as someone in a caring profession, I think it would be wrong of me to send you out into such dangerous conditions...'

Finn looked at Jessica intently and, reaching across, caressed her cheek. 'And what about you?' he whispered. 'Who's going to care for you?'

For once Jessica was speechless. Yet instinctively, she leant into him and rested her head on his chest. Finn gently stroked her hair and with every touch, her muscles relaxed just a little more.

'I'm sorry I was so off-hand earlier,' she sighed. 'And I'm not really sure why you stuck with me tonight...you must need your head examining...'

Finn lifted her chin and wiped a solitary tear from her cheek. 'Look, all I know, is that I just had to be with you. When I saw how much Mark had upset you at the party, I just wanted to pick you up and take you out of there. I just wanted to protect you...I still do.'

He leant forward and kissed Jessica softly on the lips. Nuzzling into his neck, she closed her eyes and breathed in the faint trace of cologne through his soft cotton t-shirt.

'Don't go,' she murmured into his ear. Turning his head, Finn's lips found her mouth. They kissed urgently and Jessica slowly eased her body underneath his. And as Finn gently peeled away her defences, a fleeting thought passed through Jessica's mind – maybe, just maybe, life does get better after all.

Three

Hot water rained down hard on Jessica's face. Eyes closed, she stood naked, motionless beneath the steaming cascade, her skin tingling with every drop. Fat beads of water splashing from her brow, the tip of her nose, her fingers. Her mind was still.

A sudden noise from the room next door interrupted her tranquility. It took a moment for Jessica's body to move, so immersed was she in this sensory bliss, but then swiftly she stepped out of the shower, scooped a towel around her and dashed into the bedroom, where her alarm clock was beeping loudly.

'Morning,' came a lazy groan from beneath the duvet, followed by a hand waving, searching blindly for the offending timepiece.

'Sorry!' breathed Jessica, reaching down to turn the alarm off. The hand grabbed her by the arm and pulled her, laughing, onto the bed. And there was Finn: hair ruffled, eyes barely open and a sleepy smile creasing his face.

'Oh my God!' she giggled.

'What?'

'You! You look like a caveman!' she said, playfully scratching the sandy stubble on his chin.

'Well, you look like you should be right back here with me!' Finn replied, gliding his hands over her moist skin. As he tenderly caressed Jessica's generous curves, they kissed and once again she felt a rush of exhilaration. She rested back on the pillows and gazed across at him. There was something very special about him; it wasn't just the way he looked. It was as though he radiated a kind of healing warmth. Just being close to Finn made her feel better. But what about him? How did he really feel? A niggling doubt crept into her mind -- had she been foolish to let her guard down? Who'd called him on his mobile in the wine bar last night? Jessica sat up abruptly.

'What is it?' he asked.

Uneasily, she pulled the duvet close.

'Jess?'

'It's just that...well, last night meant a lot to me,' she ventured quietly.

'It meant a lot to me, too,' he said gently. 'This caveman doesn't normally jump into bed with strange women, you know!'

Jessica managed a smile. 'No, I'm being serious.'

'And so am I.' Finn looked at her so intently that her cheeks began to burn. 'You know, I'd love to paint you one day,' he said, tracing a finger around her mouth.

'Paint me?' she laughed. 'Why?'

'Because I love to paint beautiful things.'

'Don't be ridiculous!' Jessica was slightly embarrassed.

'I'm not being ridiculous,' he replied, looking more serious now. 'You really have made a big impression on me, Jessica... I'll be honest with you, I've had more than my fair share of relationships, some more successful than others. But, thinking back, I don't know if I've ever really been...in love.' He blinked nervously, then took a deep breath. 'Look, I don't know about you, but, well, I think we were meant to meet each other last night. I believe that sometimes people meet for a reason. Fate, if you want to call it that, but...anyway, that's what I think happened. I think we were meant to meet each other...or does that sound crazy?'

'Totally crazy,' Jessica whispered softly, falling back into the pillows and pulling the duvet over the two of them.

'Hey, Jess! Do you have a razor I could borrow?' Finn called out from the bathroom. Jessica could hear water gushing from the tap as she shouted back through the door.

'On the shelf under the sink, I think!' She squirmed at the thought of her grimy little bathroom that hadn't been properly cleaned for months, with its peeling wallpaper and broken loo seat. If only she'd known that she was going to have an unexpected visitor, so that she could have bleached the room from floor to ceiling and made absolutely sure there was no trace of a line around the bath. But that was what 'unexpected' meant – unforeseen; unpredicted. And how on earth could she ever have foreseen the events of the last twelve hours?

Zipping up her nurse's tunic, she smiled softly to herself at the sound of Finn's comical opera singing that could just be heard over the hum of the running water. He seemed to be in high spirits and not at all concerned about the state of the bathroom. She wandered through to the kitchen to put the kettle on, and opened the cupboard, hoping there would be something to offer him for breakfast. Thankfully there were a few teabags left in the packet, but only a small, lone, slightly rigid crust sat at the bottom of the bread bin. Oh, well, it would probably be acceptable as toast, she thought uneasily.

Finn appeared a few minutes later, all glowing and dewy, his hair now wet and brushed back. He sat down at the little kitchen table and tried to stifle a smile when he saw the pathetic buttered crust on the plate in front of him. Slowly Jessica's tense, taught mouth broke into a grin, too, and without a word the pair began to laugh.

Finn duly ate his crust and they chatted affectionately for the next few minutes while finishing their tea. There was still so much to say, so much to find out about one another, but they both knew it would have to wait until the next time.

'Is it okay if I smoke?' he asked, pulling a pack of cigarettes out of his jeans' pocket. 'Darn, I've still got Mark's lighter,' he muttered.

'Don't you dare mention the M-word!' Jessica said.

'Ah, yes, sorry.' Finn looked thoughtful. '…well, maybe you'll get to know him one day, and then you'll see that he's a decent guy, really.'

Jessica rolled her eyes. 'Not likely,' she muttered under her breath.

'Anyway, what time did you say you have to be at work?'

'Hmmm, I should be there at nine, really,' she replied looking at her watch.

'Well, then, I suppose I'd better get going.' He sighed and pulled on his jacket, a cigarette wedged between his lips, his eyes firmly fixed on Jessica's. And then he asked softly, 'Are you going to be okay?'

Jessica tried not to contemplate the emptiness that he would be leaving behind him. She didn't know why, but just having Finn there, in the room with her, brought the same sense of peace, security and trust that she'd only ever felt with her mother. 'Of course I am,' she smiled.

'I really wish I didn't have to go,' he whispered, holding her close.

'Me, too.'

They squeezed one another tight, then Finn pulled away. 'I haven't even got your phone number,' he said.

Jessica quickly scribbled her number down on the back of Finn's cigarette packet and slid her address book across the table. 'Write yours in here for me,' she asked, handing over the tatty little grey book.

'I'll be in touch soon. Promise,' he said, flicking through the pages. 'Here's my mobile number…I'll put it under 'C' for Caveman!'

They both pretended to laugh, but it was difficult to be buoyant when they knew their time together was running out. They shared a lingering kiss, and then Finn walked out of the front door and meandered along the pavement. He stopped, and turned and, looking back over his shoulder, seemed to hesitate.

Then, with a subdued, upside-down-smile, he finally walked away.

Jessica watched until he was out of sight, then slowly closed the door behind her. She glanced at her watch. Only twenty minutes to get to work. Dashing back into the kitchen she grabbed her coat, and saw that Finn had left behind the lighter. Mark's lighter. The M-word. 'M for Moron,' she thought. Then, throwing the lighter and address book into her handbag, she set off for the hospital.

As Finn turned the corner, his pace quickened and, pulling his mobile phone from his pocket, he quickly found a number.

'Hi! Yeah...I'm so sorry, I'm running late...yeah, I know, I know...Okay, I'll meet you there...see you soon.'

He walked along the coastal road to Brighton until he reached the pier. And waited. The grey winter sky was alive with seagulls, hanging in the air, their mournful cries carried across the cold, dark ocean. At last, a black BMW pulled up at the kerb. Finn grinned awkwardly as he climbed into the car, kissing the driver, an attractive woman with long honey-blonde hair. They chatted and laughed animatedly as the car drove away and cruised along the coastal road.

After a few minutes they pulled into a petrol station and the young woman got out to fill the car up with fuel. Finn closed his eyes and rested his weary head back into the contours of the leather seat, until he was disturbed by the beeping of his mobile phone with a text message: 'U LEFT M'S LITER. WEN CAN U PICK IT UP?' He smiled but before he could send a reply, his companion had returned to the car holding a bunch of flowers which she placed carefully on the back seat. As she started the engine again, Finn opened the glove compartment and flicked through a small collection of CDs until he found what he was looking for. The Kinks. Slipping the disc into the CD player, he turned up the volume and quietly mouthed along to the lyrics of the song, 'You Really Got Me', as they drove away down the road.

The double-doors didn't seem quite so heavy that morning, as Jessica arrived at the hospital. And today she greeted Dave, the porter with a cheerful smile as he wheeled a patient out of the lift and held the doors open for her. She walked inside and pressed the button for Level 3. The doors eased shut with a smooth, automated swish. The lift was empty, save, once again, for her own reflection. Though this time it looked different. Jessica scrutinised the slightly blurred image displayed on the shiny metal surface before her. The figure stood more upright today; the creamy complexion didn't look quite so pale; even the eyes appeared more alive. Then suddenly she was swamped in darkness. The fluorescent light on the ceiling of the compartment had gone out, and the lift halted. Jessica's heart began to race. But then with a groan and a creak, the lift began to move upwards again, though still in darkness. All she could see was the red-illuminated buttons of the control panel. She took her mobile phone out of her coat pocket to check the time. Numbers 09.08, all aglow, told her she was already running late. Jessica willed the lift to keep on going, to take her safely to the next level. At last it stopped. The doors parted. With a sigh of relief, she stepped out of the darkness.

Four

Four months later

It was a bustling Friday afternoon in the leafy north London suburb of Hampstead, as two removal men hauled a large table down the steps of an imposing Edwardian property, and heaved it onto their van, already crammed with furniture. Alexandra Green tucked her ebony, chin-length hair behind one ear and loaded the last of her possessions, including a disgruntled pet cat, into her convertible mini while her Versace-clad neighbour leant on the car.

'That cat's got more sense than you,' the neighbour said disparagingly. 'Listen to the poor creature, he's crying at the thought of moving out of London!'

The frightened animal, eyes like saucers, hissed at the woman who, with feigned affection, had stuck her finger through the bars of the cat-box. She jumped back, teetering on her Jimmy Choos.

'I mean, Alex, darling, what is there to do down there? There's no Nobu, no Chinawhite...what on earth are you doing moving to a seaside town?'

'Oh, Tara,' Alex laughed. 'I never went to any of those places, anyway. There's more to life than flashy restaurants and partying, you know.'

'Well, why on earth *are* you going, then?' the neighbour continued, attempting to raise a Botoxed eyebrow.

Alex slammed the boot of her car shut and brushed her

hands together as though wrapping up a deal. She was a vision of coordinated perfection in neat chinos, crisp blue gingham shirt and tan leather loafers. 'It's time for a change, Tara, and there's a new job waiting for me, so I'm going for it,' she replied resolutely, her distinctive east coast American accent, like her, exuding determination and tenacity. 'I mean, there's nothing to keep me here.'

Her neighbour's eyes widened. 'Not even Sam, that dishy boyfriend of yours?' she probed.

'No, not even Sam,' Alex answered nonchalantly.

Tara had difficulty containing her excitement. 'Oh, it's not all over between you two, is it?' she asked deviously.

The American sighed, rather irritated by her neighbour's transparency. 'Let's just say that Sam and I are good friends.'

At that moment a burly removal man sauntered over. 'All done now, love, so we're ready to go,' he announced.

'Okay, great…I'll be right behind you. Well… take care Tara. You've been a cool neighbour.'

'You, too, darling,' Tara reciprocated, offering her cheek for a farewell kiss. 'Do send me a postcard.'

Alex waved, and drove away without so much as a backward glance.

Five

It had been a pretty uneventful afternoon in Geriatrics. Two admissions, one discharge but, thankfully, no referrals to the great consulting room in the sky. Being Friday, Jessica could still detect the lingering trace of fried haddock on the ward, as she leant on the central desk and surreptitiously eased her throbbing feet out of her scruffy, scuffed black pumps.

'Am I down for a double shift tomorrow, Bernie?' she wearily asked the staff nurse.

'You are, Jess, darlin', but you look exhausted.'

'I am. I'm knackered. Still a bit wobbly after that virus I had the other week, I think,' Jessica replied.

'Look, why don't you ask Carol if she'll swap with you?' Bernie had always harboured a soft spot for Jessica. The wilful, sharp-witted girl rather reminded her of one of her own daughters, and she'd felt especially protective of her in recent months. 'I'm sure she won't mind.'

'No, it's alright, I'm fine,' Jessica replied with a deep breath. 'Anyway, I could do with the money.'

'Well, you just take care of yourself, you hear?' tutted Bernie. 'You won't do yourself any favours if you push yourself too hard.'

'Oh, get off my case, will you!' Jessica replied with a mischievous smile, then slipping her shoes back on, she noticed a patient being wheeled back to the ward. 'Oh, good, Mr. Reynolds is out of theatre. I'll just go and do his obs, then I'll be off.'

She hurried over to the man's bedside, where his wife had been waiting anxiously. 'So how are we feeling, Mr. Reynolds?' Jessica asked, deftly tucking the stiff white sheets around him. 'You certainly gave me a fright, you know. What would I do without my star patient, eh?'

Mr. Reynolds stared ahead vacantly, his pale, watery eyes unblinking.

'Alf, love?' twittered Mrs. Reynolds.

Jessica made a note of the old gentleman's blood pressure. 'There, that's all fine…'

As she ripped apart the Velcro cuff, the crackle it made seemed to rouse her patient: 'It was so beautiful…'

'What was, dear?' frowned Mrs. Reynolds.

'The light…it was so warm and bright.'

'I think he's delirious,' she observed, glancing at Jessica nervously.

'I was looking down on the room…I could see them all working on me.' Mr. Reynolds spoke with a curious, agitated urgency. 'They were trying to bring me back, but I didn't want them to.'

'Now, now, Mr. Reynolds, come on, you'll be fine,' Jessica said firmly. 'It's just the anaesthetic.' Whilst taking her patient's temperature, she did her best to reassure the little ivory-haired lady who'd now sprung to her feet, clutching her black patent handbag tightly in front of her. 'He's had an enormous shock and a lot of medication. It's nothing to worry about. It's just the anaesthetic,' Jessica reiterated. 'Now, Mr. Reynolds, you get some rest. I'll be back to look after you in the morning.'

She gave her patient's hand a firm squeeze of encouragement, and with an affectionate wink, picked a sugary pear-drop from an open packet on his bedside table: his favourite sweets which he'd happily shared with Jessica, his favourite nurse, over the past couple of weeks. Her eight-hour shift over, she had to get away – she had something planned that evening, at 7.30, though she suspected it would be a complete waste of time.

Nonetheless she hesitated, somehow reluctant to abandon the fretful old man, with whom she'd struck such rapport. He looked so bewildered, so disorientated. But time was getting on; she really had to go. Jessica finally turned and made her way down the ward. And as she strode off, the troubled man clutched at his wife's wrist.

'I didn't want them to bring me back, Gladys. I didn't want them to.'

Six

7.30pm. Through half-closed eyes, Jessica peeped at the other members of the group; about ten in all, sitting in a semi-circle. They were a motley crew: a twitchy middle-aged chap hiding behind his beard; an acne-ridden teenager sporting a lime green Mohican and multiple facial piercings; a gaunt, youngish woman with hair cropped so badly it looked as if she'd cut it herself. What a bunch of weirdos they were, she mused, as she sat amongst them in silence, all supposedly deep in thought. All except Jessica, of course. As predicted, the meeting had turned out to be a bloody waste of time.

Suddenly overcome by an excruciating urge to laugh, Jessica bit her bottom lip and deliberately diverted her gaze through the window, focusing instead on the activity going on outside the house next door. From behind the voiles, in the twilight, she could just make out two men carrying furniture and boxes up the path.

The removal men were unloading the last of Alex Green's belongings, an easel and some canvases, from the large van parked outside the row of elegant, Regency-style townhouses. Alex walked out of number thirty carrying two mugs of tea and a plate of biscuits, her dark hair now scraped back beneath a red baseball cap.

'Here you are, guys,' she called out.

'Cheers love,' came the chirpy reply, as the two men took their refreshments across to the picturesque green, which

40

stretched out before the arc of houses. At that moment a taxi pulled up alongside the van. Alex glowered when she recognised the passenger paying the driver.

It was a dark-haired, slightly dishevelled-looking man in a suit. 'Hi, Babe!' he said, swaggering towards her.

'What are you doing here, Sam?' Alex asked tersely.

The man wrapped a heavy arm around her shoulders, almost swamping Alex's petite, finely-built frame. 'Wow!' he exclaimed, looking up at her magnificent new house. 'I've come to help you out. You can't do all this on your own.'

Alex shook off Sam's embrace. He was the last person she wanted to see, and she couldn't believe he had the audacity to come all the way from London uninvited and obviously drunk.

'I really am quite capable on my own, Sam. I want to be on my own,' she protested.

Sam hung his head and kicked a stone aggressively. Alex had bruised him, and she knew it.

'Look, Sam, I'm sorry...' she said. 'But I've changed, I need a new start now. We've talked about all this – I feel different...you must understand that,' she pleaded.

'No, I don't really. I've done everything I can for you. I even left a client meeting early to get down here to help you, Alex,' he whined.

'But I didn't ask you to Sam!'

The couple's off-again, on-again relationship had rumbled along for eighteen months, despite their many differences and his unpredictable mood swings. But as far as Alex was concerned, it had now run its course, and she felt sure she'd made it quite clear that she wanted a clean break. She hadn't failed to notice that from that moment on, Sam's interest in her had suddenly been reawakened -- which only served to confirm to her that she'd made the right decision. But as he stood there now, with his untucked, crumpled white shirt and dejected expression, he looked so pathetic, that her anger quickly turned to pity.

'I suppose you'd better come in now that you're here,' she sighed.

They walked into the wide hallway, which opened into an impressive open-plan living area, piled high with boxes. 'So this is it!' Sam nodded rather coolly. 'It's much bigger than it looks in the pictures.'

Alex had discouraged Sam from joining her on her property-search in Brighton; she'd felt there was absolutely no point in adding a new dimension to the already disintegrating relationship.

'Ah yes... very nice indeed,' he added.

In the sleek, modern kitchen Alex took a couple of bottles of beer from the already-stocked fridge. Not only was she cross with herself for giving in to Sam, but she was also irritated by his presence in her new home. It was as if she'd turned the first clean page on a brand new in her life, and he'd started scribbling all over it. She opened the beers, took a swig from one and handed the other to Sam.

'You drinking beer?' he asked. 'What's happened to you? You never used to touch it!'

'What's the harm in a girl having a beer once in a while?' Alex snapped. 'Actually, I really quite like the stuff these days.'

Sam shook his head. 'You're right, you really have changed.'

Alex busied herself unpacking boxes, while Sam rattled on about his meeting that afternoon. '...So the client was gob-smacked by our pitch for the Color-Glo ads. The copywriters came up with some great lines...'

Alex feigned interest in the latest office dispatch, but it had been a long time since she'd worked there and tonight she just wanted to unpack a few more boxes, take a shower and get into bed. Alone.

'...But they weren't as good as anything you'd have written, of course. You know, the agency just isn't the same without you, Al,' Sam continued, wandering over to the lounge area where he flopped onto the sofa with another bottle of beer. It was very clear that, in actual fact, he had no intention of helping at all.

Alex sat down next to him, gathering herself to announce once and for all that it really was over and that he should go home.

'You know, you look really cute with your hair up like that, Al,' Sam said, running a hand across her thigh.

'What do you think you're doing?' Alex shouted, pushing his hand away angrily.

Just then, one of the removal men looked in at the door. 'We're just about done, love,' he said with a smirk on his fat, ruddy face that glistened with perspiration.

Alex shot from her seat. 'Great, thanks very much,' she said, slipping a £20 note from her back pocket and handing him the money. 'Here, this is for you guys,' she smiled awkwardly.

'Cheers, love. You sure you don't need a hand shifting anything else?' he asked, with a wink and a nod towards Sam.

'No, I'm okay thanks,' Alex replied, gratefully. 'I can manage just fine.'

Back next door, at number twenty nine, Jessica had found the evening a disappointing experience, and she doubted she would return for a repeat performance. It seemed to her that despite all assurances from her colleague Bernie, counselling was just another word for self-indulgent bollocks, invented for people with nothing better to do than bore other people with their problems.

The counsellor, Melissa, a statuesque middle-aged woman dressed in black, with unruly fuchsia dreadlocks, began to draw the meeting to a close.

'Now, friends, thank you all for coming to this evening's Good Grief meeting. I hope you've all found this first session valuable. And I look forward to seeing you again next week.

Safe journey home. Love and light!'

With the removal men gone, Alex went back into the house to find Sam still lolling on the sofa. 'Okay Sam, enough is enough,' she announced, marching over to where he was sitting. Her nostrils twitched and she sniffed the air. 'You've been smoking, haven't you?' she snapped.

'No!' he said defensively. 'I gave up six months ago, you know that.'

Alex was furious. Not only had he turned up unannounced, not only had he shown no interest in helping, but now he was lying to her as well.

'Look Sam,' she sighed. 'I really think it's time to call it a day, don't you? You can get a train back to London - I'll drive you to the station.'

'Oh, Al, can't I just stay the night – I'll sleep here on the sofa, I promise?' he begged pitifully.

But Alex was adamant. 'I don't think it's a good idea for you to stay tonight...or any other night, for that matter.'

She held open the front door, waiting for Sam to follow. With a reluctant grunt, he staggered out, sulkily dragging his heels like a petulant teenager. As they made their way towards Alex's car, Sam caught sight of a pretty young redhead walking despondently down the path, away from the house next door.

'Cheer up, Ginger, it might never happen!' he shouted out with a cocky, egotistical laugh.

Jessica glared. 'Dickhead!'

Flushed with embarrassment, Alex hurriedly pushed Sam into her car. 'I'm so sorry!' she called out.

'It's you I feel sorry for!' Jessica retorted over her shoulder.

As Alex manoeuvred her car along Montpelier Crescent, she could see the redhead in her rear view mirror, cutting a lonely figure as she wandered along the quiet street. She sincerely hoped that the woman wasn't her new next-door neighbour – in fact, she hoped she'd never lay eyes on her ever again.

Seven

Another downpour, but it didn't matter to Jessica. She had no plans to step outside her front door that miserable Monday morning, probably not even for the whole day. Sitting at her kitchen table, pale and drawn, still in her tea-stained dressing gown, she stubbed out her fourth cigarette. With the telephone clenched between her ear and shoulder, she absent-mindedly flicked the silver lighter on then off again, on then off again. '...I asked for extension 521...yes, Geriatrics...yes, I'll hold.'

The kitchen was even more chaotic than usual: dirty plates and mugs were stacked around the sink, and rubbish spilled from the over-full bin.

'Answer the damn phone!' Jessica muttered, lighting yet another cigarette. 'Oh! There is life on Geriatrics! ...It's Jessica Gibson. I'm just phoning to say I won't be in today....no, some sort of bug, I think...no, I don't know if I'll be well enough to come in tomorrow...yes I'll let you know, bye.'

Putting the phone on the table, she took a long, deep drag from her cigarette and stared out through the window at the teeming rain. How could she have got herself into such a mess? What the hell was she going to do? There was only one answer. Jessica's face clouded over with sadness as her eyes fell on a small, white plastic object on the tabletop. Angry tears slipped down her cheeks. There was no mistaking the parallel blue lines displayed on the pregnancy wand. She'd been such a fool. She grabbed the silver lighter and threw it across the room. It bounced against the wall and clattered to the floor. Jessica slumped onto the table, head in hands. She cried out for her mother, hopeless, helpless cries of desperation, even though she knew she wouldn't hear her. She didn't see the silver lighter as it rolled slowly, silently across the floor towards her.

Upstairs Mrs. Campbell unplugged the vacuum cleaner and pricked up her ears. She frowned as she recognised the sound of crying coming from the basement flat below, and tutted to herself – there was always some drama or another going on down there, she thought, shaking her head and turning up the volume on her radio.

Eight

Seventy-two hours in Brighton and already Alex felt at home. She wheeled her brand new bike out into the front garden and zipped up her waterproof jacket. This evening, her exercise regime was about to begin in earnest. Setting off along the smart, leafy close, she believed she really had found the new beginning she vitally needed. Anticipation crackled through Alex's veins.

Leaving Montpelier Crescent, she zig-zagged through the darkening streets, until she met the blustery coastal road. The wind lashed through her hair and she could taste the salt on her lips. She couldn't remember the last time she'd felt so free. So alive. Certainly not in London, where life had been so claustrophobic. It was funny how fate had brought her here to Brighton, she reflected, as she gained momentum, turning off the main street and down towards the sea. She'd been in the advertising industry in her native New York since university, working as a copywriter alongside various art directors on some low-key accounts. Until her father, a renowned commercials' producer, had pulled a few strings across the pond and, before she knew it, she was fully ensconced in a new advertising agency in London. That was where she'd met Sam, an account manager with immense charm and an ego to match. But more recently, Alex hadn't really felt right in the city – she didn't know why. It was just instinct. And she felt it had been instinct that had led her to her new life here in Brighton.

Now it was a similar gut feeling that prompted Alex to stop

abruptly in her tracks. Darkness had fallen and, looking nervously about her, she realised she was lost. She was alarmed to find herself behind a high brick wall, surrounded by what appeared to be a series of deserted lock-up garages. She knew the marina must be close by – she could hear the sound of rigging clanging against masts, chiming like distant bells calling out to sea. Turning around hastily she followed the sound, her eyes searching for something, anything that looked at all familiar.

Around the corner, and Alex was relieved to see the marina, full of life with its stretch of buzzy restaurants and bars overlooking the water. Unsure of which direction to follow, she boldly cycled along the wooden boardwalk, passing a cluster of smart, modern apartment blocks on her left. In the distance, she could see the lights of the moored boats twinkling eerily like eyes in the darkness, and nervously her clammy hands tightened their grip around the handlebars of the bicycle. Although conscious that she was leaving the reassuring hustle and bustle of the quay far behind, Alex was compelled to cycle further, deeper into the cold, still night. On she went, the wooden decking pulsing like a heartbeat beneath her tyres, the audience of empty boats nodding their approval.

Suddenly, she screeched to a halt; she felt exposed and vulnerable, as though she were being watched. Her eyes frantically searched boat after boat, hoping to find a living soul who might direct her home. Weak and light-headed, Alex turned and followed a path down to the quayside. Wheeling her bike through an open gate, she found herself on a dark, shadowy pontoon. An icy chill rushed through her, and she stopped in her tracks at the sight of one small vessel, bobbing there on the inky black waves. She stared at the scruffy little fishing boat, with the words 'Guiding Light' hand-painted on the weathered blue hull. Her heart pounded so hard it hammered inside her head.

'She's a beauty, isn't she?'

Alex was startled. 'Oh! Oh...yes,' she panted, relieved to see an old man emerging from the galley of a rundown boat moored alongside the 'Guiding Light'.

'It's a shame, she hasn't been out for a while,' he confided. 'Between you and me, I reckon Mr. Finnegan will be putting her on the market before too long. You interested?'

'What? Oh, no...I just...actually, I'm lost,' she stuttered. 'Could you tell me how to get back to the main street?'

Alex tried hard to concentrate on the old man's directions, despite her giddy head. 'Thanks, thanks very much,' she sighed. 'I don't know how I managed to lose my way so easily!'

On course for home again, she couldn't get the unassuming little blue boat, 'Guiding Light', out of her head. Nor the magical marina, with its hypnotic sounds and twinkling lights, which, until tonight, she hadn't even known was there.

At last she could make out the familiar silhouettes of Montpelier Crescent just ahead. The wind whipped about her and the trees whispered, as Alex wheeled her bike along the path and leant it against the wall. She began to feel uneasy again. Her cold, stiff, trembling hands fumbled clumsily with the door key until, finally, she was able to retreat to the safety of her new home.

Inside, she saw her phone on the hall table, its red light flashing. Four voice-mail messages:

'Hi, babe, only me.' Alex tutted at the sound of Sam's voice. 'Just wanted to say I'm, well, I'm missing you – and I'm really sorry about the other night. Hope you'll give me a chance to make it up to you. I'll try you again later.'

Beep. 'Hi, Al... I'm at the rugby club bar now. The boys all say hello...so give me a call, maybe we can get together?'

Beep. 'Al...babe...I love you...'

'Drunken idiot!' Alex shook her head at the sound of Sam's slurred pleas.

'...Where are you? I just wanted to know...have you

forgiven me yet? I mean, just because you've moved out of London, it doesn't have to be the end for you and me. You know, absence and the heart, and all that? Anyway…I'll see you soon.'

Beep. 'What are you playing at! Why won't you answer my calls?'

By now Alex had slumped on to the floor in despair.

'Where are you? What are you doing? I suppose you just want to write me out of your life now you've moved. Suppose you think I'm not good enough to join in your pathetic little game, eh? Well, Brighton isn't that far away, you know. You won't get rid of me that easily.' Beep.

'Oh, just leave me alone!' Alex shouted, hastily pressing the button that would instantly delete Sam's messages.

If only it were that easy, Alex thought to herself as she wandered into the lounge and looked out of the window at the empty street veiled in black. If only she could delete Sam from her world at the touch of a button.

It occurred to her, as she stared past her reflection in the glass, how much darker the darkness seemed here than in London, let alone New York. And it was so quiet. The only sign of life outside was a small dog scratching at a magnolia tree in next door's front garden. Alex began to feel nervous. What if Sam turned nasty? She'd never heard him sound as menacing as in his last message – was he about to make life difficult for her, just when she'd finally got her feet back on solid ground?

She shook the very idea out of her head and pulled down the blind. With a smile she struck a match and lit the wick of a large fragranced candle there on the window ledge: thick, creamy wax in an opaque glass jar. English Rose. A quaint, if somewhat ironic, leaving gift from her old neighbour Tara.

Drinking in the sweet, intoxicating aroma, Alex melted onto the sofa where Cookie the cat already sat contentedly. His rhythmic purr soon lulled Alex into a state of demi-sleep: that delicious, cotton-wool world just a breath away from slumber. Somewhere in the distance, she could hear bells chime. Gently at first, then louder and louder, until the sound tore through the room and wrenched Alex back into consciousness. Her whole body lurched. As she sat rubbing her eyes, not yet fully awake, the ringing sounded out again and again.

It was the doorbell. Cookie leapt, terrified, from the sofa, as Alex bolted to the door and flung it open. But no one was there. Nothing. She looked frantically from left to right, not daring to step beyond the threshold, but her eyes were unable to focus on anything in the dense, ominous night.

'Hello? Who's there?' she called out nervously. 'Sam? Is that you?'

Hardly waiting for a reply Alex swung back into the house, pulling the door firmly shut behind her. But before she even had a chance to catch her breath, she could taste the bitter, acrid stench of burning.

'Shit!' she exclaimed at the sight of long, crimson flames licking the window blind in the living room, and she dashed to grab the fire extinguisher from the kitchen. Within seconds all that remained of the blind and the once-fragrant candle was a grey, smoking mass of ash. Cookie mewed, traumatised, from behind the fridge.

'Oh, you poor baby!' cried Alex, extracting the tightly-knotted cat from his hiding place. 'Thank God the doorbell woke us up…it's all right Honey, it's all right.'

Cookie's wide, golden eyes, round like planets, blinked at her unconvinced, as she cradled him in her arms. 'Okay, I know, everything feels pretty weird right now, but we're going to be fine here…just fine. Right then, little fella …I'd better get this lot cleaned up. But how about we get you something to eat first, hey?'

As she walked back into the kitchen, ice suddenly filled her veins. It was as if she'd stepped into an open freezer: the air enveloping her was frost-sharp and seemed almost to crystallise on her skin. She looked up at the small kitchen window. It was closed.

'Jeez!' Alex shivered. 'I suppose the damned heating's given up on me now.'

She put Cookie down and he scampered away to the safety of an armchair. Alex pressed a hand against the radiator. 'Still warm!' she muttered, confused. A strange, defiant chill hung within the walls.

Shaking her head in disbelief, she checked her watch. Then taking a variety of bottles from the medicine cabinet, she gulped down a handful of pills with a swig of water.

Just then, the telephone rang. It must be Sam, calling to continue his tirade. 'What the hell do you want now?' she barked angrily into the handset.

However it wasn't her ex-boyfriend, but her mother at the other end of the phone, and Alex had never been so pleased to hear the reassuring sound of her voice, no matter how far away.

Alex found it impossible to get to sleep that night. It wasn't just the gale raging outside, whistling through the tiles on the roof. So much had happened to unsettle her. Her restless mind refused to give in, haunted by thoughts of Sam, and the evening's events. Alex had always believed herself to be such a strong person, but tonight his messages had left her feeling defenceless and weak.

She looked at the clock: 1.45am. This was ridiculous; she had to get some sleep. She decided to go downstairs for a drink, and switched on every light ahead of her as she went.

Standing in the kitchen, she sipped a cup of hot, calming chamomile tea, breathing in the woody steam that formed clouds in the still-chilly air. At last, her head began to clear and bed beckoned once more. But Alex hesitated as she went to leave the room.

Was that the smell of cigarette smoke? Or just the last trace of that evening's fire? She inhaled more deeply. It certainly smelt like cigarettes, but then again...

'Idiot!' she berated herself, realising she'd allowed Sam to mess with her head so much, that she was unable to trust her own senses. 'Of course it's the darn fire.'

With new resolve, she collected Cookie from the sofa, switched off the lights and marched back up the stairs to bed.

But under the duvet again in the darkness, the ghosts of doubt returned to plague her. Could it have been Sam ringing her doorbell? Would he ever leave her alone? Alex reached out a hand and switched on her bedside lamp. It was going to be a long night.

Nine

Alex awoke with a sudden jolt the next morning. It was ten a.m. Habitually an early bird, it was out of character for her to sleep in so late, but after last night's disturbing events -- Sam's menacing phone calls; the fire and the mysterious ringing doorbell -- she'd resigned herself to reading her book until the early hours.

But now, as she stood on her sunny bedroom balcony over-looking the quiet street, she realised how irrational she'd been. And she was pretty sure that however intimidating Sam was, it was absurd to even consider him stalking her. Anyway, she had more important things to think about that day. She stretched and yawned and mused over what she would wear that afternoon for her first official visit to Homewood, a special needs school in a small village just outside Brighton, where she would be starting her new job as an art assistant. Deciding on a classic white shirt and smart black jeans, she went back inside to shower and dress, excited by the prospect of the day ahead.

Alex enjoyed the rejuvenating twenty-minute cycle to school along the coastal road, with the warm sunshine penetrating the back of her waterproof jacket and the clean, fresh sea air filling her lungs. She wallowed in contentment and gratitude at simply being alive and was reassured once again that her instinct to move to Brighton had been the right one. As she cycled along, she recognised a turning off to the right, which last night had led her to the deserted marina and the funny little boat, 'Guiding Light'. This morning, the sound of screeching seagulls and the multitude of boats, with their noisy diesel engines and clanking cargo, was almost deafening. But there was something about this discordant maritime symphony that strangely touched Alex deep inside. She brushed the feeling aside and pedalled on towards her destination.

At last she reached the school. Out of breath, she stood for a minute, collecting her thoughts, resolving to channel all her energies into her new job. Untucking her jeans from her boots, she checked her hair and make-up in the bicycle mirror and walked into the welcoming little school.

As she stood at the front of the class, Alex found the group of five-year-olds, all with learning difficulties, both grounding and humbling. The children's fresh, eager faces beamed at her with endearing innocence as Pamela Harrison, the class teacher, introduced them to their new art assistant. 'Now, children, this is Miss Green. She's going to help you with your artwork every morning on Tuesdays, Wednesdays, Thursdays and Fridays...'

One little girl with thick glasses and pigtails snorted with laughter.

'Maddy,' said Pamela gently. 'Can we all share the joke?'

The forthright youngster giggled uncontrollably. 'You're going to help us with our paintings and your name is Miss Green and green is the colour of paint!'

With that, the whole class erupted in hilarity and even Mrs. Harrison and Miss Green were unable to stifle a grin.

'Yes, that's very true, Maddy,' Pamela continued. 'Now, I know Miss Green has lots of lovely ideas to share with us, so now let's welcome her to Homewood with our special song. Right, one, two, three...'

The children piped up with their saccharine-sweet song that nonetheless brought a lump to Alex's throat, the purity of their little voices touching her heart.

'We'd like to say hello,
And welcome you to Homewood School,
We love and care,
We help and share,
And that's our golden rule.'

Pamela clapped proudly as the children sat down.

'That was really beautiful, children, thank you very much and well done!' said Alex. 'I can see we already have some great artists in this class,' she enthused, looking around at the colourful scribbles pinned on the walls. 'And I'm so looking forward to getting started on some really exciting projects with you.'

Maddy raised her hand enthusiastically. 'Miss Green?' she giggled.

'Yes, Honey,' Alex replied.

'What's your boyfriend's name?'

'Oh, well, actually I don't have a boyfriend right now,' Alex smiled. 'Do you?'

'Yes I do,' the little girl said proudly, surveying her fellow classmates. 'Tom's my boyfriend, Ryan's my boyfriend, Jack's my boyfriend, Conor's my boyfriend and I think I'm going to marry Ollie!'

The two women grinned. 'Nice to see she's keeping her options open!' Pamela whispered. 'Right, quiet now everyone. Go and get your coats on, it's break time.'

As the children made their way to the cloakroom, Pamela tucked their chairs under the tables. 'A lot of these kids are very bright despite their problems,' she explained. 'Things like just holding a pencil properly or cutting out a shape can be quite a challenge for them...it might not be quite the cut and thrust world of advertising you're used to, but I think you'll find working here very rewarding.'

Alex smiled as she watched the children filing out to the playground. 'I think I will, too.'

Ten

A week had passed since Jessica had sworn she would never return to Good Grief and the crank with the dreadlocks and her gloomy groupies. But now here she was, a glutton for punishment, getting ready for another evening of emotional strip-search. She decided to have a bath, and left the taps running while she looked for something to wear. Looking in the wardrobe, there wasn't much to choose from: she hadn't been to the launderette for days. As she grabbed the only clean pair of trousers and a sweater, she looked down at the collection of bulging bin bags, which she'd brought over from Linda's house only a few weeks ago. A treasure trove of the most precious memories of her mother, all wrapped up in black plastic, crammed there, at the bottom of the wardrobe. Hesitating for just a second, she slipped a hand into the top of one of the bags, and from the assortment of belongings, she pulled out an old photo album. She hadn't opened it since that dreadful afternoon when she'd started clearing the bedroom. And now she needed its precious contents as succour for her soul. She needed that bolster so much, to sustain her through the long lonely hours that lay ahead of her, and the grim prospect of what the next day held in store.

As she sat down to open the book, something fell to the floor from between its pages. She picked it up. It was a photograph of her mother that Jessica couldn't remember ever seeing before – one of those sterile photo-booth snapshots, only a few centimetres in size and obviously taken just months before her mother had died, for some membership card or other. Jessica was instantly overcome with sadness. There was something so melancholy about the sight of Linda's fixed, empty smile and expressionless eyes against the lonely white backdrop. Smiling at nothing, but a cold machine.

The dagger of grief twisted again inside Jessica. How she longed to reach out and hold her mother close. She missed her so deeply. There was so much she wanted to share with her. She wished she could tell her all about the man she'd met four months ago, the man she'd fallen instantly in love with, who'd turned her life around in just one night. But who she'd never heard from again, leaving her alone with the most difficult decision she'd ever had to make. And as she closed her eyes and took a deep, steadying breath, she thought she could detect a trace of her mother's favourite fragrance hanging in the air just ahead of her. She inhaled as deeply as she could, and tried to hold on to the faint scent which was there, and yet somehow, wasn't. But then it was gone. Just a figment of her imagination.

Slowly she opened the album at the first page to find a single photograph, sealed safe beneath the clear plastic sheet, lovingly labeled in her mother's careful handwriting with the words: 'Jessica, one day old.'

The faded colour picture showed a youthful Linda, weary-eyed but with such a joyful smile, cradling her newborn baby in her arms. The sight of the tiny, helpless bundle, held so closely to her proud mother, sent Jessica reeling. She slammed the book shut and rushed into the bathroom, drowning in a wave of nausea. Perching on the edge of the bath, she waited for the sensation to pass.

At last she turned off the taps and eased herself into the hot, bubbly bath water. She lay back and closed her eyes, trying to empty her mind of all thoughts of the past, of the present, of the future. She didn't notice the hot steam, which had filled the tiny bathroom, begin to dissipate, leaving a mist of condensation on the mirror. She didn't notice the air gradually clear, and a shape begin to form, slowly, as if by magic, in the vapour on the glass. A distinct outline, In the shape of a heart.

Just as before, the session began with closed eyes and deep reflection.

'We need to surrender to the pain before our healing can begin,' Melissa said.

But Jessica didn't want to 'surrender to the pain'; to do so would destroy her, she was sure. Once again she was the only group member defying the rules by looking around and wondering why she'd returned for another episode of this farcical peepshow.

'Now hold those thoughts, hold those feelings,' Melissa sang in her theatrical way, dreadlocks dancing with a life of their own. 'And breathe in…and out…'

Jessica had planned to go to bed early, as her procedure at the clinic was booked for eight o'clock the following morning. Maybe her subconscious had somehow forced her to come along to the meeting, to distract her from having to think about the next day? She wasn't sure. But one thing she did know was that, for some reason, she had felt compelled to show up for another dose of Melissa's 'cathartic counselling', as she'd called it. Cathartic crap, more like.

'Okay, everyone, now you can open your eyes. This evening we're going to discuss the impact that other people are now having on our lives, good or bad. Let's start with you Graham…'

But just as Graham was about to speak, there was a faint knock on the door. The handle turned and in walked a tall, thin, nervous-looking woman in her late twenties, who Jessica recognised from the previous session.

'Hello,' she said timidly. 'Sorry I'm late.'

'Don't worry, Hannah, my love,' Melissa replied. 'Just pull up a seat', she smiled, consulting her register.

With a nod, Hannah added another chair to the semi-circle

and sat down.

'Okay, then, Graham, continue in your own time.'

The small bearded man fidgeted impatiently in his seat and wiped his nose on a grubby handkerchief. 'Yes, well, as I was about to say, since my wife died last year, I've noticed that people seem to be avoiding me,' he said. 'I've even spotted them crossing the road so they don't have to speak to me. It's as if they're embarrassed or something.'

Noticing the tea stains on his tie, and what she was certain was a decomposing baked bean attached to his lapel, Jessica thought she might cross the road too if she saw Graham walking towards her.

'Yes, Graham, that's something many of us have experienced, isn't it, Friends?'

The group muttered in agreement.

'And you really have hit the nail on the head, my love. It's true, people often are embarrassed because they don't know what to say. Once they get over the hurdle of that first conversation, then they'll stop avoiding you. So sometimes we need to make the first move, we need to help them before they can help us...'

Jessica tried hard to concentrate as Melissa continued with her sermon. But her mind persistently returned to that image of herself as a baby in her mother's arms, and the increasingly painful decision she'd reached. Eight a.m.

'How about you, Hannah? Do you feel able to tell us about your experience of loss?'

'Oh, dear, I don't really know where to begin,' the young woman stuttered, nervously tugging at her sleeve.

Jessica thought she looked like a scarecrow, with her baggy checked shirt and short, lifeless hair.

'It's all been very difficult.'

Melissa tilted her head to one side melodramatically, her face morphing like putty into an exaggerated expression of sympathy. 'Of course, we understand, my love,' she cooed.

'Well, what about your family? How much support are they giving you?'

'I think it's very hard for them to give me support,' Hannah replied. 'My husband certainly doesn't understand...'

Melissa nodded vehemently. 'Ah, yes, we often find that when we lose someone, the relationships we have with those left behind can suffer. It's difficult for our loved ones to fully understand what we're going through, especially if they haven't experienced loss themselves. But if a bond is strong enough, it will survive and may even grow stronger. Has anybody else experienced friction within the family since their loss?' Melissa continued.

A rather plump, elderly woman with white hair and kindly eyes spoke up. 'Yes, Melissa...I have.'

'Ah! Joan, share it with us, my love.'

'Well, my sister – I mean, my half-sister – resents me for mourning our mother now, because I didn't get on with her at all when she was alive.'

'Go on, my love, go on,' Melissa said.

'The situation's got so bad; she's not even speaking to me. She seems to think she's the only one entitled to grieve. You see, things were always difficult between my mother and me, right up to the day she died. We were just very different people, really. But it wasn't easy for me when she passed away, and I felt guilty. You know, maybe I should have tried harder to get along with her, maybe I should have spent more time with her?' Joan sniffed into a dainty white handkerchief.

'Guilt is a very common emotion at such a time,' Melissa added.

'Then after the funeral, the solicitor handed me a letter which my mother had written just before she passed away,' Joan continued. 'In it, she told me that despite our differences, I'd always been very special to her, and she confessed to a secret she'd kept from me since the day I was born.

'She explained that I was illegitimate which, back then,

was considered a real disgrace -- not like these days - and said that her family had wanted her to get rid of the baby – me. But Mother had refused and was determined to keep me.'

'What a brave woman,' Melissa smiled.

Jessica was fascinated by this ordinary little old lady's tale, which could have come straight out of a soap opera.

'Yes, and ever since I read that letter,' Joan said, wiping away a tear, 'I've realised how special she was, and how grateful I am to her for giving me my life.'

The room was silent, but for the broken woman's sobs.

'What a touching story, Joan, thank you so much for sharing it with us, my love,' Melissa said gently. '...Jessica, you've also lost your mother, haven't you? How have your relationships changed since her passing?'

Jessica, spellbound by Joan's poignant revelation, searched frantically for something to say. 'Well...there isn't anybody, really. And, anyway, what's the point? People just let you down. You're better off on your own.'

'So how are you *feeling* now Jessica?' Melissa probed more deeply.

'How am I feeling?' Jessica snapped, taken aback by the forcefulness in her own voice. And then instantly her eyes were drawn towards Joan, whose endearing face seemed to be looking back at her so intently. Jessica didn't know how she felt -- the old lady's words had thrown her conscience into confusion. The whole room seemed to be watching her now, waiting for her reply.

'I...I...I'm not sure,' Jessica stammered. But then she saw the answer in Joan's soft, sympathetic smile. And suddenly everything became perfectly clear. Tenderly she placed a hand on her gently rounded belly, and murmured, 'Well...I... I guess I feel I have something to live for now.'

Outside on the street, Alex opened the boot of her car and carefully began to unload the array of shopping bags squashed inside. Not just the humble thin, plastic supermarket carriers, though there were several of those. But big, solid, proud rectangular bags of pristine white card, with glossy black chord handles and names like Artisan, Cuccina and Space embossed luxuriantly in monochrome italics on their sides. As a self-confessed shopaholic, The Lanes – the collection of narrow winding alleyways, home to many unique little boutiques in Brighton's most fashionable quarter – had been impossible for Alex to resist.

She noticed a small trickle of people emerging from the house next door: a mixture of ages, men and women, with no obvious connection. But just as she locked the car, she saw a face she recognised. It was the redhead Sam had insulted last week, she realised with dismay.

'Shit!' she muttered under her breath and, head down, pretended to rummage in her handbag in the hope that she wouldn't be noticed. But then, as she glimpsed over her shoulder, Alex saw that the young woman had stopped still on the pavement. With a deep breath she prepared to field some no-doubt cutting but justifiable reference to Sam and that embarrassing scene. But the woman crumpled onto the ground.

'Oh, my God!' exclaimed Alex, dashing across the pavement and kneeling by her side.

'Is she alright?' called out another woman, rushing over to join them. 'I think she's pregnant.'

Jessica groaned and began to open her eyes, squinting at the two concerned faces staring down at her. 'I'm okay…I'm okay…just need to get my breath, that's all.'

'Look, I live just here,' said Alex. 'Let's get her inside.' And the two women helped Jessica to her feet.

Eleven

Sipping a glass of water, Jessica rested on Alex's sofa. She still felt vaguely dizzy and, although shivering, could feel her sweater moist against her back.

'How about a cup of tea?' Alex asked.

'No thanks, water's fine, but if you wouldn't mind phoning for a taxi to get me home...'

'Let me take you!' Alex offered, but then cringed at the sound of her rather too-loud voice. She wanted to help, of course, but realised that guilt over Sam's behaviour was prompting her to be somewhat over-enthusiastic. 'I mean, it wouldn't be a problem,' she added.

'Honestly, I'll just get a cab,' Jessica replied amiably, conscious of Alex's embarrassment. On one of her good days she'd have gone straight for the jugular – the Yank and her asshole boyfriend were prime targets for one of her most acerbic attacks. But it wasn't just her foggy head and horribly dry mouth that held her back. No, there was something instantly likeable about the spirited American who seemed so eager to please. She looked around for the other woman who'd come to her rescue, the slightly gawky, twitchy one, with the dodgy haircut, who'd been at the Good Grief meeting next door. But she had gone.

'Taxi's on its way,' Alex said. 'How are you feeling now?'

'Much better, thanks. Just had a funny turn, that's all. I haven't eaten all day,' Jessica replied.

'Can I get you something now?'

'No, no, I'll have something when I get home.'

'I gather you're pregnant... so, when's the baby due?'

It was a question that until now Jessica hadn't allowed herself to even consider. With a quick mental calculation she answered: 'September. My baby's due in September.'

'Hey, do you mind me asking, what goes on next door?' Alex seized the opportunity to enquire about the comings and goings at her neighbour's house. 'Is it some kind of kinky cult I'm missing out on?' she joked as they sat in the comfy open-plan lounge, that looked like something out of an interiors magazine.

'I wish!' Jessica laughed, stroking Cookie the cat who purred beside her. 'Actually it's a bereavement counselling group.'

'Shit! I'm so sorry,' said Alex, shrinking with embarrassment.

'Don't worry. To be honest, it's not usually my kind of thing,' Jessica replied, 'but I have to admit, it's actually been quite an eye-opener.'

A car horn tooted outside. 'Oh, there's your cab,' said Alex. 'Now, you sure you're gonna be okay?'

'I'm fine, honestly. I've got no plans for tomorrow, so I'm going to stay in bed all day. Anyway, thanks again for everything. And, by the way, I'm Jessica.'

'Alex Green. Good to meet you.'

Back inside, Alex helped herself to a bottle of beer from the fridge and flopped onto the sofa with a weary sigh. Out of the corner of her eye, she spotted her mobile phone on the coffee table, its red light blinking. One text message. From Sam.

HI. WHERE R U? WHY HAVEN'T U RETURNED MY CALLS? STOP PLAYING GAMES. HOW ABOUT I COME OVER? WE CAN SORT THINGS OUT? XXX

Alex took a swig of beer and sank back into the cushions with an exasperated sigh, Cookie nestled on her lap. 'Oh,

Cooks,' she said. 'Why can't he just take No for an answer?'

Just then, a loud clatter in the kitchen sent the cat flying off the sofa and out through the cat-flap. 'What the hell was that?' Alex murmured as she went in to the kitchen, only to find an array of pill bottles scattered across the floor. Shaking her head in disbelief, she picked them up and replaced them on the shelf in the medicine cabinet, where they'd sat in regimented order quite uneventfully, until now. Then she shivered. Why was it always so cold in here? She glanced at the clock and, with a tut, poured a glass of water before swallowing a cocktail of the tablets. Suddenly, the lights began to flash off, then on again; off, then on again. Startled, she backed into the lounge. The lights there also flashed: off, then on again; off, then on again. And could she smell smoke?

Her first reaction was to check the fuse box. She looked in the cupboard under the stairs. Everything seemed to be in order. But then something caught her eye. She turned. In the softly-lit living room, a shadow moved. Someone was there. Was it Sam? She watched in terrified silence as the grainy silhouette moved towards the kitchen. Her heart bounced like a punch-bag within her paralysed body. Perspiration pumped from every pore. She inched along the hall in silent, nightmarish slow motion, dragging concrete legs towards the front door. Then, at last, outside in the darkness, she raced, panting with terror to her neighbour's house, and rang desperately on the doorbell. 'Help me! Please! Somebody help me!'

Alex was still trembling as she sat at her kitchen table some time later, while her neighbour, Melissa, poured her a large glass of brandy. 'Now, remember, the police have gone over the house with a fine-toothed comb. There is nobody here, okay?'

Alex nodded weakly. 'It's just, this isn't the first time there's been someone prowling around. And I'm pretty sure I know who it is.'

'Who?'

'My ex, Sam,' Alex replied anxiously. 'I'm sure he's trying to freak me out because I ended the relationship. I thought I knew him, but obviously there's a crazy side to him I didn't know.'

'Really? Did you tell the police?'

'Yes, but to be honest, as soon as I mentioned an ex-boyfriend, they seemed to lose interest.'

'Oh, dear...Well, some men do display vengeful tendencies when they've been rejected,' Melissa said, slipping swiftly into counsellor-mode. 'Generally those with low self-esteem. Although I shouldn't worry, most of them are all mouth and no trousers – they rarely do any harm. But look, if you're still concerned, you're more than welcome to stay at my place.'

'It's okay, Melissa, I'll be fine,' Alex replied. 'You've been fantastic. Why don't you get home now?'

'Only if you're sure?'

'Sure I'm sure...' Alex smiled feebly.

'Okay then, my love. Well, now you know I'm just next door, feel free to call on me any time. Goodnight. Love and light!'

Alex saw Melissa out and then locked the door behind her. She went upstairs, only to return with her duvet and pillow, and curled up on the sofa for the night, with the television switched on for company.

Twelve

Jessica lay, mesmerised by the rapid, pulsating rhythm transmitted by the Doppler monitor, pressed against her bare abdomen.

'There we are, a good, strong healthy heartbeat,' Shirley the midwife beamed. 'Everything seems fine. And you say you reckon you're about nineteen weeks?' she asked breezily.

'Yes... I didn't even realise I was pregnant until a few weeks ago,' Jessica replied, in a haze of wonderment as the midwife scribbled in her notes. '...My periods have always been erratic... I just put it down to all the stress I've been under lately.'

'Bit of a shock, then,' Shirley grinned.

Jessica smiled back. Now it was all becoming so real: daunting and yet so exciting. But she was sure that her sudden u-turn had driven her in the right direction. By deciding to keep her baby, Jessica knew that she was being true to herself and that this pregnancy would give her hope, a future. The only other time since her mother's death that she'd listened to the same instinctive inner voice was on the fateful night she'd met Finn.

'So have you felt Baby kicking yet?' asked Shirley, interrupting Jessica's thoughts.

'Um, just a kind of fluttering, really.'

'Well, I imagine you'll start to feel some more obvious kicks in the next couple of weeks. And what about the cigarettes?' Shirley added.

'Don't worry; I've given up. I just inhale other people's instead!' Jessica joked.

The midwife studied a small separate sheet of paper. 'Your haemoglobin levels are fine now, so hopefully there'll be no more fainting,' she said. 'And we'll get you in for a scan in the next couple of weeks.' Then she looked up, her face now more serious. 'Look, Jessica, I know you've been through a lot recently, but believe me, this little one's going to bring a ray of sunshine into your life. A child is a gift from God,' she continued. 'You've been blessed.'

There was a time, not too long ago, when Jessica would have seized the opportunity to demean such whimsy. But today she found herself uncharacteristically restrained, and simply smiled.

'A ray of sunshine.'

****

'Yellow!' called out a handful of children in eager unison.

'That's right!' exclaimed Alex. 'The sun is yellow...so you're going to need lots of yellow tissue paper.'

Alex wandered around the classroom, helping the children who sat in small clusters, busy making a collage. 'That's a beautiful butterfly, Lily,' Alex enthused.

'Can we have some more cotton wool for the clouds, please Miss Green?'

'Yes, of course you can, Tommy. Just a minute.'

'Miss Green! Miss Green!'

'Just a minute, Maddy!' Alex called out from the art cupboard. 'I'm just looking for something.'

'Miss Green! Miss Green!'

'I told you, I'll be there in a minute,' Alex replied, handing Tommy a mountain of cotton wool balls.

'But Miss Green, there's a man outside staring at you! Who is he? Is he your boyfriend?' Maddy giggled cheekily.

Alex immediately swung around. 'What? What man?' she asked, hastening towards the window. She half-expected to see Sam standing there, but the playground was empty. 'There's no one there,' she said, managing to hide her relief as she slammed the window shut and stared through the glass warily. 'Now don't be silly, Maddy. Just get on with making your flower.'

'Well, he was there!' Maddy persisted. By now the rest of the class had abandoned their glue sticks and paint brushes, and were crowding around the window, to take a peek themselves, amidst cries of 'Where? Where?'

'Now calm down everybody!' Alex called out. 'Back to your places at once! Right then, who needs more glue? Here you are Nathan, will you finish that tree off for me? Good boy.'

With the class settled, Alex took a seat next to Maddy, whose hands were now caked with PVA and strips of pink tissue paper. 'So, Maddy…what did he look like, this man you saw?' she probed gently.

Without even looking up at her teacher, Maddy answered casually: 'A bit fuzzy.'

'Well, maybe that's because you're not wearing your glasses. Again! Can you tell me anything about him, Honey?' Alex coaxed. 'Was he about my age?'

Maddy thought for a moment. 'Yes…he was old, just like you.'

Alex took a deep breath. 'And what colour was his hair? Was it fair like yours? Or dark like mine?'

With a mischievous chuckle, the little girl replied: 'Nooo…it was…GREEN! Like a space monster!' And with that, she scurried off to the playhouse.

Doing her best to hide her frustration, Alex peered through the small window into the make-believe kitchen, where Maddy and Conor were now playing with a toy tea-set. 'Come on, you didn't really see anybody did you?'

'I did!' Maddy replied indignantly as she poured imaginary

71

tea from the plastic teapot.

'So what did he look like, then?' Alex asked, doing her best to remain calm.

'It was just a man...' came the nonchalant reply. '... but he was smiling at you.'

Alex knew she shouldn't interrogate the child any further – she didn't want to frighten her and, moreover, she didn't want the little girl to pick up on her distress. But if what Maddy was saying were true, it could only have been one person: Sam. And any sympathy Alex had harboured for him was now replaced by anger. He'd gone too far this time. Enough was enough. She was relieved when the bell sounded for lunch.

'How dare you! How dare you come to the school?' she screamed angrily into her mobile phone. 'What the hell are you playing at, Sam? I told you it's over; just leave me alone! Just stay away from me, you hear?'

Trembling, Alex hung up, not giving Sam the opportunity to speak or defend himself. He was defenceless, in her eyes. He didn't deserve the right to reply. But as she rinsed the paint palettes and brushes under the tap, the possibility that Sam might be out there, waiting for her, began to fill her with dread.

When the school day was over, Alex walked across the school car park, her eyes searching for any sign of Sam. Feigning self-assurance, she undid the padlock on her bike then walked with it slowly, head held high, until she reached the kerb. And then she pedalled as fast as she could, darting through traffic and swerving past pedestrians, until she finally reached Montpelier Crescent. But she wouldn't feel safe until she was inside the house, complete with its new security locks and alarm system. Hardly able to breathe, not daring to look behind her, Alex scrambled into the refuge of her home, where the telephone was ringing.

'Hello!' she gasped.

'It's me, Sam.'

'Where the hell are you? What do you want? You followed

me, didn't you?' she shrieked.

'Hey, calm down, Al.'

'Don't you tell me to calm down! Where are you?'

'I'm in the office, of course. I'm in London.'

'I don't believe you! You're here, in Brighton, you came to the school, didn't you!'

'Now for Christ's sake, Al, stop and listen to me!' Sam bellowed. 'When you called earlier I was in the middle of a meeting. I have no idea what this is all about, but I've been here in London all day long. If you don't believe me, you can ask Gary or Pete Jackson. They're here, too.'

Alex closed her eyes, assimilating Sam's words.

'Look, I know I've behaved badly recently, and I shouldn't have left all those messages the other night. I know it was out of order, I'm sorry, I was pissed. But I would NEVER follow you to school, if that's what you think...'

'Sam, I don't know what to think any more. So much has been going on,' Alex replied. She felt as though she might pass out. 'Look, I'm gonna have to go now, but I'm sorry. I'm really sorry.'

In the kitchen, Alex poured herself a large glass of water and knocked back a concoction of pills. She must have been crazy to suspect Sam of stalking her, she told herself. But if it wasn't Sam, who the hell was it? she wondered, tapping a number into the telephone handset.

'Hi, Pamela, it's Alex. Listen, I thought I'd better let you know that one of the kids said she saw a man lurking around in the playground outside the classroom this morning... Yes, it would have been about eleven o'clock...I'm sorry I didn't say anything earlier, I thought it was a friend of mine, but turns out it wasn't him. I just thought you should know...yes, okay, Pamela. Thanks a lot...bye.'

Just at that moment, the doorbell rang. Alex froze. It rang again, and then a thud hit the doorstep. Legs like jelly, she crept over to the window and peered nervously from behind the curtain. It was only the postman, now winding his way back down the path. With a grateful sigh of relief, Alex opened the front door where a small parcel lay on the doormat. She picked it up and smiled, instantly recognising her mother's ornate handwriting. In a rush of excitement she tore open the package to uncover a small cardboard box. She lifted the lid and amongst layers of delicate tissue paper lay a small, slim rectangular case made of gold filigree. Alex knew what was inside the precious container – a tiny scroll of parchment handwritten in Hebrew with words from the Old Testament. A mezuzah. Alex read the note that was packed alongside it:

Darling Alex, Mazel Tov! Congratulations on your new home. May this mezuzah bring you divine guidance, love and laughter, comfort and protection. Be sure to follow the instructions and fit it properly. Love, Mom and Dad.

'Well, you never know. This could be exactly what I need,' she muttered, immediately taking the house-warming gift, complete with fixings, outside to the front door. And, just as instructed by Jewish custom, she held the mezuzah in position – up on the right-hand side of the door frame, slightly pointing inwards at just about shoulder height. But before fixing it permanently in its place, Alex whispered the solemn Hebrew blessing, the same words she'd heard her mother recite back home: 'Baruch Ata Adonoy, Elo-heinu Melech Ha'olam, asher kid'shanu bi'mitzvo-sav, vi'tzivanu leek-bo-a mezuzah.'

Without delay, using the tiny tool provided, Alex turned the screws at both top and bottom of the mezuzah until the glinting golden case was firmly held on the wooden doorframe. She stood back to admire her handiwork.

'Not bad,' she congratulated herself, and found to her surprise that the mere presence of this small piece of tradition fixed to the outside of her home was deeply reassuring. She remembered her socialist, atheist university days when she'd considered her family's mezuzah to be nothing but an empty label of their religion. And now, here she was, happily displaying a mezuzah of her own and taking grateful comfort from the promises of protection held within.

'You've reached the voice-mail for Alex Green. Sorry I'm not here to take your call, but please leave a message after the tone, and I'll get right back to you.'

Beep.

'Oh, hello, Alex. This is Pamela. I just wanted to let you know that we've had a look at this morning's CCTV footage, and there's no sign of anyone hanging around the school grounds at that time at all. Just the little darlings' fertile imagination running riot again, I should think. Anyway, nothing to worry about. See you at school.'

Beep.

Thirteen

One of the features of the new house that had initially appealed to Alex when the obsequious estate agent had first shown her around was the 'rear elevation' as he had called it. The moment she had seen the vast, empty room drenched in daylight from the floor to ceiling French windows overlooking the garden, she knew it would provide her with the perfect studio, where she would be able to indulge her recent passion – painting.

She'd hardly set foot in the room since moving in, except to stash several packing boxes safely out of sight. But this Saturday morning, all that was about to change. Alex had decided to put all negative thoughts out of her over-active mind. A spot of creativity – and something decidedly more challenging than potato-printing – would do her the world of good. She opened the French windows, inviting the fresh air into the room, and immediately began unpacking the equipment she would need.

A large, clean canvas stared at her expectantly. It had been weeks since she'd managed to find the time or the inclination to put bristle to paint, but now, sketching out her composition with sweeping, feather-light pencil strokes, Alex felt a charge of electricity at her fingertips, guiding her hand. Aquamarine. Cyan. Azure. So many shades of blue. As the watercolours gushed from her paintbrush Alex brimmed with exhilaration, channeling all of her energies into the image that, almost with a life of its own, seemed to be taking shape so swiftly.

It could have taken minutes. It could have taken hours.

Alex had lost all sense of time. But before her on the finished canvas, a landscape of seven vast chalk cliffs perched on a shoreline, waves crashing magnificently at their feet. As she stood, exhausted, gazing at the picture of the swirling, surging ocean, her mind flashed back to the 'Guiding Light', the little craft dipping on the waves of the marina. The memory seemed to make her heart beat faster. It thumped inside her head, pounding louder and louder, so loud it seemed to echo about the room. Alex inhaled deeply. Then turned icy-cold.

'Cigarettes,' she gasped. This time the smell of tobacco was so overwhelmingly close. But how could it be, when there was no one else there? She could sense the smoke coiling, gathering around her. But she wasn't afraid. It was as though she were being caressed, wrapped in a warm embrace, and she felt extraordinarily tranquil.

Then out of nowhere a strange mist seemed to float across the room, like a cloud of shimmering vapour, like nothing she'd ever seen before. Alex watched as it drifted before her and then hovered within arm's reach.

'What's going on?' she whispered. The translucent apparition slowly faded and Alex watched, mesmerised as, in its place, rained a torrent of tiny flickering white lights, like snowflakes, pouring down at a dizzying pace, making her eyes sting. Gradually the illuminations evaporated into nothing, leaving only a sharp chill hanging in the air, so cold Alex shivered.

'Who are you?' she murmured, now convinced that someone or something was there, in the room, with her. But her words were met with silence. Suddenly she was overwhelmed by the feeling of wind lashing at her face, taking her breath away. The ground seemed to move beneath her feet, as though she were sailing a sea-tossed boat. She grabbed the wooden frame of the easel to regain her balance, then the sensation instantly vanished. At once the jar of water that sat by her paints flew across the room, splattering the white-washed walls with a sea-spray of blue. Instantly the chill that had filled the room lifted. It was as though a bubble had burst. And Alex knew that, once again, she was alone.

She sat in the stillness, trying to make sense of the baffling experience. There could only be one explanation now for what was going on, for all the strange things that had happened to her. And the more she thought about the possibility that she was being haunted, the more likely it seemed. She desperately needed to clear her head and, hearing the seagulls' cries outside, knew there was one place she had to go.

Walking along the now-familiar streets, Alex found it hard to believe that she didn't feel afraid. Her head filled not with fear, but with bewilderment as she tried to piece together the many peculiar events that had taken place since she'd moved to Brighton. She knew, deep down, that they were all connected, she just didn't know how. Or why.

She could hear the bell-like clang of rope against mast again; feel the goose-bumps begin to prickle beneath her clothes. Since the night she was lost at the marina, Alex had managed to defy its inexplicable, magnetic pull; but now she knew that she should resist no longer, and she followed the path down to the waterside. Around the bend, and there was the marina. At first she was almost blinded by the brilliant reflection of the sun's rays on the rows of countless white boats moored there on this bright spring afternoon. She drifted past boat after boat, and wandered along the boardwalk towards the East Jetty. And then, looking across the array of moored vessels, she saw the little blue boat.

'Lost again, are we?' a voice called out. It was the old man she'd met there before, this time on-board and busy sweeping down the deck of the 'Guiding Light'.

'Oh! Hi,' Alex answered vaguely.

'Can't seem to keep away! Is it my good looks or this little beauty you've come to see?' he jested, his sky-grey eyes twinkling playfully.

'Er, the boat, I guess,' she murmured.

'I'm just about to take her out – just a short trip around the bay. The owners have asked me to keep her ticking over. Want to come along?'

Alex didn't hesitate. 'Thanks, yes, I'd love to,' she heard herself reply, and made her way down to the pontoon, where she took the fisherman's weather-beaten hand and stepped onto the boat.

While he prepared to set sail, Alex instinctively followed a narrow staircase leading down to the galley below. It was dark; the little portholes only allowed a small amount of light to filter in, but once Alex's eyes had adjusted, she could see that the cabin was strewn with belongings. A crate of empty beer bottles lurked in the tiny kitchenette; old cigarette ends sat stubbed in a dirty ashtray and a cluster of fishing rods lay on the floor, each carefully labeled with the name 'Finnegan'. Far from feeling like a prying intruder, invading some stranger's private property, the slightly oppressive, musty atmosphere was somehow familiar. Without thinking, Alex eased into a hammock that was strung across the far end of the cluttered den. She closed her eyes and inhaled the pungent tang of wood polish and stale tobacco. The deep rumble of the boat's engine was hypnotic, almost lulling her into a trance, emptying her mind of all concerns and simply leaving her with a sense of peace.

'You all right down there?'

A wave of diesel fumes and the old man's shout suddenly shattered Alex's tranquility. For a moment, she didn't quite know where she was but, rubbing her eyes, she quickly came to, and so took the stairs up to the deck.

The marina was already just a scribble on the horizon as 'Guiding Light' carved swiftly through the opaque waters. Alex stood alongside the old man who steered the boat further and further out to sea. The billowing wind snatched her breath and briefly carried away her troubles. The gulls seemed to call her name and Alex realised that she'd never in her whole life experienced such peace. As they sailed around the coastline now, her eyes scanned the faraway landscape; the myriad buildings painted golden in the afternoon sunshine gave way to glorious swathes of green. And then beyond, a huge white escarpment, stretched out like angels' wings, spread, skimming the ocean. Alex gasped, suddenly recognising the spectacular scene.

'Ah, yes, The Seven Sisters chalk cliffs,' her companion answered, without needing to be asked. 'Arguably the most beautiful view in the whole of England. They almost reach up to heaven, don't they? Been here before?'

'Never,' Alex said, shaking her head slowly. This was all so surreal, like some kind of dream. 'Never.'

The old man gave her a quizzical look. 'Anyway, better be heading back now,' he announced, swiftly swinging 'Guiding Light' into a u-turn. 'Don't want to be late for my tea.'

Alex shivered as they sped home, the sharp ocean breeze slapping her into consciousness. She frisked her memory for some deep-buried recollection of that vast range of cliffs, the very vision that she had recreated on canvas that morning. But there was nothing.

Meandering wearily through the Brighton streets, Alex's cheeks stung from their sea-bound battering. She had hoped to find clarity, but instead her mind was left foggy, churning with so many emotions and questions that she could not answer. And there was certainly no one she could talk to about the things that had been happening lately and the way she was feeling now. Her friends back home would think she was cracking up, while her mother would simply jump on the first London-bound plane out of JFK. And Alex was not in the right frame of mind to handle a visit just yet.

No, she would have to figure this one out all on her own, she pondered, gazing casually into a nearby shop window. The warm fragrance of sandalwood and neroli drifted through the open door, enticing Alex inside, where a pony-tailed man sat elf-like behind the till and smiled at her welcomingly. She drifted between the shelves almost groaning under huge hunks of semi-precious stone: amethyst, agate and rose quartz. A rainbow of dream-catchers hung from the low ceiling and a posse of giggling teenagers huddled around a display of books on tarot and sorcery.

Not really sure why she was there at all, Alex turned to leave, but a noticeboard at the door caught her eye. Amongst the various hand-written ads for yoga and meditation classes, one small poster grabbed her attention:

All are welcome to
'An Evening of the Paranormal'
with guest speaker
Dr. Rosalind Starke
at The Beacon, Border Passage, Brighton
Saturday May 12th, 7pm

'Help yourself to a flyer,' called out the elf. 'There's a pile just there.'

'Oh, right, thanks,' Alex replied self-consciously. And, stuffing one of the photocopied invitations into her pocket, she finally made her retreat.

Fourteen

Twenty weeks. Twenty-one centimetres.

Jessica looked like a naughty schoolgirl hiding a secret as she floated along the corridor towards Pathology, a grin unknowingly fixed to her face. Since catching sight of her baby on the screen during her ultrasound scan that morning, she'd been engulfed by euphoria, unable to concentrate on her job properly and with the image of the foetus, thumb in mouth, etched firmly on her mind. Glancing down, and pushing out her little bump, she wanted everyone else to share her secret. But then her smile faded, as her mind drifted back to Finn. Again. As it had done all too frequently. He was the only one who wouldn't know.

Over the past weeks, it had seemed that the more Jessica had come to terms with the pregnancy herself, the more she'd been pricked at by her conscious to tell him. She'd spent hours contemplating whether she had the right to deliberately deprive the man of his own child. And then, on the other hand, whether she had the right to deliberately deprive her child of a father. She'd thrown all arguments into the equation, including the concept of 'what you've never had, you'll never miss'. Indeed, she herself had experienced a wonderfully happy childhood without a father. Finally, after much deliberation and soul-searching, Jessica had come to the decision that she needed to free herself of the burden that had been weighing her down. So after allowing herself a few swigs of wine one evening, she'd bolstered up her courage enough to dial the number still logged in her phone, the number she'd dared herself to dial all those months ago, when there had been no response. But the same impassive voice had answered back: 'This number is currently unavailable.'

Jessica had even forced herself to return to the flat where she'd originally met Finn at the party, hoping that someone there would know of his whereabouts. But a family of four had recently moved into the second-floor apartment owned by the Housing Association, and there was no record at all of the previous occupier's new address. In despair Jessica had signed up to several social networking websites in an attempt to track Sarah down, or to find someone else from school who might still know her, but to no avail.

Eventually, all things considered, she had reached the painful conclusion that moving on without Finn in the picture was probably for the best. Why unnecessarily complicate the life of a guy who quite clearly wanted nothing to do with his baby's mother anyway?

Shaking off the gloom, Jessica guided her thoughts back to the here and now; back to the image of her precious little infant in vitro, and sauntered contentedly to the desk at Pathology, handing over several vials of blood.

'Hiya. These are from G3,' she said cheerily. 'We need the results ASAP, apparently.'

'Okay, Jess,' the receptionist replied, noticing that the nurse had a sparkle about her that she hadn't seen in a long while. 'Have you changed your hair or something? You look really great today.'

Naturally Jessica was flattered by the compliment from her colleague, but instead of a characteristic sharp-witted response to hide her embarrassment, she simply uttered a humble: 'Oh, thanks, Sue. No, nothing's changed!' and turned to head back to the ward.

As she spun round, she immediately collided with a woman walking towards her. 'Sorry!' they both yelped in unison.

'Oh hi!' Jessica exclaimed, recognising the dark-haired woman with the American accent.

'Jessica! I didn't know you were a nurse,' Alex smiled. 'How are you now?'

'Much better, thanks,' Jessica replied. 'What are you doing here?'

'Just came for a routine blood test, that's all,' Alex answered easily.

Jessica tapped Alex's arm fondly. 'Listen, thanks again for looking after me the other week. I really appreciate it…hey, I don't know if you're free, but I'm on my tea-break in five minutes. Fancy joining me?'

'Sure. Sounds good,' Alex grinned.

The hospital cafeteria was a sea of blue and white as the doctors and nurses took temporary reprieve from their stress-filled day. A strange calm pervaded the room, with the gentle hum of their muted voices amid the clinking of cutlery. Jessica carried over two teas, a flapjack and a cream cake to the table, where Alex was sitting waiting.

'There we are: healthy oatcake for you, and cream bun for me,' she announced, placing the tray on the table. 'I've always had a lot of flesh on me,' she laughed. 'And I'm not intending to go on a diet now – not when there's two of us to feed!'

Alex smiled. 'Are you planning on going back to work when the baby's born?' she asked.

'Yes, definitely. I have to. I'm on my own, you see, so I haven't got much choice. Just got to sort out child-care. Anyway, how about you? What do you do?'

'Well, I only work part-time. Sold my house in London and made quite a profit, so I'm not rushing to get back to nine to five. I'm just helping out with arts and crafts at a local school,' Alex replied. 'It's a complete change of direction for me – this time last year I wouldn't have dreamed of even picking up a paintbrush!'

'What did you do before?'

'I used to work in advertising – I was a writer, first for an ad agency back home in New York, then in London.'

'That sounds glamorous,' remarked Jessica, putting rather too much cake in her mouth at once.

Alex shrugged: 'Not really. Just lots of stress and long hours. Don't get me wrong, I loved it, but last year I had to take sick leave, and then I was offered voluntary redundancy. It was the perfect opportunity to get out of the rat-race. So here I am!'

'But why Brighton?' Jessica asked, wiping cream from her lips.

'It's funny, really, the job just kinda fell into my lap and when I came down here to visit, it felt right, somehow. I just felt really...at home.' Alex's words faded as her face paled.

Jessica sensed that something was troubling her. 'So have you settled in well? It's a beautiful house.'

'Yeah, I love the place, I really do...but, oh, I dunno,' Alex murmured, nervously picking at her flapjack.

'What?' Jessica asked. 'What is it?'

The American sighed. 'Well you're going to think I'm crazy, but some really weird things have been happening.'

'Like what?'

'Well, like lights flashing, things moving, stuff like that.'

'Sounds like you need more than your blood testing,' Jessica laughed.

'Yeah, I know...I never thought I'd say anything like this, but I'm beginning to wonder whether my place is haunted.'

'You're not serious! You don't believe in all that crap, do you?'

'No, I don't...well, I didn't...oh, I don't know.'

' There's got to be some other explanation.'

'Like what?' Alex answered.

'Mice? Rats? Squirrels in the attic?'

Alex shook her head. 'Believe me, I've thought of everything.'

'So what are you going to do about it?' Jessica asked with a smirk.

Alex hesitated. 'Well... the other day I picked up a leaflet about some kind of talk on the paranormal that's happening next week and...'

'The paranormal?' Jessica interrupted disdainfully.

'Yeah, not far from where I live, so I was thinking I might go along...'

Jessica raised an eyebrow, then checked her watch. 'Damn. I've got to get back to the ward.'

'...It's not that I'm scared, or anything, but maybe they'll be able to give me some answers.'

'Oh well, good luck!' Jessica said, getting up to leave while devouring the final remains of her bun.

Alex swallowed her pride while she had the chance. 'I don't suppose you'd come with me, would you?' she asked tentatively. 'I don't really feel like going on my own and I don't know who else to ask. But of course if you're busy, don't worry, I quite understand...'

'Well, erm...' Jessica stalled, frantically trying to think of an excuse. But in the end she decided that honesty was the best policy. 'Oh, sorry Alex, but no. I really hope you get some answers, but it's not really my thing. I don't believe in ghosts.'

It was almost seven o'clock when Jessica finally left work that evening, exhausted after what had seemed to be an unusually long day. Walking towards the bus stop, her legs felt weak, her head ached and she reminded herself that she should drink more water in her condition. In fact, she hadn't had anything to drink at all since her tea break earlier that afternoon. Since she'd bumped into Alex. Alex, the kind American who'd taken her in when she'd collapsed. Heat rose to her cheeks and a small, shameful voice inside tried to be heard, but it was forcefully dismissed. Jessica was far too tired to be of help to anyone else now and, anyway, she had enough on her plate.

At last she reached the corner of the street, just in time to see the back of her bus disappear out of view, into the half-light. She sighed. Taxis were an indulgence, but this evening it didn't matter and so she made her way along the street towards the taxi rank.

Trudging past a little row of shops, most locked up for the night, Jessica stopped abruptly outside one: Petit Enfant. Low lighting illuminated the window display, a carnival of designer strollers, cots, toys and soft furnishings. Jessica pressed her nose up against the glass and peered in through the window. In childlike wonderment she marvelled at every exquisite item of clothing, every handcrafted ornament and play-thing, including a highly-polished wooden rocking horse, with a real leather bridle and saddle, rocking ever so gently backwards and forwards. £999. Jessica scanned the other goods: a three-wheeled buggy for £400; a wicker crib for £150; a musical mobile, its dangling stars and moons bobbing up and down, for a mere £99. Everything was so expensive. Suddenly all the excitement she'd felt on seeing her baby on screen that morning evaporated, replaced instead by the realisation that she would never be able to give her own baby a cosy nursery with a top-of-the-range crib and dancing mobile. In fact, she didn't know how she was going to afford even the most basic necessities for her child.

Jessica's eyes were drawn to a double photo frame with two empty spaces behind the glass, edged with colourful teddy bears and balloons. In her mind's eye though, all she saw staring back at her were the faces of Linda and Finn. They had both, in their different ways, lost the chance to love her baby; they would both be sorely missing from its life. And hers. She cast her mind back to Finn. With his wide smile, deep green eyes and blond hair, he had looked just like an angel to her. An angel, he clearly wasn't but Jessica quietly hoped that one day their paths would cross again. She bit her bottom lip and fought back the tears. How would she manage on her own? Jessica felt little more than a child herself. Closing her eyes for a second, she longed for her mother and the unconditional love that had always made her feel so safe.

Allowing herself to face the reality of her loss like this was too painful, so Jessica turned around and paced briskly towards the taxi rank, where a small queue of office workers had formed. She guessed that they all worked together, confident and happy young men and women, laughing, flirting and exchanging office gossip while they waited for their taxis home. She felt conspicuous in her solitude. And so lonely. Then she remembered Alex. Why had she been so selfish, so oblivious to Alex's feelings earlier today?

Climbing into a taxi, she tried to be pleasant to the driver, though making small-talk was the last thing that would lift her mood. Grinning at her from his rear-view mirror, he assaulted her with a barrage of questions: 'Am I right in thinking you're a nurse, love?'; 'What do you make of the NHS cutbacks then?'; 'Bet you get paid a pittance, don't you, love?'; 'Got anything nice planned for the weekend?'. Politely, though briefly, Jessica answered all but the last of his questions, and instead shook her head in response. For this coming weekend, just like every other weekend, she would be in her flat alone with just the TV for company. She had nothing 'nice' planned at all. And yet, Jessica thought with another pang of guilt, she had blithely turned down the opportunity for some company on Saturday evening. It may not have been her idea of a great night out, but then, what was? Jessica was beginning to realise that she was her own worst enemy. For Alex had offered her the hand of friendship and, more importantly, she had asked for her help.

Suddenly Jessica knew what had to be done.

'I'm sorry but could we turn round, please?'

The driver looked confused.

'I've just remembered that I need to go to Montpelier Crescent instead.'

Fifteen

The Beacon was just a small, insignificant-looking old building hidden along a dark alleyway called Border Passage. The chipped front door opened into a quaint, musty hall, adorned with flickering candles and vases full of faded artificial flowers perched on every available surface. A keyboard stood in the corner. At the head of the room, a pair of heavy golden drapes provided an incongruous, rather theatrical backdrop for the small platform, where only a lectern and a pair of uncomfortable-looking chairs were positioned. And at the back of the room, was another table, crowded high with bric-a-brac – books with yellowed pages, chipped ornaments and once-loved cuddly toys.

When Jessica and Alex arrived, there were at least twenty or so visitors seated on rows of plastic chairs, most of them in their twilight years and obviously regulars at the little meeting house. Almost like being back on the ward, Jessica thought to herself wryly.

Spotting two empty seats at the back, Jessica and Alex edged their way past an excited gaggle of blue-rinses and sat down in the corner.

'So what do you reckon's going to happen tonight, then?' Jessica asked, turning her nose up at the vases of synthetic chrysanthemums and paintings of Red Indian chiefs adorning the room.

'I'm not sure, really. I just hope someone will be able to help me. I guess it's some sort of lecture about the paranormal, ghosts, spirits, things like that.'

'Well, I could do with some spirits right now,' Jessica smirked. '…Like a large rum and Coke.'

The two women giggled quietly.

'Hey, Jessica, I know you've probably got better things to do on a Saturday evening, but…thanks, thanks so much for agreeing to come with me tonight. I really appreciate it.'

'Oh, it's nothing!' Jessica said. 'Anyway, I couldn't miss out on the opportunity to buy a lovely crocheted toilet roll cover, now, could I?' she teased, pointing to the array of bric-a-brac nearby. Displayed amongst the gaudy figurines and willow-patterned crockery was a hand-written sign: BRING AND BUY IN AID OF MUCH-NEEDED FUNDS FOR A NEW ROOF.

'…And a spice rack! Why is there always a spice rack at every second-hand stall?'

'It must be a British thing,' Alex smiled, not really knowing what Jessica was talking about. 'Maybe we should make a contribution, though,' she added, scanning the table top for something to buy.

She flicked through a collection of CDs: dusty and slightly sticky; mostly albums by long-forgotten Eighties bands or singers she'd never heard of. Suddenly, one of them slipped between Alex's fingers, and clattered onto the floor, its plastic case snapping in two. 'Shit!' she hissed, bending down to pick it up. The opening chords of a song signalled that proceedings were under way. 'I'd better take this, then,' she muttered, before dropping a couple of pound coins into the collection box and hurriedly pushing the CD into her handbag.

The small gathering stood to sing. Discordant, wavering voices rang out with the sombre lyrics to what Jessica thought sounded like a funeral hymn. She nudged Alex in the ribs and nodded towards the organist – a frail-looking elderly lady wearing ill-fitting spectacles and a pained expression, who was readjusting her hearing aid with one hand while creating musical havoc with the other. Jessica clenched her jaw, struggling to hold back her laughter.

With the last, excruciating notes of the song, everyone sat down and an elderly lady wearing a powder pink two-piece took to the platform. She stood behind the lectern and with a deep breath, began to address the group.

'Good evening friends, and welcome. As most of you know, I am Mary Watkins, the President of our little church, The Beacon, and I'd like to welcome you all here this evening. Now I'm sure everyone was looking forward to our special talk on the fascinating subject of the paranormal, and hearing the experiences of our invited speaker, Dr. Rosalind Starke. Unfortunately, however, due to unforeseen circumstances, she cannot be with us tonight. But she sends her sincere apologies and promises to visit us some time in the near future...'

Alex couldn't help but tut with disappointment. It certainly didn't look as though she was going to get any answers tonight, after all.

'...However, ladies and gentleman, I'm pleased to invite onto the platform one of our very own members, spiritual medium Ernie Lambert, who has kindly offered to step in at very short notice, and with no preparation, to give us an evening of clairvoyance instead...'

As the congregation clapped appreciatively, Jessica groaned and rolled her eyes.

'...Send him your love,' Mary Watkins continued, 'so that he may be able to link up with those in spirit and bring you their messages of love and reassurance.'

A stooping, frail old man with trembling hands, got up onto the podium with the help of his walking stick and cleared his throat. 'Hello, everyone,' he stammered. 'Before I start, I'd like you to bow your heads in prayer, and send thoughts to anyone you know who's in need...'

Jessica and Alex bowed their heads and exchanged bemused glances.

'...Great Spirit, we ask you to shine your light on all those who are suffering around the world,' Ernie implored. 'To bring peace wherever there is discord...and to protect our friends in the animal kingdom. We ask that this service be in your safekeeping and that all that is said and done here tonight be in truth and love and light. Amen.'

Ernie took a sip of water and cleared his throat again. 'Right, then,' he began. 'I'm being drawn to a gentleman sitting in the front row, wearing the green shirt.'

A man fitting the description smiled eagerly.

'...I have a lady here with grey hair, can you accept that?' Ernie asked.

The man shrugged. 'Er, possibly.'

'Well, she's saying she's your grandmother, do you understand this?'

'Both my grandmothers are still alive,' came the flat reply.

'It must be a great-grandmother, then,' Ernie persisted. 'Anyway, she's showing me a cat. It must have been important to you at some stage.'

'Actually I'm allergic to cats.'

'Ah, that must be it then, that's what your great-grandmother's trying to say.'

Jessica didn't dare look at Alex, knowing that if their eyes met she would be unable to contain her laughter any longer.

'She's telling me she had trouble breathing towards the end,' Ernie continued. 'And she's saying that she left some jewellery for a member of your family. Does this make sense?'

'I'm sorry, not really. I didn't know my great-grandmother.' The man in the green shirt was clearly unimpressed.

'Well, remember what I've said and ask around the family...God bless you, I'll move on now...'

As the old man squinted, looking around the room in search of his next target, Jessica shrank into her seat so as to avoid his gaze.

'I'd like to come to the lady over there in the flowered blouse,' he said, pointing to a woman seated next to Alex.

'Oh, hello,' she called out nervously.

'I can see the number sixty-two. This must be significant to you.'

'Sixty-two?' The lady looked puzzled.

'What about twenty-six? Is your house number twenty-six?'

'Er, no, it isn't,' she answered blankly.

'Well, is it number two?.. Or six?'

The lady shook her head slowly.

'Well somebody you know or you yourself will be moving to a house where either of those numbers appear on the door…'

Jessica looked up at the clock on the wall. 7.50pm. She wasn't sure how much more of this she could endure.

By 8.30, the whole congregation was fidgeting and squirming in their seats. And despite battling on like the old soldier that he was, it became clear that Ernie's many attempts at communication with 'the other side' were defeating him and failing to satisfy his audience.

'…and before I go, she's just telling me that you're very tired at the moment, but you'll be going on holiday and this will be an opportunity to recharge your batteries. All right, dear?'

Ernie waited for a reaction from an old lady in the fifth row, who was snoring quietly. Her companion roused her with a sharp nudge and she looked up, dazed and blinking, unaware of anything that Ernie had said to her.

'Thank you so much, Ernie,' Mary Watkins announced, taking the opportunity to intervene. She sprang to the podium from her front-row seat. 'I'm afraid we've run out of time now, but you've certainly given us plenty to think about this evening. Now, before we go, let's join together in singing a closing song. Thank you Jean.' She smiled and nodded at the organist who, taking her cue, grimaced and tweaked her hearing aid again before playing the opening chords of Amazing Grace.

Jessica winked at Alex and the pair sidled hastily out of the building and tumbled into the darkness.

'Oh, my God, that was so painful!' giggled Jessica, like a truant schoolgirl. 'I thought we'd never get out!'

'Oh, Jess, Honey, I'm so sorry for dragging you along. What a complete waste of time. You must have hated every minute.'

'Don't be silly,' Jessica replied generously. 'I thought it was hilarious, especially when that old dear started snoring!'

The pair burst out laughing, the climactic release of the evening's countless stifled sniggers. And as they tottered back up the alleyway towards the car, it felt like the most natural thing in the world for Jessica to link arms with her new-found friend.

'And what about poor old Ernie?' she continued. 'He just couldn't get a thing right, could he? I reckon I could have done a better job of contacting the dead than him!'

Just then a woman's voice called out from the darkness behind them. 'Excuse me!'

Jessica and Alex turned to see a woman hurrying after them. 'Excuse me!'

'Oops,' hissed Jessica. 'We've been rumbled!'

'I'm, er, sorry we had to leave.' said Alex, frantically trying to conjure up an excuse for their premature departure.

'No, no, dear, don't worry about that. I know, it wasn't one of our best nights - mediums have good days and bad days. You should think about coming to the Sunday morning service for a proper demonstration,' the woman panted as she caught up with them and wiped the sweat from her brow with a chubby hand. 'I don't want to hold you up, but I just had to speak to you. Can you spare a minute?'

Jessica and Alex looked at one another. There was an urgency in the woman's voice that made it hard to refuse.

'Okay, sure,' Alex replied tentatively.

'Oh dear, it's starting to rain.' The woman looked up at the starless sky. 'Where shall we go? I really do need to talk to you.'

'Well, we could go and sit in my car?' Alex suggested. 'It's just around the corner.'

The woman squeezed her rather large frame into the passenger seat; Alex sat behind the wheel while Jessica climbed in the back. By now fat, round raindrops were plopping onto the windows with a juicy thud.

'Right, well, I have to tell you that all evening I've had a young man from the spirit world with me,' the woman began, still a little breathless. 'And he was adamant that I should speak to you. Can I just ask, first of all, are you sisters?'

'No,' replied Jessica dismissively. Her stomach was rumbling and she was in no mood for more time-wasters.

'Really?' The woman seemed surprised. 'Well, there's a very strong link between you two. Anyway, I'm not sure which of you this message is for...' she continued hesitantly, then turning to Alex she added: 'I feel it's for you, dear. This young man has wanted to get through to you for some time. He's very anxious, poor soul.'

The woman seemed increasingly agitated, then spoke as if to another, unseen passenger in the car. 'Yes, yes...I'll tell her...he's saying you have a connection with him, you both do.'

Jessica shook her head. 'Doesn't mean anything to me,' she sighed, drawing doodles with her fingertip in the condensation on the window.

'Come on, come on...yes... yes... okay, I'll tell her.' The woman muttered to someone, somewhere, before announcing to Alex: 'He's been trying so hard to contact you, dear. Have you been aware of a presence? Have you felt someone around you?'

'Maybe...' Alex was suddenly intrigued.

'He says there've been times when you've been frightened, dear. He didn't mean to scare you, but he so wanted to get through. Can you accept that?'

'Yes, yes I can,' Alex murmured.

'Well, he's so pleased that you both came along tonight, there's such a lovely vibration here for both of you.'

Jessica shifted uncomfortably in her seat and looked at her watch. There was still time to make it to the Bengal Brasserie.

'Now, he's saying there's someone you know who's very unhappy. A woman. This young man wants you to give her a message…he says she mustn't blame herself. You must tell her that. Do you know who this lady is?'

'No, I don't think so,' Alex replied. Her mind had gone blank.

'Well, he's tried to get through to her, too. But she's not as receptive as you are…come on, come on love, give me a name…Anne? Annie? He's saying a name… sounds like Annie.'

Alex's heart sank. 'No, I don't know anyone called Annie.'

'Well, you'll have to ask around,' the woman said adamantly. 'Anyway, this person is going to need your help.'

Jessica tutted impatiently in the back of the car.

The woman turned to look at her, then paused for a moment. 'There's a lot of love for you here, too, you know?' she said thoughtfully. 'And now I'm feeling a very strong maternal vibration. Is your mother in spirit?'

Jessica didn't reply; her eyes fixed, unflinching, on the misty window.

'I sense she passed fairly recently and she's here with us now. She's saying everything will be all right. Don't worry…'

Jessica's chest tightened; she could barely breathe, but stubborn as ever, she refused to respond.

'…Don't worry about the future. She is with you all the time, and she's reaching out and putting her arms around you now. She says she'll always be with you… you'll always be her little girl.'

As raindrops streaked down the windowpane, casting shadows that danced across Jessica's paralysed face, it was impossible to distinguish between the rain and the tears trickling down her cheek.

Sixteen

After the woman had gone, Jessica sat quietly in the back of the car, still staring through the steamy wet glass while Alex started the engine without a word. Each locked in their own thoughts, they individually dissected the bizarre conversation that had just taken place.

At last Alex broke the silence. 'I think I feel a little freaked out.'

'Don't be silly!' Jessica replied, rather too forcefully. 'She was talking a load of bollocks.'

'But that woman described everything that's been going on!' Alex's fearful eyes gaped anxiously at Jessica in the mirror. 'I mean, you tell me, how could she possibly know about a presence in my house? How could she know I can feel someone there?'

Alex waited for some caustic response. But nothing. Instead she saw Jessica's head bowed in her hands. 'Jessica, are you okay, Honey?'

Alex pulled over and turned the engine off.

'Are you all right, Jessica?' she asked, remembering the words about her friend's mother. She leant around and took hold of Jessica's hand. 'You didn't tell me your mom had died.'

'I'm okay,' she sniffed. 'She died just over a year ago.'

Alex handed her a crumpled tissue from her pocket.

'Thanks,' Jessica said, blowing her nose.

'How are you feeling, after what that woman said to you?'

Alex asked hesitantly.

'I don't really know what I feel...' Jessica replied shaking her head slowly. '...but I'm not convinced...I've never believed in this sort of stuff.'

'But how else did she know about your mom?' Alex asked.

'Lucky guess? She didn't say much else, did she?'

The American looked at her fiery companion. Through the bravado she could somehow recognise the vulnerability, and felt a sudden urge to protect her, to help her.

'You've been through a lot, haven't you, Honey?' she said warily.

Jessica shrugged. 'Well, it's not going to get much easier with a baby, is it?' she said, struggling to blink away her tears.

'You'll be okay... Look, I know we've only just met, Jessica, but I really hope we can be good friends. It's not the same as having your mom around, of course it isn't, but I'd love to help you with the baby – I love kids. And anyway, I don't know anyone in this town, so I'd be grateful to have a friend, too.'

The two women had not been too late for that curry after all, and after sharing a chicken madras, they drove home feeling relatively upbeat. And with the belief that no one wished to harm her, and the comforting thought of her mezuzah fixed to her front door, Alex felt more reassured. As she pulled up outside Jessica's flat, she thanked her once again for coming with her.

'You know, I really do appreciate it.'

'It's okay... it's certainly been an interesting evening,' Jessica grinned, opening the car door.

'But what am I going to do if this spirit keeps hanging around?' Alex asked, a worried frown returning to her face.

'Just see what happens... It might all come to an end now,' Jessica replied as she got out of the car, no longer sure whether she was humouring her friend or not.

An unexpected, almost-tangible air of calm greeted Alex when she returned home. As she wandered from room to room in trepidation, half-expecting lights to start flashing or objects to start flying off the shelves, all that she found was peace. It might have just been her imagination, but Alex believed she could detect a sense of release in the atmosphere. And somehow she instinctively felt that the spirit, whoever he was, would trouble her no more.

Jessica stood in her kitchen that night, her head bubbling with confusion and bewilderment. Happy or sad – she didn't know. Uplifted or battered by the bizarre experience – she couldn't tell. All she knew was that she felt something. It wasn't the numbness and emptiness of those darkest days, months back. And it wasn't the sense of hope she had felt on meeting Finn, and again more recently with the anticipation of the baby. No, this was different. Something extraordinary had happened tonight. Something that had sparked off a skirmish with her radical, dogmatic outlook. Something that was a challenge to her whole mindset. And even though it had only made the tiniest of chinks in her rigid armour, try as she might, Jessica was unable to ignore the significance of the evening's implications. But how could she possibly begin to believe the unbelievable? How could she possibly have had contact from her deceased mother?

She poured some milk into a pan with three heaped spoonfuls of drinking chocolate and dropped a slice of bread into the toaster. Even after the curry, she found herself craving a sweet cocoa with toast, but then Jessica could usually find room for food, especially when something was tormenting or upsetting her. She switched on the radio for company, the melancholy minor chords of a sorrowful ballad immediately stinging her soul.

'…This is Radio Sussex…' came the DJ's honeyed tones. '…and Saturday night's Songs For The Broken-Hearted.'

Out sprang the toast with a pop. Jessica drove her knife into the block of butter and began spreading, her vision blurring as her eyes welled with tears.

You'll always be her little girl... You'll always be her little girl...

As the voice in her head intensified, each stroke of the knife became slower and slower, and teardrops fell one by one onto the toast. Then she turned, swiftly, to see the foaming, forgotten milk cascading over the sides of the pan, like angry lava.

You'll always be her little girl...

Hurling the knife onto the floor, Jessica ran desperately towards the bedroom. Throwing open the wardrobe doors, she tugged in a frenzy at the bulging black bags containing her mother's belongings, lodged so tightly together. One tumbled out of the wardrobe and onto the floor. She tore it open and, scooping up a bundle of clothes, buried her face in them, sobbing and spluttering, awash with mucus and tears.

Seventeen

Jessica was woken by the deep, guttural sound of her own sobs the next morning. She could barely prise apart her swollen, sticky eyelids as she rolled over, the spasms which shook her body beginning to subside. There was no distinct memory of a dream. Just the most awful, over-powering sense of sorrow.

She stared ahead vacantly, her head swimming in the agonisingly familiar haze that swamped her like an emotional hangover. For a moment, she even wallowed in it, wrapped safe from the outside world in her comfort blanket of grief. As she closed her hot, heavy eyelids again, Jessica could hear the gentle peal of church bells away in the distance. Ringing out, calling the flock to worship. The bells would also be ringing across the churchyard where her mother was buried, she realised: ringing out across her mother's grave.

Perhaps they were calling her, summoning her there to the graveyard? Perhaps they knew that Jessica had only once had the courage to lay flowers at the spot where her mother lay? She pictured her mother's lovely body there, beneath the black, crumbly soil, and then came a flash of the unthinkable – how might it have decomposed? Her skin, her eyes, her hair – had it all disintegrated now, rotted away, been devoured by worms, to leave nothing but a bare, faceless skeleton?

She sat up abruptly, shaking the grotesque images from her head; smearing away the tears of desolation that now sprang from her eyes.

None of that could have happened. None of it.

As she tried to pull herself together, thoughts of the night before began to creep into Jessica's mind. The woman sitting in the car, her faint odour of perspiration, her voice. So strong, so sure. Jessica could hear it again now.

She's with you all the time...she's reaching out and putting her arms around you...she'll always be with you...

Jessica took a gulp of air. 'Are you really there, Mum?' She coaxed herself to say the words out loud. 'Are you there?'

There came no reply. The only sound, the church bells in the distance.

But what the hell – if there was a chance, just the slightest chance, that she might be able to make contact with her mother, Jessica decided she was going to take it.

The Sunday morning meeting was in full swing when Jessica stole surreptitiously into The Beacon half an hour later. She slid onto a seat just by the door and scrutinised the room with eyes still hot and raw, instantly recognising the portly frame of the woman they'd met last night amongst the flock of chattering pensioners.

Jessica was relieved to see that the clairvoyant standing on the platform today was a smartly dressed woman of around her own age. In fact, she looked quite normal, Jessica noted, and unlike poor Ernie's disastrous performance, she seemed to be having some success with a gentleman in the front row.

'She's telling me that August 23rd is a very important date for you,' the clairvoyant said to him earnestly.

'That's right, it was our wedding anniversary.'

'Yes...yes...and every year you would give your wife a bouquet of her favourite flowers...freesias...the purple ones, with the incredibly strong perfume. My goodness, I can smell them now...'

The man nodded enthusiastically.

'...Now she wants you to know that she's fine...' the clairvoyant continued, pacing the platform as she spoke. 'She was met on the other side by...her brother? Does she have a brother in spirit, name beginning with the letter B?'

'Brian!' came the swift reply.

'Well, she's having a wonderful time catching up with Brian, and lots of old friends and family...she just wishes she could see you smile again...'

Jessica watched, enthralled by the possibility that this ordinary-looking woman in the chain store jacket might actually be communicating with the dead.

'...So she's sending you lots of love and...what's this?' The clairvoyant began to laugh. 'She's saying that you've been thinking about buying a new car...well, you should treat yourself, but choose the Lexus not the Ford. She says the ladies won't be able to resist you in that one!'

'Thank you, thank you so much,' chuckled the widower appreciatively.

'God bless,' the clairvoyant smiled. 'Now...I think I've got time for one more message...where am I going?'

She surveyed the small gathering of faces beaming keenly up at her. But her eyes rested on Jessica.

'I'd like to come to you,' she said softly.

Jessica's heart lurched.

'Now, there's an old gentleman standing by my side...he's not a member of your family, but he wants to be known to you.'

Disappointment instantly drenched Jessica like a bucket of cold water.

'...He wants to say thank-you...I feel that this is a very recent passing...' The clairvoyant frowned. 'I also feel that he did cross over to the other side briefly once before, but it wasn't his time to go then. Can you accept this? Do you recognise this person?'

'No, sorry,' Jessica replied uncomfortably.

'I'm getting the letter R now,' the clairvoyant continued, her brow furrowed in concentration. '...And a hospital situation. Are you a doctor, or a nurse?' she asked.

'Yes, a nurse!' Jessica spluttered.

'...He's showing me his hospital bed and, for some reason, pear drops! My goodness, I can taste them...I can feel them on my tongue! Pear drops...do they mean anything to you?'

It was as though every kindly, creased face in the room was turned towards Jessica. She felt the blood rush to her cheeks, and her memory rewound back to the sweet old man in the Geriatric Ward.

'Mr. Reynolds... a patient of mine, Mr. Reynolds...but I didn't know he'd died,' she uttered incredulously.

'Well, he wants you to know that he's passed and he's happy, he's very happy...and he wants to say thank you again. He liked you a lot, you know...he's laughing now and saying you and he often shared a good joke together. And he's telling me you always pinched his sweets!'

Jessica smiled sadly.

'What a lovely man,' concluded the clairvoyant. 'But now, I'm afraid, my time is up. So, ladies and gentlemen, thank you all so much for sending me your vibrations of love this morning...'

Jessica slipped out of the hall as quietly as she'd entered it, dizzy with emotional exhaustion and, now, wonder. She hadn't really expected to get a message from her mother. She hadn't really expected to get anything credible at all. But what she'd been told that Sunday morning was enough to persuade her that maybe it was possible to contact the dead. Maybe there was such a thing as life after death. And maybe, just maybe, her mother wasn't so far away after all.

Eighteen

At number twenty nine Montpelier Crescent, Friday evening's Good Grief session was coming to a close.

'Ah, and finally, Hannah,' Melissa sang across the room. 'We haven't seen you for a while. It's wonderful to have you back. How are you doing, my love?'

Jessica's gaze fell on the scrawny young woman with the terrible haircut, the one who'd helped her the night she'd fainted outside. The night she'd made the momentous decision to keep her baby. Since then, she'd come to realise the importance of listening to others, and she'd even found herself quite enjoying the regular group meetings.

'Well, things have been rather difficult...with my husband, actually,' she replied quietly, tugging anxiously at her sleeve. 'Everything seems to have got on top of me, that's why I haven't been able to get here...'

Just then Melissa's little West Highland Terrier trotted into the room, a sock in his mouth and a triumphant wag propelling his white stub of a tail.

'Oh, Freud! You know you're not allowed in here!' squealed Melissa, ushering the disappointed dog out through the door. 'I wonder if his anal glands need squeezing again?' she muttered to herself, grimacing, before switching her attention back to the matter in hand. 'Ah, yes, how dreadful...I'm very sorry to hear about your problems at home. Do you think your marriage could be suffering because of your grief?'

'Well, yes, I suppose so...I think, because of my...my loss...I'm just not able to be the wife my husband wants...the wife I was. I can't be there for him in the way I used to be.'

Melissa interrupted with a flick of her dreadlocks: 'When we lose someone we love, our whole world turns upside down, and we need time to heal. As we've discussed, there is such a diverse range of emotions we experience – guilt, depression, even anger. And, crucially, the people around us need to understand this.'

The group members nodded earnestly.

'If possible, we need to surround ourselves with positive, caring people,' Melissa continued. 'People who will allow us to work our way through the various stages of grief, listening and sharing whenever we need them...And now, friends, I'm afraid we've run out of time, but we'll touch on this further next week, and discuss other ways in which we can all refocus our lives and help ourselves move forward.... As I always say, life is all about learning to say goodbye...and it is possible to keep our dearly departed loved ones in our hearts, while at the same time acknowledging that they would want us to progress and be happy again...So, on that note, thank you all for a very valuable session. And I look forward to seeing you again next week. Love and light!'

With that, Melissa spun over to her bureau in the corner, and the group began to disperse. Jessica watched them all hurry away, some heading home to comforting arms and warm beds, others to emptiness and cold, cruel silence. And there was Hannah, winding her gangly, angular frame into her cardigan as she went out the door. Jessica realised that she hadn't thanked her. Now was her chance.

She caught up with her out on the street. 'Hi! How are you doing?'

The young woman turned around in surprise. 'Oh, hello! Yes, I'm, er, fine thanks.' She blinked nervously, pulling her cardigan tightly around her. 'How are you now?

'Much better,' Jessica replied. 'Actually I just wanted to say thank you for helping me when I fainted the other week.'

'That's alright.'

The pair continued strolling a little further in polite conversation, Hannah sympathising with Jessica's experiences of early pregnancy. 'Actually, I've got loads of baby clothes you could have, if you like?' she offered, as they were about to go their separate ways.

Jessica was rather taken aback. 'Wow...that would be fantastic, thank you, if you're sure you won't be needing them?'

Hannah shook her head. 'No, definitely not. Please, take them; it would be nice to see them go to a good home. '

'Well if you're sure?'

'Of course. I'll bring them along to the next meeting.'

Jessica couldn't believe her luck as she sat on the bus on her way back home to Hove. That one kind gesture, that offer of practical support from somebody she barely knew, made Jessica feel all the more excited at the prospect of her baby's arrival. It was a start. A wonderful start. She placed a hand on her belly and, as if in reply, felt the reassuring kick of her baby inside.

Nineteen

As Alex drew up outside Jessica's basement flat, she parked her car with typical precision and, flipping down the sun-visor, checked her reflection in the mirror. With a quick slick of lip gloss and a ruffle of her bob she was ready. Almost. Just as she reached across to grab the bunch of exotic tiger lilies nestled on the passenger seat alongside her, Alex spotted the small plaster dressing peeking out from beneath her short-sleeved t-shirt, and ripped it off her skin immediately. No one would notice the tiny pin prick which had been hidden beneath the blood-stained swatch of cotton wool. And that was just how she wanted it. Nobody knowing. Nobody asking. Nobody scrutinising her every move.

Alex could still detect the sterile hospital smell hanging on her hair, her clothes. Hardly surprising, as she'd just spent two tedious hours sitting in the waiting room to have yet another blood test. Rummaging in her bag for her perfume, the ever-present bottles of pills rattled their nagging, discordant tune, an irritating jingle that had almost become the soundtrack to her life.

There at last, her favourite, Chanel No 5. Alex breathed in the fragrant mist like an ex-smoker inhales somebody else's cigarette smoke. And, having finally concealed all evidence of her hospital visit, she grabbed the thirsty flowers and swung out of the car.

'Aaah!' The two women swooned in unison at the sight of a

little polka dot romper suit that Jessica was holding up by the arms.

'It's adorable!' she cooed. 'You know, I can't quite believe there's a small person in here who's actually going to be wearing these clothes soon.' She sat back in the sofa, hands rested on her now sizeable bump.

'I hope you're having a girl, there's an awful lot of pink!' Alex remarked. 'Where did all this stuff come from?'

'Oh, from one of the women at Good Grief. She's got daughters apparently…anyway, if it's a boy, he'll just have to be in touch with his feminine side!'

The coffee table almost groaned under the weight of all the baby paraphernalia that swamped it in a frenzy of pastel terry-towelling and Winnie the Pooh.

Jessica pulled a clumsy-looking contraption from a carrier bag.

'What the hell is that!' Alex asked.

'It must be a breast pump!' Jessica chuckled naughtily, placing the ugly plastic device over one of her enlarged breasts.

'You gonna use it?'

'Definitely not!' she retorted. 'Not unless it makes a decent cappuccino!'

The two women giggled.

'Oh, God, I must tell you about last night's ante-natal class!' Jessica gasped, as she bit hungrily into a biscuit. 'All the other women were there with their partners – me on my own, of course – and we had to practice breathing. But the midwife wanted us to heave and grunt as if we were actually in labour. So there we were, sitting in a circle on the floor, making the most horrendous noises like a herd of constipated heifers. Then the woman next to me, who is so goddamn perfect she looks like she's just stepped out of Mother & Baby magazine, suddenly farted. And everyone just carried on grunting, as if nothing had happened!'

Alex laughed.

'What is it about pregnancy that makes people so open about their bodily functions?' Jessica continued. 'I mean, I wouldn't normally talk to complete strangers about yeast infections and haemorrhoids, so why should I do it just because I'm expecting?'

Jessica noticed that Alex suddenly seemed rather distant.

'Oh dear, I'm not putting you off having a baby one day, am I?' she grinned.

'Well, you certainly make a great case for celibacy, Honey,' came the breezy reply. 'But to tell you the truth, I can't have kids. Well, not exactly can't, just shouldn't, I suppose.'

'I'm really sorry, I…'

'No, no, don't worry, Honey. It's okay. It's not a problem,' Alex interjected. 'It's just that, to tell you the truth, I was born with a heart condition. I'm healthy enough now, but I have to take a lot of medication, so having kids wouldn't be a good idea. But I'm cool with it, really…'

Jessica studied her face for the slightest trace of emotion. But there was none. Not a trace. Just well-practiced inscrutability.

'…Anyway, I've got the kids at school, who are quite a handful, believe me, and, of course, I'm going to have lots of fun with your little one, too!'

'Quite right,' Jessica replied. Clearly Alex didn't want to discuss the matter further and so, for her sake, Jessica diverted the conversation back to her impending motherhood. '…Which is why I pronounce you official nappy-changer, nose-wiper, baby-sitter and bottle-washer! Cheers!'

The two women clanked mugs in a toast. 'Cheers!' they laughed.

'After all, what more could I need?' continued Jessica, adding with a wicked smile, 'Apart from the baby's father, of course!'

Jessica could sense that her flippant remark had made Alex

uncomfortable. As she watched her fiddling with the poppers on a tiny romper suit, too polite to ask the obvious question, Jessica felt a sudden tug of affection for the woman. She had to put her out of her misery.

'I don't think I've told you…' Jessica began casually, 'but I'm not in touch with the baby's father. In fact, he doesn't even know I'm pregnant.'

'Well, you had mentioned you're on your own,' nodded Alex.

'I did try to tell him…well, kind of…but to be honest, it wasn't the longest relationship in the world…One night, actually,' Jessica grimaced.

Alex didn't really know what to say next. She could see that Jessica's whole demeanour had now changed; suddenly she looked lost and alone. And it occurred to Alex that her friend's frivolous banter had probably been no more than bravado.

'I must admit, I don't really know how I'm going to cope on my own,' Jessica murmured, carefully smoothing out the creases of a tiny white romper suit on her lap. And then the tears began to flow. 'I'm scared, Alex. I'm really, really scared.'

Alex reached out to the now sobbing Jessica and wrapped her arms around her. 'Don't worry, Honey. I'm here for you. You'll be fine. You'll be just fine.'

Alex couldn't sleep that night. She couldn't get the thought of Jessica, and her predicament, out of her mind. She felt great admiration for this brave young woman, who was about to face motherhood on her own, without the support of a partner, or any family at all. Alex had meant what she'd said to Jessica, but wondered now whether it had been enough to make her realise that she really would be there for her. Deciding that actions speak louder than words, she concocted a plan for the next day.

'So what's the urgency?' Jessica asked as Alex opened her front door the following afternoon.. '...I hope you realise that I've missed a leaving do at work to get here. The fact it's for Nigel Ladbroke, who I loathe and despise, is beside the point. There would have been free cake!' she joked.

'Well hopefully the surprise I've got for you will make up for it,' Alex smiled, as she ushered her friend inside, where loud rock music filled the room. 'And don't worry, I've got cake, too.'

'What's going on?' Jessica asked.

'You'll find out in a minute, just be quiet and sit down,' Alex instructed, and disappeared into the kitchen.

Jessica did as she was told and looked around at the pristine open-plan living room, admiring Alex's sleek, minimalist style.

'What do you think of the music?' Alex called out.

'It's The Kinks, isn't it?' Jessica replied.

'Yeah, it's that CD I picked up at the paranormal evening we went to...I'd never heard their stuff before, but I love it, I can't stop playing it,' Alex said. 'Anyway...this is for you, Honey.'

Jessica turned to see Alex wheeling in a top of the range, designer pushchair. The very one she'd seen in the window of Petit Enfant only the other day. Festooned with balloons and bows.

'I'm sorry you missed out on the celebrations at work, Jess, but I just couldn't wait to give it to you,' Alex smiled. 'I hope you like it.'

'I just don't know what to say...' Jessica gasped, and the pair hugged. 'Apart from thank you. Thank you so much.'

Just then, there was a loud thud from upstairs. The two women jumped.

'What the hell was that?' Jessica asked, wide-eyed.

'Oh, don't worry, it's only my brother,' Alex laughed. 'He arrived from the States late last night.'

And on cue, in sauntered a tall, dark-haired young man in

nothing but a pair of boxer shorts. 'I'd forgotten you were upstairs, Ben,' Alex said. 'You gave us a fright...anyway, meet my friend Jess.'

'Hey, Jess,' Ben smiled. 'Please excuse my state of undress.'

'There's really no need to apologise,' Jessica said. 'The pleasure's all mine...how long are you staying?'

'Oh, a couple of years, at least.'

'That's a long holiday!'

'I wish... I'm an attorney and my firm has shipped me out to work in the London office. Once I've got over this God-awful jet-lag that is.'

He poured himself a glass of water and took an apple from the fruit bowl. 'Well, it's back to bed for me,' Ben yawned. 'I'll leave you ladies to carry on. See you again some time, Jess.' And with that he gave a friendly wave and disappeared back upstairs.

Twenty

Hannah Parker had been awake since four a.m. She'd lain in bed for hours, just listening to the sound of the rain battering her bedroom window. And Richard snoring beside her, his white, freckled back turned coldly towards her, rising and falling with every breath. Her gaze fell onto her own weary frame: bones protruding beneath fleshless skin; the ugly purple birthmark on her forearm; bitten-down fingernails bleeding and raw. How she hated herself.

Eventually she crept out of bed and set to work. She packed the children's things first – pretty pastel t-shirts with coordinating trousers for her two daughters who, even at the tender ages of four and seven, had very fixed ideas on what they would or, more often, wouldn't wear. There was no time for tantrums this morning. For herself, Hannah packed a pair of old jeans and a clean sweatshirt. She'd lost all enthusiasm for fashion a while back. And anyway, two nights at her parents' house had all the appeal of a 48-hour visit to the dentist. With a heavy heart, she threw a ball of socks into the hold-all and zipped it up as quietly as possible, but Richard stirred. He groaned and squinted at the clock, then rolled over and went back to sleep. As manager of a local estate agents, he was due in the office by nine, so he could afford a little longer in bed. He obviously had no plans to wave his family goodbye.

The clouds opened again, and Hannah pulled the front door shut with a muted thud before bustling the children, complete with armfuls of books, comics and cuddlies, into her car, out of the rain. Turning on the ignition, she tried hard to swallow the boulder that had formed in her throat. The girls immediately began to bicker in the back, but she did her best to block out their high-pitched squabbles and carefully edged the car out of the drive.

Nearly two hours after leaving Hove, Hannah pulled into Hollybush Way, a winding country lane on the outskirts of Bournemouth. A sickness borne from both apprehension and nostalgia welled in the pit of her stomach like dark, sticky treacle, as the car approached her parents' home, the only house the unworldly Hannah had ever lived in before marrying Richard. Hastily she wound down the window and breathed in the cool fresh air. It had been a stressful journey, having to act as referee between her two incessantly quarrelling daughters. But as she turned the car into the sweeping gravel driveway, she knew that worse was yet to come.

She glanced around at Lisa and Carrie who had been sleeping for the past twenty minutes, now no longer at loggerheads, but head to head, peaceful and resting against one another in familial trust. Then she saw her kindly father, Joe, walking slowly over towards the car. He waved at Hannah meekly, and she waved back, noticing how much older he suddenly appeared than his seventy years. He used to stand so straight and tall, she thought, but more recently he seemed more hunched, more frail and it hurt her to witness the decline. She remembered the days when her mother Terri used to greet her at the door with a wide smile and a warm, maternal hug. But so much had changed, and those days were well and truly gone.

'Wakey wakey,' Hannah said, gently shaking Lisa and Carrie from their slumber. The girls stretched and yawned and looked around, momentarily disorientated. But when they saw their doting grandfather, they raced out of the car and he received an ebullient double-hug from them both.

'Oh, it is so lovely to see you!' he said in his warm Irish lilt.

Hannah stepped out of the car and began unloading the paraphernalia from the back seat. 'I'm so sorry we're late, Dad, there were road-works everywhere and Carrie needed the loo...'

She turned around jauntily but her father and the girls were already heading inside. Deflated, she carried the bags and toys to the house single-handedly, the gravel crunching beneath her shoes. As she scanned the grand colonial-style residence with its wide verandah and immaculate gardens, there was no warmth or happiness emanating from its bricks and mortar. The irony of the Gaelic word, 'Failte', meaning 'Welcome', etched on a highly-polished brass plaque there by the door, was not lost on Hannah. For this, her childhood home, was the place that, these days, she felt least welcome in the whole world.

'Isn't this lovely, girls?' Hannah said with forced enthusiasm. She had joined her children and parents in the formal dining room, where they now sat around the large mahogany table for breakfast. 'Mother, you really shouldn't have gone to so much trouble. '

'I wanted my grandchildren to have a decent meal,' Terri snapped.

'Here you are, Hannah dear,' Joe said, depositing a thick glistening slab of pink fatty bacon onto his daughter's plate, alongside the huge mound of scrambled eggs already sitting there. Hannah stared down at the meal in front of her. Although empty, her stomach felt full; her deprived body heaved with nausea. Poking at the food on her plate, she desperately searched for something to say, something that might thaw the frosty atmosphere.

'So, how are the ladies at the bridge club, Mother?' she asked tentatively.

Her question was met with an uncomfortable silence, broken only by the clatter of fork against plate. Joe stepped in:

'Your mother hasn't been for some time, Hannah. She hasn't felt ready.'

'That's a shame,' Hannah murmured, pushing her plate away furtively.

'Not hungry *again*?' Terri spat accusingly.

Suddenly, there was a loud crash from the far side of the room. They all turned.

'Oh, no!' cried Terri, as she hurried across to retrieve the framed photograph that had fallen from the wall, and now lay face-down amongst shards of splintered glass. 'Oh, no,' she repeated tearfully, clutching the cherished family portrait tightly to her chest as she scuttled from the room.

'What's the matter with Granny?' Lisa asked.

'Oh she's just not feeling very happy this morning, that's all,' Joe replied softly.

'But Granny's never very happy,' said the younger sister, using a stubby little finger to draw a smiley face in the puddle of tomato ketchup on her plate.

'Well, Granny's had a lot on her mind lately, and we have to be kind and gentle with her...so how about we go into the garden and pick her a lovely bunch of flowers? And if you both promise to be extra-quiet, I'll show you where I've discovered a hedgehog hibernating.'

'Yay!' the two girls squealed in unison, and followed their grandfather eagerly into the garden.

Left alone in the dining room, Hannah swept up the broken glass from the floor, then scraped the cold food off the plates into one sticky, congealed mass. The sight almost made her retch, but she felt duty-bound to clear the table and leave the dining room as pristine as possible, so as not to upset her mother further. Job done, she then made a hasty retreat to her childhood bedroom. Opening the window, she rested her weary elbows on the sill, and breathed in the spring air, heavy with the scent of hawthorn blossom. Her empty eyes slowly, steadily filled with tears that trickled down her cheeks and on to her lips. Inadvertently, she licked the briny tang of sorrow that she had tasted all too frequently over recent months, and was immediately taken back to a moment in time that she neither wanted to remember, nor forget. A dull ache welled in Hannah's stomach as she fought off images and memories that would haunt her always. And the notion that perpetually tormented her returned. If only she could turn the clock back, if only she could change the turn of events, if only things had been different. If only.

Twenty-One

Ben glanced at the clock on the wall. It was exactly two minutes since the last time he'd looked. He'd always hated hospitals: the smell, the sterility, the air of uncertainty. For him, a hospital was a place of fear and dread. Sitting in the empty waiting room, he distracted himself by flicking through a dog-eared issue of Man & Motors magazine. As a self-confessed petrol-head, he was looking forward to treating himself to a new sports car, to replace his beloved vintage Mustang, which he'd had to leave back home in the States. But a gulp of lukewarm, acrid liquid from a plastic cup was an unpalatable reminder of exactly where he was. You could only get coffee like that in a hospital. Then, just as he was comparing the engine size of a Maserati Grancabrio with that of an Aston Martin DB7, Alex returned. Looking up at his sister, he was glad to see the reassuring smile that told him all was well.

'Lunch is on me,' she beamed.

'It sure as hell is - have you tasted this stuff?' he said, tossing the plastic coffee cup into the bin.

They were lucky enough to get a table on the terrace at the Hotel Seattle, overlooking the picturesque marina. It was an unseasonably warm, sunny afternoon, and the seagulls squawked with delight at the abundance of tit-bits left by the many al fresco diners.

'Well, I can see why you like it here so much, ' Ben said,

pushing back his Raybans and reclining in his seat. 'Brighton's a great place.'

'Yeah, I love it here…it's so different from New York, and London, but there's still a real buzz.'

'You sure you don't mind me staying with you? I don't want to cramp your style.'

'Course not,' Alex replied, taking a sip of beer. 'It'll be nice to spend some time with my big bro. I've missed you. And, to be honest, it'll great to have the company.'

'Cool…I just hope you've got all the sports channels? I need to keep up with the Knicks, they're doing great in the basketball league.'

Gazing out to sea, Alex's eyes followed the silhouette of a small boat making its way back towards the mouth of the marina.

'You have, haven't you?'

His sister looked back at him blankly.

'Got the sports channels?

'What sports channels?'

'I guess I've been talking to myself!' he laughed. Then added, 'You seem a little preoccupied, Al…you sure everything's ok?'

'Oh, I'm sorry Ben, yeah, everything's just fine. Actually, no… there is something. Something I haven't told you.'

Her brother looked worried.

'You'll probably find this hard to believe but, what the hell…there's been some kind of ghost, or spirit, in my house.'

'What?'

'I've been told that the spirit of some dead guy has been trying to make contact with me.'

'Says who?'

'A medium.'

Ben snorted in disbelief. 'You've got to be kidding!'

Alex shook her head. 'Nope. I know it sounds ridiculous, that's why I didn't tell you before, but it's true.'

As they shared a plate of calamari, Alex recounted the mysterious events that had unfolded since moving in to Montpelier Crescent. And they were still discussing her encounter with the medium, and the woman's explanation for what had happened, when they returned home.

'Well, I'm not so sure I want to stay here with you now!' Ben joked as they walked in through the front door. 'Not if this place is haunted.'

'Don't be silly,' Alex said. 'There's nothing to be scared of. Anyway, if there is someone here, they're peaceful now. Nothing's happened for ages.' She went into the kitchen to take her usual dose of tablets.

'I think we should try to find out who this spirit is,' Ben announced when Alex joined him in the living room.

'And how do you suggest we do that then?' she asked, flopping onto the sofa.

'With an ouija board, of course. It's a way of contacting the dead.'

'I know what it is, but you're not doing it in my house!'

'Oh, come on, it'll be fine. I did it once at university with Jake and Spencer after a few beers, just for fun,' Ben explained, grabbing a notepad and pen from Alex's desk. Then, kneeling at the coffee table, he tore pages from the notepad into smaller pieces, and began writing the letters of the alphabet and numbers from one to ten on the scraps of paper. '...We didn't really believe anything would happen, but we made contact with Jake's dead grandfather. He spelt out Jake's car registration number, and then, when Jake left to go home, his damn car wouldn't start! I'm still not sure what to believe, but it was one hell of a coincidence.'

Alex gave a shrug of defeat and sat down on the sofa, as Ben arranged the pieces of paper in a circle on the coffee table and placed a glass in the centre. 'Now, we both put a finger on the glass and ask out loud if there are any spirits present,' he explained, sitting down next to his sister. 'If there are, the glass should move to spell out the spirits' answers to our questions.'

Alex frowned. 'Ben I'm not sure about this…surely we could be letting in any spirit, maybe even an evil one?'

'Nah, it'll be fine Sis, let's just give it a go. Maybe we'll find out who this guy is?'

With a tut, Alex placed a finger on the top of the down-turned glass.

'Is anybody there?' Ben asked out loud. Nothing happened. 'Is anybody there?' He asked again.

The glass remained still. The pair sat in silence. Despite her initial reluctance, Alex willed it to move now. For maybe they could find out more about the spirit who had apparently been trying to make contact with her?

'Come on, fella…we know you're there…give us something,' Ben said.

Still nothing.

Suddenly the scraps of paper went flying and the glass shot onto the floor with a crash. It was Cookie, Alex's cat, who'd launched himself onto the table in a bid to attract his owner's attention.

The brother and sister burst out laughing. 'Oh Cookie!' Alex said, scooping the cat up into her arms. 'Are you trying to tell me it's dinner-time?'

'Well, I guess it was worth a try,' Ben shrugged, picking up the scraps of paper and leaving them in a neat pile on the coffee table. 'Maybe the guys and I had more beer than I thought that night.'

'Yeah, I reckon you did too,' Alex said with a smile, taking Cookie into the kitchen. She emptied the cat's food into his bowl and he munched away greedily.

'I'm off for a shower, Sis!' Ben called out.

'Okay,' Alex replied, and flicked on the kettle for a cup of tea. Waiting for it to boil, she leant wearily against the unit. And as she watched the hot steam swirl and gather, the words of her favourite song, by The Kinks, drifted into her head:

'How very much like me you are, when you come to me, truly, truly trust your heart...'

She carried her tea into the living room, and slumped onto the sofa, the song lyrics still playing in her head. And then she went cold. The scraps of paper Ben had used to make an ouija board were still there, stacked on the table top. But one piece of paper had moved. Only one. It lay face up in the centre of the tabletop, its letter on display... H.

Twenty-Two

Sunday morning, and the large, chintzy bedroom was awash with delicate early light, as Terri sat poker-faced at her dressing table, methodically unrolling curlers from her hair. Joe stood in front of the wall mirror slowly knotting his tie in awkward silence, looking in the glass before him at his wife's reflection. He wondered what had happened to the woman he'd married more than forty years earlier – the woman who had bowled him over at the Killarney youth club dance, with her radiant smile and infectious laugh; the woman who, even back then, had been unashamedly straight-laced, but whose sharp sense of humour had won him over.

But now this woman was barely recognisable and Joe could almost feel the leaden weight of his heart in his chest as he mentally superimposed Terri's once sunny face over her now cold, wretched features. Her lips seemed permanently pinched and Joe couldn't remember the last time he'd heard her laugh. The only smile she ever wore these days was a feigned veneer painted on solely for Father Matthews.

He broke the silence. 'It's nice to see the weather's picking up, isn't it, dear?' he smiled uneasily, slipping on his blazer.

Terri hung a string of pearls around her neck and mumbled some inaudible response.

'Are you sure you're up to going, Terri, dear?' Joe probed cautiously.

'I've got to show my face there some time,' she replied sharply, applying chalky white face powder to her nose and forehead. 'It's Palm Sunday and I do not intend to make this the first Palm Sunday that I fail to turn up for Mass!'

'Well, whatever you think is right,' Joe said, walking towards the door.

'Actually, I think we should all go,' Terri added.

Joe hesitated, then gave a resigned nod and closed the door behind him.

Once he was safely out of the way, Terri unlocked a drawer at the bottom of her wardrobe and took out an old wooden box. Lifting the lid, she rummaged around for something inside, then pulled out an old envelope, which had been opened many times before. Inside was a letter and a photograph of a pretty young woman, a red baseball cap sitting on her dark bobbed hair. Terri unfolded the letter, dog-eared from so many readings and re-readings, and stared at the snapshot of the smiling, carefree woman. Terri's face slowly hardened as she wiped away an angry tear. Then hastily, she threw everything back into the box and slammed the drawer shut.

Hannah had slipped outside on to the verandah, for some rare time alone. It had been a long while since she'd sat there in her favourite spot, a place that held so many memories. She perched on the edge of the white swinging seat, looking out over the patchwork countryside.

'Ah, there you are, dear.' It was Joe. He sat down next to his daughter and put his arm hesitantly around her shoulder. 'It's a shame Richard couldn't make it. I suppose this is a busy time of year for estate agents,' he said.

'Mmm? Oh, yes...poor Richard. He works so hard,' Hannah replied, oblivious to the hint of sarcasm in her father's voice.

'And how are you doing, dear?' Joe asked.

'Oh, you know,' she answered quietly. 'The girls keep me busy.' She turned to look at her father intently. 'But what about Mother? She doesn't seem any better?'

Joe lowered his voice. 'Well, I'm afraid she's still having her panic attacks. I had to call out the doctor last week, he said she mustn't be unnecessarily upset, so we've got to tread very carefully.' Joe seized the moment. 'Actually she's asking if you'll come to Mass. She thinks we should all go.'

Hannah sighed in dismay. 'Well, if you really think it will help her, I'll go...but it won't change anything, will it, Dad? What good has sixty years of praying done for Mother?'

Joe was essentially a mellow, easy-going fellow, who had dealt with life's blows with stoicism and restraint. However, he was finally beginning to feel a little downtrodden, even irritated, by his wife and daughter, and decided that it was time he started to be more assertive in his own home. 'You know that the church has always been an important part of her life, Hannah...' He stood and walked towards the door. 'We'll be leaving in half an hour.'

As the five of them entered the silence of the vast Church of the Sacred Heart, their footsteps echoed on the stone floor, attracting a number of over-curious stares and nods as they were ushered to their pew.

'It's a shame you couldn't have found something smarter to wear,' Terri hissed at Hannah, their eyes meeting for the first time that morning.

The organ piped up as the liturgy began, with the solemn ceremonial procession – the priest, clergy and choirboys all robed and cowled, carrying the large gilt cross and swinging incense.

Hannah watched, detached from the ritual being played out before her. She felt like a guilty intruder who, despite having membership, no longer wished to belong to the club. As the congregation began to sing the first hymn, Hannah's eyes wandered around the huge, modern building with its golden font, ornate chandelier and giant crucifix suspended over the altar. She scanned the rows of pious worshippers who today seemed more like herds of cattle, blindly going through the motions, than intelligent, thinking, rational human beings. And she wondered how she could have been brainwashed like the rest of them for all those years.

Terri stared at the words in her hymn book, nervously dabbing the corners of her eyes. Unable to find a voice, she mouthed the words, vacantly, unaware of Lisa and Carrie giggling and chatting next to her.

At the end of the service the members of the congregation shook Father Matthews' hand one by one as they filed outside through the open doors.

'It's good to see you here again, Theresa,' he said warmly, sandwiching her hand between his. 'God Bless you.'

Without the strength to speak, Terri managed a frail smile and, carrying her pain like a cross on her back, headed out towards the daylight.

Next in line stood Hannah. Pushing the children ahead of her, she was eager to offer a polite nod then make her escape. But as she glanced up into Father Matthews' face, she saw such innate kindness; in his eyes a pure, unquestioning love. There was no judgment, no bitterness, no scorn. She could scarcely move, despite Joe's firm hand guiding her from behind.

The priest said nothing. But under his gentle gaze, before finally moving on, Hannah felt – for a few, long seconds – the one thing she believed she so desperately needed: forgiveness.

Twenty-Three

The summer got off to a busy start. Alex's working days were long, but she gladly gave extra time to helping out with sports' day, the summer fete and various school excursions. Meanwhile, Jessica found the courage to move out of her rented basement flat and into her mother's house, where she was finally able to complete the gruelling task that she'd begun all those months ago. She bagged and boxed all of her mother's possessions, but absolutely nothing was discarded or given away. It was still too soon for that. Instead, it was carefully stored, close at hand, in the spare room.

And there was also time for fun. Alex and Jessica mooched along Brighton's 'Lanes' together; went to see a movie at the cinema at least once a week and, one Saturday caught a train in to London, where they took a ride on the London Eye. Apart from the expense of the trip and Jessica's torture at needing the lavatory whilst trapped inside a transparent capsule, 443feet above sea level, it was a thoroughly enjoyable outing.

Today they hit the beach, which was as busy as ever. With true British gusto, groups of holidaymakers – families, teenagers, loved-up couples – sat in clusters across the shingle, determined to benefit from any break in the clouds.

Not such a typical sight was the American bunting, draped across a couple of deck chairs beside one particular picnic blanket, stars and stripes billowing in the breeze. As Alex sat quietly, staring out at the ocean, sketchpad in hand, her brother Ben and Jessica finished a game of beach tennis further along the shore. The air was cool, sharp and salty, and Alex filled her lungs. This wasn't the way she usually celebrated the Fourth of July, but it felt good nonetheless.

Jessica and Ben picked their way across the pebbles and back to the picnic blanket. 'God, I'm exhausted!' puffed Jessica, easing herself into a deckchair.

'I hope you haven't overdone it, Jess,' Alex said. 'You're meant to be taking things easy, not thrashing my brother at ball games!'

Ben laughed as he stretched out on the blanket. 'There's no chance of that, don't you worry!... How long now till the baby's due?'

'Oh, approximately 10 weeks, two days and twelve hours. And I don't mind admitting, I'm terrified. It's alright for you men.'

'I know! I know!' Ben smiled. 'All of the pleasure, none of the pain!' And with that he pulled on a pair of trainers. 'Just off to get something out of the car,' he called out.

The two women watched as Ben jogged away towards the promenade.

'There is something about a man in faded Levi's and a white t-shirt that is just irresistible...' Jessica remarked.

'I think you need to cool down, Jess!' Alex laughed.

'I am simply appreciating the view!'

'Hey, Jess, listen... I've been meaning to ask, have you thought any more about having a birthing partner there with you when the baby comes?' Alex asked earnestly. 'You know, for some moral support.'

'Nope!' came the succinct reply. 'And I wouldn't want anybody there, either. I've never understood these women who see giving birth as some kind of spectator sport. I mean, why would you want to have your partner there, watching you burst at the seams? How unsexy is that?'

'Well, I guess a lot of women need the support,' Alex shrugged.

As Jessica rummaged in the picnic hamper, she could feel Alex watching her. 'What is it, Al? You seem a bit, I dunno, *serious*. Lighten up, I thought this was a big party day for you Americans. Independence Day, and all that.'

'I'm just a bit worried about you, Honey. That's all,' Alex replied. 'Why don't you at least try to find the baby's father and tell him? You never know, he might really want to be involved. Or don't you want to see him again?'

'Of course I do,' Jessica retorted. 'But I only ever had his mobile number, and I've tried that. He's obviously changed it. I met him through a friend, who seems to have disappeared off the face of the earth, so what else can I do? Anyway, he's probably got a wife and kids somewhere.'

'How about the web, Facebook or something? Surely you can track him down somehow?' Alex persevered.

'No…you see…' Jessica hesitated. She could hardly believe she'd been so stupid – the truth wasn't something she found easy to admit. '…I didn't know his surname.'

'Good God!' spluttered Alex, then quickly added, 'Sorry, Jess. I didn't mean to sound judgmental, it's just, well, Honey, I hope you knew his first name!'

'I'm not that bad!' Jessica laughed self-consciously. 'His name's Finn. It might be hard for you to understand, Al, but it was a bloody awful time for me. I'm not normally like that, it's just that, after my mother died I was so incredibly low… and then suddenly there he was - this amazing guy, who just kind of appeared and picked me up and made me forget everything. Of course I knew about the risks I was taking and what the consequences might be – I am a nurse, for God's sake. But I didn't care. For that moment, for the time I was with him, nothing else seemed to matter at all.'

'Any regrets?'

Jessica stopped to consider. Regret certainly had featured in the kaleidoscope of emotions she'd wrestled with over the past months. And being a single mother had never been top of her

To Do list. But she was sure of her answer.

'No, I don't regret what happened. You see, even though Finn didn't turn out to be the guy I thought he was, and even though I do feel kind of used…meeting him literally turned my life around. He proved to me that I could be happy again, and that I could actually carry on…I'm not sure I'd even be here now if I hadn't met him.'

Jessica was suddenly interrupted by a male voice, breathless with enthusiasm.

'Right, ladies!' It was Ben. 'Time for us to do some serious celebrating.'

Watching the American peel the foil from the top of a champagne bottle, Jessica's heart dipped and her mind drifted back to New Year's Eve when she and Finn had shared a bottle of champagne. Just the two of them, oblivious to the rest of the world, as they'd ambled home, arm in arm.

If she tried hard enough, she could still, just about, recapture the scent of his cologne warm on his skin; the dimples in his cheeks; his deep green eyes…but as the months had passed, this had become harder and harder to do, and Jessica realised sadly that one day soon the finer details of these memories would probably be lost for ever.

The sudden crack of the champagne cork jolted her back to reality.

'Here's to the Fourth of July - Independence Day!' Ben exclaimed, bottle held high.

'And to the future,' cheered his sister, giving Jessica's hand a reassuring squeeze.

Twenty-Four

It was evident from the moment Hannah stepped through her front door after Friday evening's Good Grief session that Richard had not done as she'd asked. He'd been reluctant to let her go to the meeting in the first place, and had only confirmed that he'd be home in time to babysit at the very last minute.

She walked into the living room to find Lisa and Carrie rolling around on the floor watching cartoons and eating sweets, while Richard was slumped in his armchair, stony-faced, glaring at the newspaper.

'Oh, Richard, couldn't you have put them to bed just this once?' Hannah asked, looking around at the shambolic room. 'Go along girls. Off to bed now, it's very late. I'll be with you in a minute.'

The children knew they'd got away lightly and quickly disappeared.

'You said you'd be back just after nine, and now it's nearly ten!' Richard growled, without averting his eyes from the sports page. 'How do you know I wasn't waiting to go out myself?'

'Oh, I'm sorry, Richard, but the session started late and then…'

'You're so selfish,' he interrupted. 'So wrapped up in yourself. And now it's bereavement counselling to talk about, guess what? You! You and Sean.' Richard stood up, throwing his newspaper on the chair. 'Well, I just can't take any more of your fixation with Sean's death. It's got completely out of hand.' Now his face loomed at her, the veins on his forehead pulsating with anger. 'You don't live in the real world any more, Hannah, you're obsessed! Just look at you – you're a bag of bones. You've let yourself go, you've let this place go...well, I've had enough. I've thought about it and I'm leaving until you sort yourself out!'

With that, he stormed out of the room; Hannah felt whiplashed. 'You can't do this! Please, Richard, please!' she cried, following him into the hallway where he was pulling on his coat. 'I don't believe you, you're just using all this as an excuse,' she cried. 'You just don't love me any more, do you? I can understand that you might not find me as attractive as you used to, but I thought you might still care.'

Richard snatched his car keys and strode with deaf ears towards the door.

'You do care, don't you?' Hannah begged, grabbing at his coat-sleeve in a desperate attempt to make him stop and listen.

But her husband simply shook his head and walked calmly out of the house, leaving Hannah staring ahead in disbelief.

She staggered to the sitting room and collapsed into an armchair. How much worse could it get? Her mother despised her. Her husband had left her. Sean was dead. What was the point in living, she wondered. She closed her eyes and sobbed uncontrollably, lost in an agonising haze of sorrow.

Sitting on the edge of her single bed, hands cradling a small white porcelain urn, Terri had spent the last hour lost in a merciful state of limbo. Not thinking. Not feeling. Just there.

The telephone rang downstairs.

'Hello?...Oh, Hannah! You don't normally phone so late. How are you?'

Terri could hear Joe's warm greeting as he answered the phone in the hall. Sweet as Irish Mist, she'd used to say affectionately of her husband when they were newlyweds. These days she hardly said anything at all.

'What? Why on earth? Hold on, let me just get your

mother…Terri! Terri!'

She hastily replaced the urn in its designated place on the mantelpiece where it stood alongside her small collection of holy icons and a number of precious photographs, each ornate silver frame polished to within an inch of its life. Terri's eyes lingered on the smiling, jolly faces; moments in time, captured forever; images now destined to torment her for the rest of her days.

Footsteps hammered their path up the stairs. 'There you are!' sighed Joe, finding his wife standing guiltily by the shrine. 'Didn't you hear me call you?'

'I did not,' Terri uttered, turning away to reorganise the neatly arranged trinket boxes and ornaments on her dressing table.

'That was your daughter on the phone. Why can't you just speak to her?' Joe was losing patience with his wife's unflinching severity. 'You can't carry on like this Terri. She phoned to say that Richard's left her…left her and the girls.'

Terri said nothing: her eyes empty; her thin nervous fingers occupied with their futile task.

'In the name of Mary, Mother of God, this is your daughter we're talking about here, woman. Your daughter!' Joe shouted. And with a final disparaging glance towards his wife's rigid silhouette he left the room, slamming the door behind him.

Terri barely flickered. Then slowly, she retrieved the urn from the mantelpiece and sat down with it once more on her bed, a solitary tear winding its way down her care-worn cheek.

Twenty-Five

Melissa looked terrible. Even her dreadlocks, normally full of a life of their own, lay limp and listless on the pillow.

'Are you sure you don't mind, my dear?' she croaked. 'You'll find my register on the bureau downstairs. All the names and numbers you'll need are there.'

'Don't worry, I'll take care of everything,' Alex said, standing at her neighbour's bedside. 'Now is there anything else I can do? Can I get you some more tea? Maybe some soup?'

'No, I'll be fine, but if you wouldn't mind taking Freud just for a short walk, I know he'd be grateful.'

'Sure. No problem. Now you get plenty of rest, and I'll be back to see you again later.'

Once she'd taken Freud around the block, Alex returned home, where Jessica and Ben were still sitting where she'd left them, at the kitchen table having coffee. She quickly enlisted their help, and together they methodically worked their way down the list of Good Grief members, telephoning them all to let them know that, due to a bout of flu, Melissa was bed-bound and tonight's meeting would be cancelled.

'Right, that's my lot finished,' Alex said with a sigh.

'Just one left for me,' said Jessica, chomping on a kosher dill pickle, the only appealing snack she had been able to find in Alex's kitchen cupboards. 'I'll try calling Hannah Parker again.'

She dialled the number.

In the Parker household, the telephone rang.

'Lisa!' Hannah called out in a feeble, but exasperated voice. 'Please answer the phone!'

The two children immediately detected their mother's distress and ran, pushing and shoving, into the cluttered hallway littered with boots and toys, in a race to reach the phone first.

Carrie grabbed the handset. 'Hello, who's calling, please?' she asked, delivering her well-rehearsed greeting slowly and deliberately. 'Oh, Mummy's in bed.'

Her older sister snatched the phone. Carrie burst into tears. 'Is that Daddy? Hello?' Lisa asked, and then, after a disheartened pause, she answered, 'Oh, no, Mummy's not well. She's been in bed all morning. Okay. Goodbye.'

'I answered it first!' Carrie shouted, her cheeks flushed with fury.

'Well, you're just too young to talk to people on the phone, I'm afraid,' Lisa barked condescendingly.

'Well, I always talk to Daddy on the telephone!' Carrie howled. 'And I want to talk to Daddy now!'

Hannah appeared in her dressing gown, weary and incensed. 'What on earth is going on?' she shrieked, her rare display of anger startling Carrie into silence. And then she looked around at the mess the children had made while she'd been trying to rest. 'You girls just cannot be trusted,' she bellowed through angry tears. 'Go outside at once!'

Jessica replaced the handset. 'Hannah's little girl said she's not well.'

'What's up?' asked Alex.

'I've no idea,' Jessica replied. 'But she seems very fragile and she's painfully thin. Wouldn't surprise me if she's got anorexia or something. And it sounded pretty chaotic over there...I think I'll phone back.'

Jessica dialled the number again. 'Hmmm, there's no

reply,' she frowned. 'I'm a bit worried to be honest...and she really needs to know that tonight's being cancelled.'

'Well, why don't you just go over there?' Ben suggested.

'We could do, I suppose...We've got her address here on the list,' mused Jessica.

'Let's go, then, shall we?' Alex said, grabbing her keys.

Fifteen minutes later the two women stepped out of Alex's car and walked along the pavement of Wayfield Avenue, a small cul-de-sac in Hove. There stood Hannah's dilapidated estate car, parked on the drive of the modern, unassuming house. And there were her two young daughters playing in the front garden: the eldest steering a bicycle round and round in circles, while the youngest was pulled along in a doll's pram attached to the bike by a skipping rope.

'Hello girls,' Jessica said, opening the garden gate. 'I'm Jess. I phoned earlier. Is Mummy feeling any better now?'

'I don't know,' Lisa shrugged sheepishly. 'She's indoors.'

The front door had been left ajar, and Jessica gently pushed it open. The two women looked in on the untidy hallway, and beyond the hall to the kitchen. There was Hannah standing with her back to them in her dressing gown. Or was it Hannah?

The woman hunched over the sink, washing up, certainly had Hannah's petite build and broken demeanour. But as Jessica attempted to compute the image before her, something wasn't right and for the briefest of moments, her mind could only register confusion.

How could the smooth, hairless scalp belong to Hannah? After a few moments, Jessica could stay silent no longer. But, in her shock, all she could muster was a pathetic, 'Hi!'

Hannah spun around abruptly, a china mug crashing to the floor. 'Oh, my God!' she mouthed under her breath, trembling hands reaching for the edge of the counter, to steady her frail, weak frame. Then flustered and embarrassed, she quickly knelt down and began picking up the broken pieces of crockery.

'Hannah, I'm so sorry! We should have, we should have called...' Jessica stammered awkwardly. 'Well we did call, but your daughter said you were ill, which is why...'

'It's all right,' Hannah sighed, looking up, a defeated smile thawing her features. 'Honestly, it's all right, come in...'

Jessica and Alex felt uncomfortable, but hesitantly they entered the cluttered hallway, strewn with toys and books and muddy shoes. They followed Hannah upstairs to her bedroom, where an almost tangible sadness hung in the air of the gloomy room with its dark wood and dark walls.

'I'm afraid this is the only tidy place in the house,' Hannah said, quickly straightening the duvet. 'Please, sit down.'

'Hannah, er...this is Alex,' Jessica said, perching on the end of the bed.

'Hi, I live next door to Melissa,' Alex added sitting alongside her.

'Yes, I remember.'

'We actually came to let you know that this week's meeting has been cancelled,' Jessica said. Neither she nor Alex knew what to add. 'I'm really sorry that we called round unannounced,' Jessica repeated. She couldn't believe that they had intruded on this woman they barely knew, at her most vulnerable and exposed.

'Please don't apologise,' Hannah insisted. 'To be honest, it's a bit of a relief. It's about time I faced up to it all.' She sat at her dressing table and took the lid off what looked like a hatbox. 'It's not a bad specimen,' she said, fiddling with the glossy, lifeless hairpiece. 'My husband Richard thought the cheap synthetic ones looked too awful, and wouldn't be seen dead with me wearing one of those.'

Jessica remembered how she'd often thought there was something not quite right about Hannah's appearance when she'd seen her at the Good Grief meetings. She just hadn't been able to work out what. 'I hope you don't mind me asking, Hannah, but what happened? How did you lose your hair?' she asked cautiously.

Hannah sighed. 'It was the shock of my brother's death. I just woke up one morning, and there were great big clumps of hair on my pillow,' she said. 'After a week, I had none left at all. Richard was horrified – he'd always loved my hair, I don't think he saw me as the same person without it.'

'Well, that's crazy!' Alex said. 'He's your husband; it shouldn't matter whether or not you've got hair! And anyway,' she continued, 'You don't need that wig, you look great without it -- you've got such a pretty face.'

'Thanks, but how I look is so unimportant to me these days,' Hannah sniffed. 'And as for Richard, well, he's walked out on me, so his opinion doesn't count for much now…You know, in a funny sort of way I'm pleased I lost my hair. Every time I look in the mirror I'm reminded of my brother's death, and I hate myself. I want to hate myself,' she said, running a hand over her bare scalp. 'It feels like a punishment, a punishment I deserve.'

'Of course you don't deserve it,' Jessica frowned.

'Yes I do!'

'But why?'

'Because it's a fact, that's why.' She cupped her hands over her blotchy, tear-stained cheeks.

'I can't believe you've kept all this bottled up inside,' said Jessica. 'Why haven't you mentioned your brother at counselling?'

'I wanted to, that was the whole point of going… but for some reason I just couldn't.'

Jessica felt helpless listening to the emotionally battered woman whose raw, candid words reminded her that not so very long ago she, too, had felt totally alone and dejected. She recalled how she had been unable to talk about her pain and, instead, had lived in silence, denial and anger. And now she recognised a similar suppression in Hannah, for she, too, had clearly been alone with her agony. Jessica blinked away a tear of hurt; hurt, this time, for someone else.

'So talk to us now,' Alex said. 'Tell us about him now.'

'Well, what can I say...?' Hannah smiled. 'He was just a great person, really. He was four years older than me, but that didn't matter...and when I got married, he was still really supportive, even though I knew deep down he didn't really like Richard.' She looked thoughtful. 'I suppose he thought Richard was going to change me. Maybe he did? But Sean was so easy-going and philosophical about life...he used to say to me, 'Hannie, everything happens for a reason'. But hard as I try, I just can't find a reason why he had to die.'

'Mum-meee! Daddy's here!' a small voice called out from downstairs.

'Oh, no, I forgot Richard was coming to pick up the girls,' Hannah sighed. 'Just bear with me, will you?' she said, grabbing her wig and putting it on. 'I won't be a minute.' And she rushed downstairs leaving Alex and Jessica alone in the bedroom.

Alex grabbed Jessica by the arm. 'Did you hear what she said?'

'Yeah, such a sad story.'

'No! Not that! She said she blames herself for her brother's death! Just like that medium said to us in the car. You remember! She asked us if we knew a woman who was very unhappy. Who was blaming herself for something!'

Jessica raised an eyebrow. 'Yesss...but, she gave you a name, didn't she? And it wasn't Hannah.'

'No...no, it wasn't...she said it was something like Ann or Annie...Didn't Hannah say her brother called her Hannie?'

'Well, I suppose it's close...' Jessica rolled her eyes.

'So, if it's her...then that means...the spirit who's been trying to contact me is Hannah's brother!' Alex gasped.

'Ssssh, she'll hear you,' Jessica whispered. 'You're getting carried away, Alex.'

'No I'm not. Come on, it explains everything.'

Jessica shook her head. 'I'm not so sure. You're just looking for an explanation.'

'I can't believe you're saying this,' Alex said, with an exasperated sigh. 'You told me yourself that you'd had a message from one of your patients who you didn't even know had died. You said yourself, you were gob-smacked!'

'Alright, alright,' Jessica said, shaking her head. 'So what do we do? Tell her? Tell her that her dead brother visited us in your car and told us that she's got to stop blaming herself? I mean, come on! She'll think we're mad!'

With the children now away for the rest of the evening, the three women sat around Hannah's kitchen table, nursing much-needed mugs of tea. And as the incredible tale unfolded, Hannah shook her head weakly.

'So you're saying that my brother's ghost has been haunting you? But why would he come to you, someone he never even knew, rather than me?'

'I honestly don't know, Honey' Alex answered, 'but seemingly he has tried to get through to you.'

'I know it sounds unbelievable, Hannah,' Jessica added. 'But please, please come with us to see a medium, and see for yourself. I was exactly like you, I thought it was all a load of bollocks, but honestly, I'm not sure it is any more. Come with us, Hannah, please – what have you got to lose?'

Hannah wanted to protest; she wanted to say that since Sean's death she'd lost all belief in a God, in a Heaven, in anything. But even if she'd had the nerve to speak out, the last thing she wanted to do was offend Jessica and Alex, virtual strangers who seemed to be offering her such genuine support. Moreover, somewhere deep within, an ember of hope was beginning to ignite, to flicker, and she just couldn't dismiss their suggestion out of hand.

Looking across the table at the two pairs of eyes gaping back at her expectantly, she found herself replying, 'Nothing, I suppose, though my mother would be horrified.'

'Well, does she need to know?' asked Jessica.

Hannah didn't reply.

'Your brother wouldn't want to see you so unhappy, Honey, would he?' Alex added gently.

Hannah shook her head.

'And, that's exactly what the medium said,' Alex continued. 'She said he's really worried about you, because he knows you're in so much pain.'

'Look, there are no guarantees,' Jessica said. 'But surely it's worth a try, isn't it?'

Hannah clenched her sparsely-lashed eyelids together. A tear escaped from the outer corners of each eye, and ran over the contours of her angular cheeks, as she absorbed their persuasive words.

'So, when are you next going to see the medium?' she sighed.

Alex's face lit up. 'Well, as it happens, there's a special evening of clairvoyance on next month at The Beacon, with two celebrity psychics,' she replied.

'Would you like to go?' Jessica asked eagerly.

'Yes,' Hannah nodded slowly. 'I think I would.'

Twenty-Six

The atmosphere hummed with anticipation above the high-pitched chitter-chatter of the blue-rinsed regulars, some of whom sat knotted in head-nodding conversation, others milling between the aisles of plastic chairs crammed into The Beacon, in Border Passage. But tonight there was also a conspicuous group of boho students, and a smattering of assorted solitary individuals among the excited throng.

Jessica could hardly believe the evening had finally arrived, but here it was at last – a Demonstration of Clairvoyance with TV's 'Super Psychics' Darren and Julie England. She had never caught their mid-morning television show – she was usually either at work or still asleep – but judging by the turn-out that night, they clearly had an avid following. And, looking along the row at Hannah, blinking nervously and nibbling the skin around her fingernails, she certainly hoped they would put on a convincing performance.

Suddenly Jessica grimaced.

'Jess, you okay?' asked Alex, who was sitting between Jessica and Hannah.

'Just a twinge,' Jessica replied with a gasp. 'Is it just me, or is it really hot in here?'

'It's you -- here have a swig of this,' Alex offered, holding out a bottle of mineral water.

'No, I won't, thanks. With this baby pressing on my bladder, I'll probably have to get up to go to the loo as it is.'

Hannah gave a sympathetic smile and swallowed a deep,

steadying intake of breath. She was surprised by her racing heartbeat and moist palms. Although she hadn't admitted as much, she now realised how desperately she wanted to believe in some kind of life after death. While the idea of the supernatural was something she felt a little afraid of, she was more frightened of finding that there was no truth in it after all.

And yet, if it were just a lot of nonsense, why were there so many people here in this hall? So many normal, ordinary-looking people. People you would walk past in the street. Did they all make contact with spirits of the dead? Did they all believe?

'Good evening, ladies and gentlemen. How lovely to see so many of you here with us tonight.' Mary Watkins had taken her place at the podium and the room fell quiet, but for the scraping of chair legs on the hard flooring as the scattered congregation quickly took to their seats.

Jessica smiled to herself as she thought how much the elderly woman with her powdered cheeks and blush-coloured suit resembled one of the big blousy English roses in the vase up there on the table in front of her. She tried to imagine her own mother as a little old lady, dressed in a two-piece and sporting a demi-wave. But the picture simply wouldn't build in her mind, so far was it from the realms of possibility. With an intense pang of sadness, Jessica remembered that she would never see her mother's hair fade snowy-white. Never see her grow old. Never see her become a grandmother.

'Now, we are very proud to be hosting such a special occasion here at the Beacon...' Mary continued. 'But before I welcome in our guests, I'd like to open with a short blessing...'

Alex noticed that Hannah looked bewildered.'Don't worry,' she whispered. 'It won't be heavy. Wait and see.'

'Dear God, please bless all who are gathered here tonight and the families they represent. May all that is said and done here in this sanctuary of light be in truth and love. Amen...Right then, it's the moment we've all been waiting for, as they say!' Mary chirruped eagerly. 'Let's surround our guests with love and positivity. Ladies and gentlemen...please welcome, all the way from Manchester, Darren and Julie England!'

A door behind Mary opened, and out walked the grinning husband and wife team. With their mahogany tans, whitened teeth and similarly-bouffanted hair-dos, they looked more like retired shopping channel presenters than mobile mediums, Jessica observed. The pair shook Mary's hand warmly, then spread their smiles across the room.

'Well, good evening everyone,' said Darren, unbuttoning the jacket of his silver-grey suit. 'First of all, I'd like to say how wonderful it is to be here tonight, isn't it, Julie?'

His wife nodded emphatically.

'...I can already feel that we're going to have a very successful demonstration. But before we get started, I'm just going to perform a little ritual which I like to carry out...'

As he spoke, Darren walked around the hall, ringing a small, cymbal-like instrument, its chime floating like a beautiful ball of light. 'As some of you may already know, bells symbolise communication between the earth plane and the spirit world, so I always think this is a nice thing to do on an evening like tonight...it helps to raise the vibrations and welcome in our loved ones from the other side, doesn't it, Julie? For, remember, when we pass into the spirit world, we are not dead and gone. We have gone back to life, but in another realm.'

By now he was at his wife's side again on the platform. 'There we are, my dear, over to you.'

'Thank you Darren,' smiled Julie, resplendent in a rather unforgiving silver pencil skirt and turquoise satin blouse. 'Now then, for those of you haven't seen our demonstrations of clairvoyance before, I'll just explain. I'm a psychic artist, so while Darren receives messages from the spirit world, I shall be drawing what I pick up. Usually we are both tuned in to the same spirit, but we have been known to have two on the go at the same time, haven't we Darren?'

The audience tittered as her husband gave a theatrical nod, and a wink, his mouth open wide in silent laughter.

'Anyway, my hand will be guided by those on the other side who wish to make themselves known to you this evening. So, if you're ready, Darren?'

'I'm ready, Julie, and I hope your charcoal's at the ready too, my dear, because I'd like to begin straight away by coming over to this side of the room...'

Gesturing with a broad sweep of his arm, the medium walked towards the area where the three women were sitting. 'Now...I'm getting the feeling that I'm on a boat...out at sea...I'm a young man...Can anybody take this?'

He surveyed the faces, row upon row, gazing back at him, nobody responding. Undaunted, he continued: 'Okay, let's see...well, this young man is anxious, very anxious that I make contact with somebody here...' Darren closed his eyes. 'Come on, mate, tell me where you want to go...'

A heavy silence, dense with expectation, swamped the room; ominous and still, like the moment before a thunderbolt strikes its earth-shattering blow.

'Thank you!' Darren sang. 'It's somebody over here.' He pointed to the middle of the room, where Hannah, Alex and Jessica were sitting. 'I feel he wants to come to someone in this area...can anybody understand a young man, who loved the sea...but I don't feel he died at sea...?'

Hannah's throat tightened; the room seemed to spin; the medium's wide, shiny face loomed at her from across the hall.

'You, my dear!' he declared, now pointing directly at Hannah. 'I feel he wants to come to you.'

Suddenly she felt as though she were drowning, as though she couldn't breathe. It was as if everything was in slow motion; she could see Darren England's mouth move, but she had to strain to decipher his words.

'I have to tell you, there's a young man in spirit standing directly behind you!' said the medium with a hearty laugh.

Up on the podium Julie was nodding and sketching furiously.

'...Now, I feel this is a family link,' he continued, pacing from one side of the hall to the other. 'I can feel the love is very strong, so it's somebody close to you, my dear...I feel he was quite young when he passed, and I believe that his passing was fairly recent as I can see the newness of his spirit.'

Jessica and Alex smiled excitedly. '...He's showing me that boat again...he must have loved sailing...I want to say he's your brother, my dear. Am I right?'

Hannah nodded, biting hard into her lower lip in order to hold back her tears.

'I need to hear your voice, my dear,' called out Darren. 'It's very important you speak up. I need your energy so that I can keep the connection going. After all, I am merely the telephone line between the spirit world and the earth plane. Can you accept this, my dear? Is this your brother?'

'Yes...yes, I can, I mean, it is,' she replied in the loudest voice her constricting throat she could muster.

'Thank you my dear! Now, then...he's showing me a letter here...the initial S...did his name begin with the letter S? Don't forget, speak up!'

Hannah couldn't quite believe what was happening; her body felt numb to the core, yet somehow she managed to answer: 'Yes...my brother's name was Sean.'

'Sean! Right, thank you, my dear.' Darren was triumphant. Then he stopped in his tracks. 'My goodness! Well, I have to say that the love he feels for you, my dear, is absolutely overwhelming.' The medium took a handkerchief from his pocket and wiped his tanned, glistening brow. 'Overwhelming it is...I can feel his emotion...in fact, I'm feeling quite choked up...'

By now teardrops brimmed from his eyes. 'There's an

enormous amount of sadness here, my dear. But he's quite philosophical about it, you know. He's saying it was his time to go...it's not your fault... it was just his time.'

Hannah was unable to hold back the tears any longer, and as she wept quietly into a tissue, the whole room seemed to breathe a sympathetic sigh.

'Sean's still standing there, my dear, but now his arms are outstretched around you and the two ladies sitting with you,' Darren said. 'It's as if he's giving you all a big, warm hug. Are the three of you related?'

'Er, no,' sniffed Hannah.

The medium didn't seem to hear. 'He's got a message for you, my dear.,' he continued, pointing now at Alex. 'He's saying you mustn't worry. He's there for you.'

'Oh, but he never knew me.' Alex shook her head.

'Well, he's telling me that he sends you healing at night while you're asleep, so he's certainly looking out for you from the other side,' Darren insisted with a smile, then turned back to Hannah again. 'Now he's talking about your mother, my dear. She's here on the earth plane, isn't she? He's showing me some kind of container...in fact, it's an urn...she keeps looking at it...he says he watches her looking at it every day, and he wants to wipe away her tears...there are so many tears. He wants you to tell her that he's fine, that no one's to blame, and that she must start living again...and so must you. Look after yourself, my dear...Now then, we'd better find out what young Julie has been up to, hadn't we?'

Darren hurried over to his wife on the platform. 'How have you been getting along?'

'Yes, well, I'm just about finished,' Julie replied, adding the final touches to her large sketchpad before making her way towards Hannah. 'I'm sure this is the same young man you've been communicating with this evening, Darren...he's such a lovely, vibrant soul...here, what do you think?'

Hannah stared down at the large sketchpad that was swiftly

thrust before her. As her eyes scanned the pattern of soft grey lines and heavy shading, her mind flashed blank, her brain unable to register the image which looked back at her from the page.

'Is it him?' whispered Alex.

But Hannah could barely hear the words above the sound of her own heartbeat pounding inside her head. Then, goose-pimples began to prickle beneath her clothes and her chest tightened as suddenly the face was unmistakable: the shape of the eyes; the dimpled cheeks; the hair.

Hannah nodded forcefully. 'Yes...it is...it's Sean!'

A gasp of relief rippled around the room and Alex gave Hannah's arm a squeeze, as Jessica craned her neck, trying to see the evidence in black and white.

'Let me just go and spray this for you, so the charcoal doesn't smudge,' Julie said, whisking the pad away before Jessica was able to catch a glimpse of the sketch.

'He's leaving just one more message before he goes, my dear,' Darren continued. 'He's showing me a lighter...a silver lighter. Does that make any sense?'

Hannah shrugged. 'Er, no, I don't think so,' she replied. 'I don't think he had a silver lighter...but he did smoke.'

'Yes, well, I can smell cigarettes,' Darren nodded. 'But he really wants to talk about this lighter. It seems to be very important to him...think, my dear. A silver lighter...'

Hannah shook her head.

'No! You're right, it didn't belong to him, did it?' Darren exclaimed. 'It belonged to someone else...a friend...'

'I really don't know, I'm sorry,' Hannah said.

'Well, ask around the family, because he's telling me that he wants whoever's got it now, to give it back to the owner... Now, let me just see if I can get any more information for you...' the medium persevered. 'Come on, mate, she doesn't understand, give me more...'

Darren paced up and down the aisle, pulling out his

handkerchief again to blot a sheen of perspiration from his forehead. 'Aah…good…there's a name inscribed on the side of this lighter…but I can hardly make it out, the connection's getting weak, his spirit's tired now…I'm sorry, my dear, I can't see it, I can't get any more. But I can feel there is so much love here…'

As he spoke, Darren turned to look at Jessica. His eyes locked with hers, and seemed to penetrate deep into the core of her soul. '…He wants you to know that there's so much love.'

Jessica flushed self-consciously under the medium's unwavering gaze. Why was he suddenly staring at her like that? After all, this was nothing to do with her, was it?

The medium's words began to replay in her head. *Cigarettes. Silver lighter. Love.*

Her breath quickened. Her pulse raced.

Just then, Julie returned, brandishing the finished drawing of Hannah's brother. 'Here you are, my dear,' she smiled.

Jessica was too afraid to look across at the piece of paper that now lay on Hannah's lap. It couldn't be.

She glanced at the medium, who stood at the head of the room, watching her. He seemed to be willing her to take a look. Jessica could resist no longer, she had to know. And when she finally allowed her eyes to take a glimpse, to see the portrait for herself, every cell in her body froze.

Twenty-Seven

Outside, the streets of the seaside town swarmed with holiday-makers, their spirits undampened by the fine mist of rain filtering through the darkness. Starry-eyed children, aglow with additives, cheeks sticky with candy-floss, darted between groups of parents, plucking chips from paper cones while the smarter set spilled from trendy pavement-side restaurants. Normally the tantalising cocktail of aromas – exotic Indian spices, deep-fried fish and freshly-dipped toffee apples – would send Jessica's senses into overdrive. But tonight was different. As she trailed behind Alex and Hannah on their walk home, she was oblivious to it all.

The other two had hardly stopped chattering, frantically picking over the evening's remarkable events again and again, like magpies hungrily pecking at a carcass on the side of the road. Jessica, though, had remained silent. Her head felt muggy and her blood pressure soared.

'It's just amazing!' breathed Hannah, holding out the sketch of her brother. 'Unbelievable! Honestly, Alex, this *is* him!'

Jessica wanted to tell them to shut-up. Every word seemed to stab at her like a knife.

'I believe you, Honey, I really do, and I'm so glad you came along tonight. I knew something would happen! I just knew it!'

By now the women were approaching Alex's house. 'When do you think we could go back again?' asked Hannah eagerly as they walked up the path. 'What do you think? You'll come, too, won't you, Jessica?'

Hannah spun around to see Jessica leaning against the garden wall, looking at them in desperation.

'Oh my God! What's wrong?'

The two women rushed to Jessica's side. 'What's the matter, Honey?' Alex asked.

'It's the baby,' Jessica panted, her face contorted with agony. 'My waters have broken.'

'Are you sure? But you've got weeks to go yet,' said Alex.

'Yes! Yes! I'm sure!'

'We'd better get her to the hospital, quick!' Alex exclaimed, putting a supportive arm around Jessica.

'There isn't time!' Jessica wailed, leaning on her friend. 'I can feel the baby's head, it's coming now!' she cried through mouthfuls of air.

Hannah grabbed her mobile phone from inside her handbag and dialled 999.

'Let's get you inside, Honey.' Alex said, slowly guiding Jessica through the front door. 'You're going to be fine, Jess, don't worry. You're going to be just fine,' she said, cautiously manoeuvring her towards the sofa.

'No!' Jessica gasped and began lowering her body to the floor.

Hannah dashed into Alex's house to find Jessica on all fours. She hesitated. After all, she barely knew Jessica, and here she was, witnessing one of the most important and personal moments in the woman's life. Should she stand aside, and leave it to Alex to help her friend? Or should she help too? She dropped to her knees and began rubbing Jessica's back. 'Try not to push,' she urged. 'Just hold back, just pant!'

'You're doing great, Honey,' Alex added.

'Oh my God!' Jessica moaned. 'You just don't understand!'

'I do, Jessica,' said Hannah. 'I do understand…'

'No...no...you don't, you don't...' Jessica rambled incoherently, droplets of sweat trickling down her temples. 'I think he's dead!'

'Don't be silly, the baby's going to be fine.'

'...No, no, no...you don't understand!'

'Emergency Services!' a voice called out from the hallway, as two paramedics arrived and let themselves in through the open front door.

'Thank God!' said Hannah.

'I'm a bit worried, she seems delirious,' Alex whispered to the men, as they crouched down by Jessica's side.

'It's all right, love, we're here now,' said one of them, carefully easing Jessica onto her back. 'Okay, let's find out what this baby's up to, shall we?'

'I need him so much...Why can't he be here now?' Jessica groaned.

'Don't worry, the baby will be here very soon,' Hannah smiled, stroking Jessica's forehead.

'Right, love, time to push,' said the paramedic. 'Now, take a deep breath.'

As Jessica inhaled, Alex clasped her hand.

'Come on, Jess, you're nearly there now. You can do it. Come on, push!'

Jessica bore down into the disembowelling spasm; the burning, cleaving physical pain; her mind swimming in a delirium of disjointed images. Darren England. The silver lighter. Hannah's sketch. Finn.

'That's it, Jessica!'

'And again!'

Distorted voices boomed about her.

'One last push!'

Tears streamed down Jessica's face. She couldn't go on; she simply couldn't confront another wave of agony.

And then, she recognised a voice in her ear. A soft, gentle, loving voice.

Come on, Jessica. You can do it.

Her mother's voice.

Jessica's head spun.

She could hear Alex and Hannah encouraging her to keep going.'Good girl. Keep pushing. Nearly there!'

At last the paramedic cheered and the room filled with squeals of joy and relieved laughter. 'You've done it. Well done. Congratulations!' the paramedic announced. 'It's a boy...you have a beautiful baby boy!'

The midwife arrived just in time to cut the cord and clear the airways of Baby Gibson: a perfectly formed, pink and podgy little boy with a crown of gold, downy hair.

'Three and a half kilos! That's a very good weight, especially when you consider he's more than five weeks' early,' she chirped. 'What a clever girl you are! And only a couple of stitches! What are you going to call him?'

'Harry...after my grandfather,' Jessica replied softly.

The hysterical child was less than impressed at being forced to lie in the cold, hard portable scales. His tiny fingers spread like starfish, clutching the air; his desperate quivering rosebud lips searching for comfort as his forehead furrowed with increasing anger. Deftly scooping the baby up, the midwife restrained his wrestling arms by swaddling him in a towel, and as if by magic the crying instantly ceased.

'There we are. He feels more secure now,' she clucked, planting the little bundle into his mother's arms.

A combination of shock, exhaustion and wonderment had silenced the little boy's mother, too. As she lay on the floor snuggled in a blanket, her head propped up on a cushion, she gazed down in bewilderment, transfixed by her newborn child.

Alex found her camera and captured the first glorious moments of the small family unit – two bundles of contentment staring into one another's eyes, embarking on their unique journey together.

'Well done, Jess, he's just gorgeous,' she cooed, and stroked the baby's velvety cheek. It wasn't every day that one was witness to a new life entering the world. And for Alex it had been a particularly poignant experience, especially as she would almost certainly never have a child of her own.

Hannah marvelled at the beautiful picture of the baby absorbing his mother with his eyes. It was as though he knew how special she was, her red, wavy hair tumbling onto her shoulders. It was as though he knew how lucky he was. Hannah swallowed hard to fight back her tears – it had been such a remarkable evening. She had been so full of joy at 'finding' her beloved brother again, and then so honoured to be able to support and comfort her new friend in her hour of need.

Jessica looked up. 'Thanks, you two. Thanks so much for being there,' Jessica said. 'I couldn't have done it without you. I'm sure you were both meant to be with me!' she smiled.

'Wouldn't have missed it for the world!' Alex beamed.

Hannah and Alex went into the kitchen, conscious that mother and son might need some quiet time together. Jessica's eyes followed them, and she watched from a distance as the two women chatted and busied themselves making tea. She urgently needed to tell them; they needed to know. But how? And when?

Bittersweet impressions spun around Jessica's head as she glimpsed the father in her infant's sapphire eyes. Enveloped in primal, unconditional love for her son and brimming with elation, she could barely believe that she had brought this beautiful soul, this 'ray of sunshine' into the world.

But as she guided the helpless infant to her breast, a torrent of gloom surged over her as the full implications of her suspicions began to sink in. If, indeed, Hannah's brother *was* the man Jessica had met that night, the father of her child, then that meant she really would never see him again. He was dead. He would never feel the softness of their child's body against his skin; never ruffle his hair or hold his hand, never laugh with him or play with him. Then, as the baby pulled his mother's flesh into his mouth and began suckling contentedly, Jessica drifted into the realms of what might have been - the three of them.

An hour later, with the midwife gone, Alex drove to Jessica's house to collect the Moses basket, blankets and clothes for baby Harry. She had kindly offered to look after Jessica for a few days, until she was strong enough to go back home, while Ben was staying with friends in London. Jessica was so very grateful for the care that had been bestowed upon her by her thoughtful, compassionate friends, and as she sat up in Alex's comfy guest room bed, watching Hannah gently rocking Harry to sleep, she said a silent prayer of thanks to someone, to God, to whoever, for her precious friends and her precious boy.

But now that she and Hannah were alone, she knew it was time. Her palms moistened with trepidation as she summoned up the courage to ask the question. 'Hannah...does the name Finn mean anything to you?'

Twenty-Eight

'I just can't get my head around this. It's not that I don't want to believe it's true, Jessica, it's just that...Oh, I don't know.' Hannah's voice trailed away, as she wrestled with the astounding revelation she'd just been told.

'I understand, Hannah, I really do,' Jessica said. 'But it's a shock for me, too. I mean - your brother could be the father of my child. And he's dead! Don't you see?' she pleaded. 'Maybe he didn't abandon me? Maybe it wasn't just a one-night stand? Maybe it was as special to him as it was to me? And I'll never see him again!' she whispered, 'Think how that feels.'

'I know exactly how that feels,' Hannah retorted. 'But I'm still not sure we're talking about the same person. Okay, people did call him Finn,' she conceded. 'And Mother absolutely hated it!' For a brief moment her mind lapsed with nostalgia. 'I remember her saying to his friends, "Actually, I'll have you know, my son's name is Sean Finnegan!"' Hannah's deep green eyes even hinted at a smile as she enunciated every word. And then, just as quickly, the smile slipped away. 'But that's just not enough, Jessica,' she protested. 'It's going to take a lot more than that to convince me.'

Jessica screamed inwardly. She'd spent so little time with Finn, how could she possibly convince Hannah – or, for that matter, herself -- that he was Hannah's brother?

And then she remembered. 'You know what Darren England said about the lighter? Well, it's me! I've got it! It belonged to Mark – you must know him. Finn's business partner? I think they worked in computers or something? ' she blurted out triumphantly.

Now she was sure, it had to be Finn. It had to be.

Hannah turned her back to Jessica in some kind of instinctive defiance. Dumbstruck, she stared out of the window, squinting into the darkness, the glare of the streetlamp stinging her tired eyes, making them water. Or maybe they would have watered, anyway. Outside she saw Melissa, the counsellor, taking her dog for a midnight stroll and watched enviously as they meandered along the empty pavement, without a care in the world. How could life out there carry on as though everything were normal? She remembered the dreadful day of her brother's funeral, when she'd heard the milkman whistling merrily as he sauntered down the path, carrying the usual two pints of milk. How could he have been so oblivious to the emotional turmoil that had erupted inside the house?

Baby Harry wriggled in her arms, and immediately her mind lurched back to the present. She looked down at the new life she was cradling, at the baby's warm, pink cheeks and tiny toes, and suddenly felt an enormous rush of love. How amazing it would be if little Harry were her own flesh and blood. But, no, surely all of this was just some incredible coincidence? How could her brother possibly be the father of this child? The very idea was absurd.

She turned to see Jessica sitting up in bed, gazing back at her expectantly.

'Prove it to me, then, Jessica. Just prove it.'

Eyes scrunched tight, Jessica cast her mind back, once again, to the time she'd spent with Finn, and she desperately searched for clues that might persuade his sister to at least consider the possibility. A stony silence wedged itself between the two women, now distanced by the notion that they might be inextricably linked.

'Get my hand bag!' Jessica suddenly shrieked.

Hannah carefully handed Harry back to Jessica and, sensing the urgency, quickly ran off to look for the bag. She was back a few seconds later.

'This it?' she asked.

'Yes!' Jessica gasped. 'Now open it up.'

Confused, yet curious, Hannah did as she was told.

'Give me my mobile phone.' Jessica punched a couple of keys and then triumphantly handed the phone back to Hannah. 'See! There's his number.'

Hannah stared at the number displayed on the screen. It certainly was her brother's, but somehow it just wasn't enough. The look on her face said it all.

Jessica was exasperated. How else was she supposed to prove that she'd spent the night with Finn and that he was the father of her baby? After all, they'd had so little time together. There was nothing more she could do. But then suddenly her face lit up. 'I've got it!' she squealed. 'Look in my bag. In the front pocket. My address book.'

Hannah pulled out a small, scruffy book. 'Do you mean this?'

'Yeah...now look under C.'

'C?' Hannah asked quizzically.

'For, er, Caveman,' Jessica replied awkwardly.

'What on earth are you talking about?' Hannah snorted.

'Just look, will you!'

Hannah flicked open the book with her thumb at the letter C, and ran her finger down the short list of names and addresses:

Carter
Collins
Counsellor
Chester
Chinese Takeaway
Caveman

She stared in disbelief. There it was again, that number she knew so well, but this time written in her brother's familiar spidery scrawl. Tears formed a glistening line along her lower lids.

'He wrote that on the morning of New Year's Day, just before he left my place, about nine.' Jessica said, hardly able to get her words out quickly enough. 'He told me he was going to his parents' for the day...and that was the last time I saw him, walking down the street...'

Hannah sat, stunned, at the end of the bed. 'I phoned him on New Year's Eve,' she murmured. '...He said he'd been at a party, and was out at a wine bar with a friend...he said he'd phone the next morning, and I said I'd take him to our parents' for lunch...He called just after nine in the morning, and I picked him up near the pier in Richard's car. We were running late.'

Hannah stared ahead, trance-like, as she began to piece the jigsaw together. '...He gave me a kiss and said he was feeling a bit fragile...We were laughing,' she continued, 'and he said he had lots to tell me...Richard and the children were at home, but we had to get some petrol first...I remember, Sean waited in the car while I filled it up with petrol, and bought some flowers for Mother.'

Jessica listened intently, insatiably, devouring every detail of Finn's movements after their first and final parting.

Hannah continued almost in a trance.'...When I got back in the car Sean put on some music and was asking about the girls. He hadn't seen them for a while, and wanted to know what they'd been up to...' Her eyes glazed over as she recalled her last precious moments with her brother. 'It must have been a minute after we'd left the petrol station...we were talking and laughing...'

She stopped, almost gagging on the words she couldn't bring herself to say.

Jessica willed Hannah to continue. She had to hear the

truth, she needed to know the facts. Only then could she find some kind of peace, some kind of closure.

Hannah's voice cracked. 'The last thing I... I can remember is slamming on the brakes and swerving to avoid an on-coming car.' She clenched her eyes tightly together and angrily brushed away her tears. 'Apparently, the other driver was a teenager, four-times over the limit. He got away with a broken collar bone and stitches, and we ended up wrapped around a lamppost...' She took a deep breath. '...Then, a few days later, when the doctors thought I was strong enough, they told me Sean was dead.'

Jessica inched towards Hannah, drawing her friend in close to her and the baby. 'Do you realise what all this means, Hannah?' she sniffed.

Hannah looked down at her nephew, his eyes flickering open and shut as he slept. 'It means...it means you and I are family...' she smiled through her tears. '...We're connected by this little boy.'

An impish grin spread across Jessica's face. 'And it means you're stuck with me forever,' she teased. 'Whether you like it or not!'

The two friends, still shell-shocked, laughed together and cried together, locked in love for the baby and for his father. Both aware that this biological bond would now glue them together forever.

'Oh, Sean, if only you knew,' Hannah sobbed, stroking the baby's soft, downy hair.

'I'm sure he does know,' Jessica answered quietly.

The days following Harry's birth were warm and safe, rolling by in a calm, comfy cotton-wool cloud which enveloped itself around all three women and the baby. Jessica surprised everyone by proving to be a natural mother – so gentle and nurturing without being over-protective or fussy, and so generous with her little boy, who spent more time in the arms of his 'aunties' than in his Moses basket.

But sadly Hannah's joy was tarnished; something pricked at her conscience whenever she bathed her nephew, dressed him or rocked him to sleep.

Her mother.

Hannah hadn't seen Terri for some time, not since that dreadful weekend she'd spent at her parents' house with the girls. Of course, since then, she'd been desperate to tell them about the incredible evening at The Beacon, when she'd seen remarkable evidence of life after death. Her own brother's life after death. But she knew that any attempt to share her experience with them would have been a complete waste of time. So they'd spoken, if you could call it that, in awkward monosyllables over the phone, and Hannah had felt as neglected as ever by her parents. Consequently, it had been easier to cease striving for her mother's affections and, instead, Hannah had attempted to block her parents from her thoughts altogether. And in recent weeks, she'd taken Melissa's sensible advice and had successfully focused her time and energy only on the people around her who cared – her daughters, and Jessica and Alex.

But now there was someone else to consider – Harry, Sean's child – her parents' only grandson. And as the information she was withholding began to torment and fester, Hannah found it increasingly difficult to remain detached. They had to be told.

September 6th was the start of the autumn term and the date Hannah's eldest daughter had been longing for – her first day in the junior school. Excitedly Lisa climbed out of the car and pulled her bag over her shoulder. Throwing her mother a fleeting wave, she strode off confidently towards a group of friends in the playground.

For a moment Hannah felt superfluous, as she watched her independent self-assured daughter chattering animatedly with her playmates, oblivious to her mother's disquiet. Then, turning the key in the ignition, Hannah smiled to herself, for in her heart she knew that both of her children were not only confident with their friends, they were also confident in the knowledge that they were loved by their mother. If only she could say the same about her own mother, she sighed and, pulling away from the school, braced herself for the drive ahead.

The roads were predictably busy that morning but, with no major hold-ups, Hannah found herself crawling through the winding lanes of her parents' village and turning into Hollybush Way less than an hour later. As she negotiated the speed bumps and passed the grand neighbouring properties dotted along the exclusive private road, she felt the familiar tightening of her throat again. The sensation became tighter and tighter as she neared her parents' house and envisaged her mother's reaction to her unannounced arrival and imminent disclosure.

As she drove between the open wrought iron gates, Hannah saw that her father's car wasn't there on the driveway.

'Oh no, please be in, please be in,' she muttered out loud to herself, praying that the long journey – and her anxiety – had not been in vain. Quietly, she shut the car door and made her way tentatively towards the verandah, her mind spinning and hammering, bombarded by a multitude of words she might use to ignite, as gently as possible, the bombshell she'd come to drop. But each of them seemed as equally shocking as the next; there was no gentle prelude. With a deep breath, Hannah slowly lifted the large brass knocker and banged cautiously. Then waited. The silence was intolerable. She willed someone to answer the door, but at the same time, willed them not to. And then at last, she saw a murky silhouette, through the frosted glass, as a figure loomed towards her. The door opened.

'Oh!' Terri was stunned to see her daughter on the step. 'What are you doing here, Hannah?'

'I've come to talk to you, Mother. I hope you don't mind.'

'Well, your father's not here, he's gone to golf,' Terri said, uncomfortable at being alone in her daughter's presence, without Joe's loyal allegiance. 'You really should have phoned before you left,' she frowned. 'I might have been out as well, you know.'

'Look, I won't stay long,' Hannah pleaded.

The door opened wider as Terri reluctantly ushered Hannah in through the hallway and into the sitting room. 'You'd better take a seat if you've got something to say,' her mother said. 'Though I can't imagine what on earth is so urgent that there wasn't even time for a phone call to warn us you were coming.'

Terri folded her arms over her spotless apron and stared skywards, her face frozen in its usual pinched expression.

'It...it's Sean,' Hannah stuttered, staring at the patterns in the carpet, not daring to make eye contact with her mother. Silence swamped the room; Hannah drew in a breath of courage. 'I really don't know how to tell you this, but...'

'But *what*?' Terri demanded.

'He's made contact with me'

'What on earth are you talking about?' her mother barked, nostrils twitching with irritation.

'He's communicated ...through a medium,' Hannah whispered, allowing her eyes to leave the carpet and slowly rise to meet her mother's. They locked in pain, but not in empathy.

'How dare you!' Terri suddenly bellowed. 'How dare you come into this house and talk like this? After everything you've done, how could you insult your poor brother's memory like this?'

Hannah leapt up. She wanted to shake her mother; shake away her blinkered, bigoted beliefs; her stubborn small-mindedness.

'No, listen!' she begged. 'You've *got* to listen!' Hannah

reached out her hand to Terri in desperation, but her mother marched to the other side of the room.

'I'm not going to listen to anything you've got to say, and I'm certainly not interested in, in witchcraft!' she spat.

'I knew you wouldn't understand...'

'Don't you patronise me!'

'Look, Mother, you've got to listen to me!' Hannah implored. 'There's a baby too! He's fathered a baby!' And then her voice trailed off as her eyes fixed blankly again on the intertwining twists and swirls of the carpet. 'You've got a new grandchild, a little boy...'

'Oh no! Oh no!' Terri panted, short of breath. 'Leave me alone!' she cried. 'You've got no idea, have you? No idea of the pain I've been living with? And now you think you can just come round here with some ludicrous story and that it'll make everything all right again. Well, you can't!'

Hannah could feel Terri's agony, but she had to persist, had to seize this opportunity to make her listen, to make her believe. Pulling a sheet of paper out of her bag, she walked slowly across the room..

'Look,' Hannah begged, hands trembling as she held the sheet of paper out in front of her. 'Look, Mother, the medium drew this picture of Sean.'

The elderly woman refused even a fleeting glance at the portrait, closing her eyes firmly and brushing her daughter aside. 'Take it away! They might have fooled you, but you can't fool me!' she bellowed.

'Please, please, Mother, you must, you must just look at it. The woman who drew this had never laid eyes on Sean before, and it's him! It's definitely Sean! Look!'

Terri snatched the sketch from Hannah's hands, and violently scrunched the piece of paper into a tight ball, then hurled it across the room. 'Look what you're doing to me!' she screamed at her daughter. 'Are you trying to give me a panic attack? Sean's dead and it's all your fault! Now, just go... just go and leave me alone!'

'But, Mother, he knows how you feel,' Hannah persevered frantically. 'He sees you...he sees you with his ashes...but he wants you to know he's fine now, and he wants you...'

'I said I want you to leave!' Terri shrieked.

Enough was enough. Hannah knew her chance had been bled dry, and she walked towards the front door, somehow managing to maintain her composure in spite of her trembling lips and tear-stained cheeks. Once outside she gasped for air, choking on her sorrow, and ran sobbing uncontrollably towards the safety of her car.

Alone in the sitting room, Terri sat in stunned silence. Paralysed and unblinking. Staring at the patterns in the carpet.

Twenty-Nine

'So, how have you been?' Dr. Khan asked, peering over his glasses at the file of papers in front of him.

'Good, I guess. A little tired, maybe, but I have been pretty busy,' Alex replied stiffly. She watched the consultant as he read through her notes, scrutinising his face for a flicker of a reaction to the results of her latest blood tests. She'd had so many tests and check-ups over the years, but her nerves always managed to get the better of her.

At last, Dr. Khan removed his spectacles and, leaning forwards on the desk, focused on his patient. 'Well, your most recent results don't show any cause for concern, but if you're feeling under par, we'll run a routine biopsy, just to be sure. But, please, don't be alarmed. As you know, this is just a precaution. It might just be that you're over-doing things.'

The doctor reclined in his chair. 'Remember, Alex, you're precious. I'd like you to slow things down just a notch, perhaps even think about cutting back the hours you work at school, at least for the time being. Again, it's just a precaution.'

Alex stared back at Dr. Khan. How could this be happening now? Now, when all the pieces in the jigsaw of her life seemed to have finally slotted into place?

'Do try not to worry,' the consultant smiled reassuringly, and scribbled on a green slip. 'Now take this along with you to Pathology, I want you to have some more blood taken today, and my secretary will call you to arrange the biopsy. Take care of yourself, and I'll see you again in the next couple of days.'

Thirty

It had been one of those awful mornings when nothing had gone right, from the moment the alarm had failed to go off at seven to the car engine refusing to start an hour and a half later. Not to mention the fireworks in between: lost shoes (Carrie); forgotten homework (Lisa); burnt breakfast (Hannah); and temper tantrums (all three). But, with Lisa safely deposited at school, there was just one final hurdle: to get her pouting, petulant younger sister through the bright red nursery door which now beckoned to them as they approached along the path.

'Hurry up, sweetheart, we don't want to be late.' Hannah did her best to sound calm and in control as she endeavoured to quicken their pace, despite being pulled in the opposite direction by a distinctly stubborn four-year-old.

'I don't want to go to nursery today,' whined Carrie. 'I want to go home.'

'But you love nursery! And you're going to plant beans today!'

'Don't want to plant stupid beans. I just want to go home.'

'Oh, come on, Carrie, don't do this to me!' Hannah could feel herself losing it. How easy it would be to give in; to turn around, go back to the house and cuddle up together under the duvet in front of the television. Cosy and warm.

Just then a small voice squeaked from behind. 'Carrie! Carrie! Mummy, can Carrie come and play after nursery today?'

169

Hannah turned to see a turbo-charged munchkin in pink fake fur and fairy-wings, bolting towards them: it was Alice, one of Carrie's classmates, dragging her mother behind her.

'Can she, Mummy? Can she?'

'Well…yes…of course…if she'd like to,' gasped the exasperated woman, as she struggled to balance a bundle of rainbow-coloured books with an army of cuddly toys and a bulging leopard-print rucksack. 'Would that be okay?' the mother begged, turning to Hannah.

'What do you think, Carrie? Would you like to go and play with Alice?'

'Yes!' came the instant reply, as if that morning's painful pleadings simply hadn't happened at all. And the two little girls, hands clasped, skipped off along the path with overloaded parent in close pursuit.

'I'll give them tea…pick up about five, if that's okay?' she called to Hannah over her shoulder, as she tottered behind them.

Hannah waved in reply. That was close, she thought with a sigh and, she had to admit, more than a tinge of disappointment – she rather missed Carrie's company on the days she was at nursery. Making her way back towards the gate, a sudden swarm of late-comers surged along the path; a stampede of delightfully chubby little legs in brightly-coloured woolly tights and bleary-eyed mothers thankful for the opportunity of a few hours' peace. Hannah stepped aside to let them go by, acknowledging the familiar faces with a nod and a knowing smile. But as the group passed, one solitary figure remained, standing almost motionless there at the entrance, squinting in the morning sun.

Hannah's heart sank. 'Hello, Mother.'

Sitting at a table in the window of the small steamy coffee shop, Terri unbuttoned her navy cashmere coat and folded her silk headscarf neatly into her small handbag. Then, with a sharp glance towards her daughter, who by now was paying for their drinks at the counter, she took from the bag a piece of paper which she lay out flat on the table. She did her best to iron away the many creases with her hand, as she had already done several times before, and noticed with dismay how the soft grey smudges had begun to cloud the charcoal sketch.

'You kept it, then?' Hannah observed, with uncharacteristic testiness, placing two large mugs of coffee on the table and taking a seat opposite her mother. Despite the crumpled paper, the image of her brother, as drawn by psychic artist Julie England, was as recognisable as ever.

After a brief pause, Terri replied, 'Your father wouldn't let me throw it away.'

'Oh, so you told Dad, then? And what did he think?'

'Well, you know your father...he's very impressionable,' Terri replied dismissively, the steely Irish timbre of her voice still as strong as the day she left Killarney more than forty years ago. 'Is this what you young women do all day while your children are at school?' she hissed, with a disapproving glance around at the groups of mothers huddled gratefully around precious skinny lattes. 'Don't they have homes to run, for goodness' sake?'

'So you've come all this way to sit here and tell me -- what, exactly?' Hannah snapped. 'That I'm to blame for everything that's happened AGAIN? That this sketch is rubbish, AGAIN? That I'm a completely worthless, shameful, crap daughter AGAIN?'

Terri twitched, conscious that all eyes in the café were now upon her. 'Well, I've obviously wasted my time trying to talk to you.' Her words squeezed out through tightly-pursed lips. 'I don't know why I bothered, I really don't...'

She stood to leave, humiliated by the indignity of Hannah showing her up in public, in front of this silly gaggle of women. But as she began to button herself back into her coat, she realised that she was angry, not with her daughter, but with herself. How could she have handled the situation so incompetently? This wasn't what she'd wanted. This wasn't what she'd planned at all.

With a sigh, Terri sat down again. 'Hannah... listen to me, will you?' It had been such a long time since she'd spoken so softly to her daughter, she'd almost forgotten how. 'The answer is No...I haven't come here to tell you any of those things...any of those stupid things. I kept this picture because I wanted to keep it. In fact, I've kept everything that reminds me of your brother...everything. And yes, I've got the urn with his ashes in my bedroom, just like that medium, or whoever it was, told you. And every single day since he died, I've held it tight, as close as I could get...just like when he was a baby in my arms.'

Terri's heart gashed with guilt as she looked across at Hannah. Why had it taken her so long to see the pain in her own child's eyes? 'Just like when *you* were a baby in my arms, too,' she added, reaching over to clutch Hannah's hand. 'You know, since you came by last week, I've spent a lot of time thinking. That's all I seem to do these days – think,' Terri almost laughed – another rarity. 'But that's beside the point...I've spent a lot of time thinking, and I've realised one thing: the day I lost my son, I lost my daughter, too. Oh Hannah, I'm so sorry I pushed you away. I'm so sorry I blamed you. I was wrong. You are not a shameful, worthless daughter. I'm the shameful one. I wasn't a mother to you when you needed me. And I apologise. That's all going to change now -- if you'll forgive me. I'm here today because I want you to know how sorry I am. And because I want to listen to what you've got to say. I need to listen.'

Terri reached across to her daughter and held her tight in her arms. Hannah's bottom lip shuddered; her cheeks pulsed fiery-hot. And then the tears came.

Awkward eyes in the café averted their stare from the two women huddled together in the window seat; closed their ears to the breathless, heart-wrenching sobs.

This time Terri didn't care. She knew exactly where she should be. She was exactly who she should be: Hannah's mother.

'It's all right, darling,' she whispered. 'I'm here now.'

'Come along, little man,' Jessica cooed gently, scooping Harry out of his Moses basket, in preparation for a mid-morning stroll. Since moving out of her rented basement flat and into her mother's house, Jessica had quickly settled into a comfortable routine, and was relishing life as a mother. She kissed her son's warm, plump cheek, then attempted as carefully as possible to thread his short, stout limbs into a cosy all-in-one. But Harry was having none of it. Instantly, his miniature pink lips drew downwards, and tiny whimpers quickly turned to full-throttle howls of indignation. 'It's okay, precious...it's cold outside...we just need to get this arm through here...' Jessica said. 'Damn! Now the phone's ringing!'

Carrying the disgruntled infant with her, Jessica hurried into her kitchen to answer the call. 'Hello?...Oh, hi, Hannah, how are you?' she puffed. 'Oh, can you hear him?...No, he's fine, just exercising his rights already, that's all...I was just popping out, actually. What's up?'

Jessica strained to hear her friend's words above the wails. 'What? Oh, God, is she? Poor you...what? Now? Shit! The place is a real mess, and so am I...God, she'll probably hate me! Oh, Hannah, please don't make me do this...I know, but...yeah, I suppose so...okay then...all right, see you later. But you owe me a drink – a large one!'

Hanging up the phone, Jessica surveyed the front room in dismay – the changing mat and packets of nappies sprawled across the floor; the laundry piled high on the coffee table; the stack of unopened removal boxes waiting patiently in the corner. 'Well, my love,' she told the now-snuffling Harry.

'Guess what? Grandma's coming to visit!'

The two women could hear Harry bawling from the other side of the front door when they knocked twenty minutes later.

'How can you be so certain that he's Sean's child, anyway?' Terri asked, raising an eyebrow at the peeling paintwork and dusty, leaf-strewn doormat. 'I mean, what sort of young woman goes to bed with a man as quick as look at him, the first night they meet? It could be anybody's baby for all we know...'

'Mother!' Hannah exclaimed, shooting Terri a warning stare.

'All right, all right,' her mother replied, shifting defensively beneath her coat.

Just then the door opened.

'Hello.' Jessica smiled sheepishly at her visitors.

Hannah noticed, almost proudly, how pretty her friend's flushed, full face looked; completely bare of make-up, yet still flawless, like china. 'Thanks for letting us come over at such short notice,' she said, wrapping Jessica in a big warm hug. Nuzzling into Hannah's shoulder as they embraced, Jessica closed her eyes tight, to avoid meeting the gaze of the white-haired woman who stood just behind them.

'...Jess, I'd like you to meet my mother, Terri. Mother, this is Jessica.'

'How do you do?' Terri offered an outstretched hand.

'Oh! How do you do, Mrs. Finnegan?' Jessica replied timidly, rather taken aback by the formality of her introduction. 'Come in...'

As they followed Jessica into the house, Hannah gave her a reassuring wink.

'...I'm sorry, Harry won't stop grizzling this morning,' Jessica continued nervously, as she guided them towards the Moses basket where the baby lay, and flinched as she noticed her underwear drying on the radiator. 'I just don't know what's the matter. He's been fed, I've changed his nappy…he must be exhausted, but he just won't settle. It might be wind, I suppose, but…'

'Let me.' Terri interrupted, and tenderly cradled her grandson for the very first time. 'You are beautiful.' She held the little boy close, breathing in that unique, delicious baby smell from the folds of skin on his neck. '…Beautiful.'

Now silent, Harry's glassy blue eyes gazed back at his grandmother.

'You've obviously got the magic touch!' Jessica joked quickly. 'He's a very good baby generally, except at night, of course. And he's a big boy, considering he was early. He was three and a half kilos when he was born, and he's putting on weight nicely. He's in the top centile of his chart. Oh, and I am breast-feeding, of course…'

'Come on Jess, let's get the kettle on,' Hannah said, putting her friend out of her misery and manoeuvering her into the kitchen.

Rocking the contented child in her arms, there wasn't the slightest doubt now in Terri's heart that Harry was her grandson: his almond eyes, his square toes, the dimples in his cheeks – everything about him resembled Sean when he'd been a baby. And as his lids flickered shut and he drifted into sleep, Terri felt a pang inside. Not the usual stabbings of sorrow that, for so long, had lunged at her on a daily basis. No, this was different: primal, maternal, instinctive. Love. And she hoped that this new life would mean a new beginning for them all.

Hannah couldn't remember the last time she'd heard her mother laughing properly. But there she was in the armchair, baby Harry glued to her arms, regaling the two friends with memories of Sean's childhood. And laughing. Properly.

'…And he came to me crying, "Mummy, I've got a pea stuck up my nose!" Well, it was jammed so far up his nostril we had to take him to hospital to have it removed! That was the last time I gave him peas until he was much older, I can tell you!'

'What about the time he was dressed as Spiderman, and got stuck on the roof?' Hannah prompted her mother, wiping away tears of laughter. 'Remember? He climbed up the drainpipe, but he couldn't get down again, so Mr. Downes, the gardener, had to get the ladder and help him!'

'Oh, goodness me, yes!' roared Terri. 'He must have been aged, what, about eight? I was sure he was going to kill himself...' Suddenly, her face clouded over, her pain resurfacing momentarily. '...He always kept me on my toes, your daddy did,' she added wistfully, planting a kiss on Harry's nose.

Jessica sat back on the sofa, smiling. She was still wary of Terri, after everything Hannah had told her, but this remarkably good-humoured insight into their past – into Sean's past – had quickly put her at ease.

Just then, Hannah's mobile started ringing.

'Hello? Oh, Mrs. Clarke! Oh no! I'm so sorry...yes, I'll be there as soon as possible. Ten minutes. Bye...' Flipping her phone shut, she turned to Jessica. 'Sorry, but we have to dash. I can't believe how late it is! That was the school -- I should have collected Lisa ages ago.'

'Oh, what a shame!' Terri clucked, placing Harry in Jessica's arms for the first time since their arrival. 'We were just getting to know one another, weren't we?'

'You can come over any time you like,' Jessica said, walking with her guests to the door.

'Well, yes, thank you. And my husband would love to meet you both. Perhaps you could bring them over, Hannah? Come for the weekend.'

'Yes, Mother, I'll arrange it. But come on, we really must fly. Thanks, Jess, it's been lovely, really lovely.'

'It has,' said Terri, with a hand on Jessica's arm. 'You don't know what happiness you've brought me, young lady.

Thank you.'

'Well, it's good to know that Harry will be part of his father's family after all.'

'And so will you, my dear,' Terri added warmly. 'So will you.'

Funny how surprising a day can turn out to be, Hannah thought to herself, as she collected a trail of toys and wet towels from the bathroom floor later that evening. Despite a mild headache, she actually felt pretty good. Better she realised, than she'd felt in a long time. With the children settled in bed, she might just open a bottle of wine. And she was sure there was a ready-meal in the freezer that wouldn't take too long to heat through...

On her way downstairs, she hesitated outside the girls' bedroom. All quiet. Hannah half-closed the door, then tiptoed along the hallway. But something made her pause: the slightest sound, but distinct nonetheless. Hannah listened hard. A soft, quiet sniffling drifted from the children's room. Slowly, she stole in.

Stifled sobs were coming from the bed by the window. Head buried deep in the Barbie blanket, small fingers clamped tight onto a battered Teddy bear, it was Carrie.

'Whatever's the matter, darling?' Hannah whispered, so as not to wake the girl's sleeping sister. 'What is it?' she added, perching on the bed.

Carrie just sniffed in reply.

'Come on, you can tell Mummy,' Hannah coaxed. 'Did something happen at nursery today that upset you? Or have you fallen out with Alice?'

A pair of watery eyes shone from beneath the duvet. 'Uncle Sean gave me Teddy, didn't he?' came a distraught, trembling little voice.

'Yes, my love, that's right...he gave you Teddy when you were born.'

'I miss him!' Carrie suddenly wailed. 'I miss Uncle Sean!'

'Oh darling, of course you do.' Hannah swept her daughter up into her arms, and wiped her tears from her hot, wet cheeks. 'Of course you miss him...I miss him, too...but he wouldn't want you to be sad, would he?'

Carrie shook her head slowly.

'...He loves you so much, and he wants you to be happy...You know, just because you can't see Uncle Sean, doesn't mean he's not around you. Because he is. He's here, he watches over you, he's looking after you, you must remember that.'

'Is he?' Carrie asked, her wide eyes darting around the darkness of the room.

'Yes, darling, he is.'

'Did he see me plant my bean at school today?'

'Definitely! And he must think you're a very clever girl. Just look at it!'

Hannah picked up the dented plastic cup that sat on the bedside table. Her daughter smiled proudly at the pot of dark, crumbling soil and the word 'Been' scrawled on the side in red felt tip pen.

'Now, you snuggle up to Teddy and have a good night's sleep. And just remember, Uncle Sean is always with you, okay?'

'Okay,' nodded Carrie with a sleepy smile, and settled back down in her bed.

Hannah kissed her daughter tenderly on the forehead, and crept out of the bedroom.

She'd quite surpassed herself, she thought with relief, now pouring herself that much-needed glass of wine. In fact, she hadn't really known where those words of comfort had come from; maybe she hadn't quite realised the depth of her belief? Then, swallowing a mouthful of cold, sharp wine, she opened the drawer under the kitchen sink. Rifling through a mass of takeaway menus, bills, children's drawings and letters from school, she finally found what she was looking for. A grainy black and white picture of Darren and Julie England grinning back at her from the photocopied flyer she'd picked up at their performance.

DARREN AND JULIE ENGLAND
TV'S SUPER-PSYCHICS
AVAILABLE FOR DEMONSTRATIONS
OF CLAIRVOYANCE
AND PRIVATE READINGS
CALL 0222 335 763

Thirty-One

As Alex lowered herself into the warmth of the deep, bubbly water, every taut muscle seemed to loosen and every aching joint eased. Resting her head back on the rim of the bath, she closed her sore, strained eyelids and took full, slow, grateful breaths.

She guided her thoughts away from her demanding day at the school, and instead cast her mind back home, back to New York. She pictured her mother busily preparing for Rosh Hashanah, baking challah bread and her famous barbecue chicken with cornbread topper, no doubt. It would be a strange holiday for her parents this year, she mused somewhat guiltily, without either of their children with them to observe the holy days of Elul. But they would all talk on the phone, and raise glasses over the web-cam, so they would be together, in a distant, virtual, cyber kind of a way. And what is distance anyway? Distance is merely physical, she reflected. If you are close in your hearts, close in a spiritual sense, then no matter how far the distance, you are still together – always. This was something Alex now knew for certain to be true. Then, as she skilfully twisted the hot tap with her big toe, she sank deeper into the heat of the water and wallowed in the warmth of the moment.

But the tranquility was soon abruptly shattered by the sound of a car horn beeping outside. Alex rolled her eyes and smiled. She knew exactly who it was. Quickly stepping out of the bath, she wrapped herself in a large, soft towel and padded down the stairs to the front door, leaving a trail of petite footprints behind her. And there was Ben, leaning comically on his new Porsche sports car.

'Ta-dah!' he sang with pride, introducing his sister to his new purchase.

'Awesome!' Alex smiled through chattering teeth, water dripping from the ends of her hair and soaking her bare shoulders. 'I'll get dressed and you can take me out for a spin,' she said with as much enthusiasm as she could muster. 'In fact, I'm going to Hannah's, so you could drop me off if you like.'

Although Alex had been looking forward to the girls' night in at her friend's house, now she wasn't so sure -- she didn't feel all that great and was preoccupied by the thought of her next appointment with Dr. Khan, where she would learn the results of her recent biopsy. All she really wanted to do was go to bed. But it wouldn't be a late night, she told herself -- and anyway, she wasn't working tomorrow so she could rest as long as she liked in the morning. Her shoulders and knees ached and her eyes were battling to close, but somehow she managed to pull on her comfy velour joggers and a t-shirt, and scrape her damp hair back into a ponytail. There was no time or inclination for make-up tonight so, grabbing her handbag and smudging a little balm onto her lips, she walked out to the car.

As they drove along the coastal road with the roof down, Alex was grateful for the buffeting, blasting sea breeze whipping around her head; bringing her back to life. She glanced over at her brother in the driver's seat, and smiled inwardly at his delight in his well-deserved new toy. As the lights of Hove twinkled in the dusk and reflected on the incoming tide, Alex gazed out to sea, listening to the gulls sing their melancholy evening lullaby.

'You okay?' Ben asked, as he pulled up outside Hannah's house. 'You've been real quiet.'

'What? Oh, no, I'm fine. It's just your car's left me lost for words!' his sister teased.

'Seriously, Al, you look exhausted.'

'Stop fussing! It's just been a busy week, that's all.'

'Yeah, well, I hope you're not overdoing things,' he said.

'Now stop it, I'm just fine,' Alex insisted playfully, unfastening her seatbelt. 'Anyway, thanks for the ride – great car! You'll be getting a lot of female attention in this, I'm sure!' she laughed, slamming the door behind her.

Ben watched as his sister walked towards the house. He watched Hannah open the door, and take Alex's bottle of wine with a kiss. Alex had told him all about Hannah and her problems, but this was the first time he'd actually seen her. She was attractive, tall and very slim. He waited, and watched until Hannah turned and looked towards him with a polite wave. Then she closed the door.

The tidy, cosily-lit sitting room welcomed Alex in. Jessica, curled up on the sofa, had already made herself at home, and Lisa and Carrie stood expectantly, in matching pyjamas and fluffy slippers, 'bursting' to see their cousin Harry. But the baby was sleeping soundly in his car seat, head tilted at right-angles on his shoulder, oblivious to the activity around him.

'What are you drinking, Al? You going to have a glass of wine, or your usual beer?' Hannah asked.

Alex didn't feel like drinking alcohol at all that evening, but nor did she want to draw attention to the fact that she was feeling under par. So she answered obligingly, 'A beer would be great.'

In the kitchen Hannah poured the drinks and started unpacking the cartons of Chinese takeaway. She was surprised to find her mouth watering at the sweet and spicy aromas; her empty stomach gurgling impatiently at the thought of the fiery chilli sauce and the fluffy golden rice inside those foil containers. She had denied herself the pleasure of food for so long, that her appetite had been strangled; hunger had become a stranger. But tonight it seemed that her body was rebelling, her senses reawakening. And she wasn't going to put up a fight.

While their mother was in the kitchen, Lisa and Carrie did their utmost to rouse Harry from his slumber with surreptitious tickles and tugs. But by the time Hannah had returned they'd conceded defeat and were skulking off to bed.

'Night-night Lisa! Night-night Carrie!' their mother called out behind them with a sigh of relief.

'Now, where was I? Oh, yes!' she exclaimed, handing round plates and chopsticks. 'Before you arrived, Al, I was just saying that I've managed to book an appointment for October 17th at three. It's a Wednesday. Hope that's okay?'

'We could even do Oxford Street beforehand!' Jessica grinned, delving into a carton of crispy duck.

'I hope you'll be able to get the day off work, Alex,' continued Hannah.

'I won't need to...' came the casual reply. 'As from next week, I'll be working fewer hours.'

Jessica was surprised; she knew Alex adored her work with the children at Homewood School. 'Why's that?' she asked, gnawing on a sticky spare rib.

'The job's exhausting, and I've become passionate about my painting, so I'd like to concentrate on that more. Two days a week will suit me better,' she smiled breezily. 'Anyway, I've got to help Ben find an apartment now that he's decided to stay in Brighton.'

'Oh! Has he?' Hannah said. 'That'll be nice for you.'

'Yes, much as I love him, he can't live with me forever. And it's so easy for him to commute to the City from Brighton,' Alex continued. 'Anyway, Wednesday 17th is fine...Maybe I should drop in at the agency to see Sam again?' she pondered, prodding at her rice with the chopsticks. 'I reckon I owe him lunch, big-time...But are you sure you guys don't mind me tagging along? I never even knew Sean. I don't want to get in your way.'

'Course not...there's safety in numbers!' Jessica insisted.

'What do you mean?' Hannah asked.

'Well, I'm sure Darren England had the hots for me that night at The Beacon!'

Hannah and Alex let out a peal of laughter.

'He did! Didn't you see the way he was looking at me?'

'Oh, Jess!' Hannah giggled. 'I think he's more interested in your soul than your body.'

'Yeah,' Jessica huffed, pouring herself another large glass of wine. 'Along with the rest of the male population, unfortunately. It's gonna have to be a tummy tuck and liposuction before any man looks at me!'

Just then two little girls, hair tousled and eyes bleary, appeared in the doorway.

'What do you think you're doing?' Hannah asked sternly.

'I can't get to sleep,' Carrie whined. 'You're making too much noise!'

'Can't we just stay up a little while?' Lisa pleaded.

'No, you can't. Back to bed!' scolded their mother.

Alex gently intervened. 'I'll tell you what, girls… if you go back to bed like Mummy says, I promise you can come round and do some painting in my studio with me very soon.'

'Yay!' shouted the children, and eagerly raced back upstairs to their bedroom.

'You're a genius.' Hannah said shaking her head. 'I'm afraid they walk all over me now that Richard's not around, especially at bedtime.' She sank her teeth into another spring roll. The taste, the texture, it was as though she were eating for the very first time.

'Have you spoken to him lately?' Alex asked.

'To be honest, I've been avoiding him,' she confessed. 'He's made a few comments to Lisa and Carrie about how he wishes we were all together again, but I'm just beginning to stand on my own two feet. Anyway, when he collected the children the other day, there was a woman in the car and apparently they've seen her a few times.'

Jessica and Alex braced themselves for an outpouring of emotion, expecting Hannah to crumple and the tears to fall.

'...But it won't take her long to discover the real Richard,' Hannah continued. And, with a wink, she held up a tiny pink shrimp between her chopsticks. 'She'll soon find out the truth!'

With that the three women screeched with laughter.

'Hannah! You bad girl!' Jessica squealed. 'Is this the new you we're seeing?'

'Actually,' Hannah grinned. 'I'd say it's the old me. And, do you know what? I think I'm beginning to quite like myself again.'

'That's fantastic,' Alex said, taking a small sip of beer and hoping that her friends hadn't noticed how little she'd drunk and how much food she'd left on her plate.

As the evening went on, Alex felt increasingly tired and queasy, it was all she could do to stop herself from falling asleep. So when Harry woke for his feed, she took the opportunity to retreat to the bathroom – a splash of cold water might do the job, she thought.

Leaning on the basin for support, head bowed, she recognised that she'd been foolish to defy her body's warnings to slow down. Since moving to Brighton, she'd become fanatical about her early-morning cycle rides; she'd stayed late at school, preparing and displaying work long after everyone else had left, and then most evenings she had been compelled by an insatiable desire to sit up painting until the small hours. It was no wonder she was feeling below-par. Maybe Dr. Khan was right; maybe she'd just been over-doing things, that was all.

She splattered her forehead, cheeks and neck with water and, patting herself dry with a hand towel, stared back at her reflection in the mirror. There were dark circles under her eyes and her normally-radiant complexion was now sallow and lacklustre. With a sombre vow to take more care of herself from now on, she dusted her cheeks with blusher and applied a pastel shimmer to her pale lips. Then she stood back for inspection: not great, but definitely an improvement, she thought to herself with a breath of resignation.

Harry was sitting hunched over Hannah's left hand, his plump cheeks wobbling as she rubbed his back when Alex breezed into the room holding her cosmetics bag. 'I've had an idea!' she exclaimed. 'How about a make-over, Han, to celebrate the new – or, should I say, old – you?'

'Oh, God, I haven't worn make-up for ages,' her friend grimaced.

'Well, it's about time you did,' Jessica added.

Alex laid out her make-up on the table – only the basics, but all sleekly packaged designer labels: Chanel, Dior, Yves Saint Laurent. 'Come on, I am an artiste after all!' she grinned.

'Oh, I don't know…' Hannah groaned.

'Oh, go on, just a little to make the most of those lovely eyes.'

Hannah blushed and reluctantly perched on the coffee table beside the brushes and applicators.

Alex was glad of the distraction from her fatigue, as she dispensed a dollop of honey-beige foundation onto her palm and dotted it onto Hannah's face, before blending with nimble fingertips.

Jessica watched in awe as the masterpiece took shape. Hannah's face became a smooth, flawless canvas, as Alex carefully defined the contours of her enviably high cheekbones with shimmering powder, and made her pretty eyes magnificent with magical gold-flecked shadow. But Jessica couldn't help thinking that the unconvincing hairpiece would always ever-so-slightly mar her friend's appearance. 'Have you ever thought about wearing one of those bandanas, Han?' she asked carefully. 'I mean, without the wig?'

'Can't say I have…' Hannah answered through a taut, immobile grin as Alex painted on another coat of lip gloss. '…But I'm willing to give it a try. I'd do anything not to have to wear this thing,' Hannah continued, suddenly a little subdued.

Jessica untied the black and grey cotton scarf that was looped around her own neck. 'Well then, why don't you try this?' she offered. 'You can keep it, if you like.'

'Let's see how it looks, shall we?' Alex said, and knelt in front of her friend to gently remove the wig.

Hannah blinked, conscious of her baldness, as Alex began to drape the folded scarf around her head. But then she stopped.

'What is it?' Hannah asked nervously, raising her penciled-in eyebrows, but still sitting as rigidly as a tailor's mannequin. 'What's the matter?'

Alex didn't answer. She simply stared at Hannah's head as the scarf fell to the floor.

'Look, Jess,' she beckoned. 'Look at this.'

Jessica peered over. 'Shit!'

'What? What is it?' Hannah yelled.

The two women screamed one word in unison: 'HAIR!'

A subconscious fear of disappointment meant that Hannah was unable to digest the meaning behind the excited squeals, and she gawped up at her friends in confusion. 'What are you talking about?' came the slightly belligerent response.

'Hair, you silly cow! You've got *hair*!' Jessica retorted. 'Look!' she shrieked, dragging the bemused woman up close to a mirror on the wall. Hannah gazed back at her reflection in silent disbelief. Then very slowly she raised her hand to touch her head, and gently brushed her palm over the tiniest bristles of hair sprouting defiantly from her scalp.

'Hair,' she whispered.

Hannah was still glued to the mirror half an hour after her companions had gone home. Fingers locked beneath her chin, as if in prayer, she stared back at herself, half-smiling in the stillness. Two simple words – thank you – reverberated around her head, but she didn't really know who they were meant for, or why. She just felt a sense of overwhelming gratitude for the way her life had turned around. And she would never wear the wig again – it was obsolete - just a symbol of her past. Now she was looking to the future.

Hannah was suddenly disturbed by a knock at the door. She looked at her watch. 12.45. Who on earth could be calling at this time? Hurriedly she tied the scarf around her head and walked to the door.

'Who is it?' she called out anxiously.

'Richard,' came the sheepish response. 'I know it's late. But I really need to talk to you. Please, Hannah. Please.'

Like a kick in the stomach, Hannah's contentment was immediately eclipsed by a raw, sorrowful pain. The mere sound of her husband's voice, now without a hint of egotism or conceit, so gentle and so seemingly full of regret, plunged Hannah right back into the depths of heartache and longing. Slowly she opened the door just a few inches and caught Richard's eyes in the darkness.

'Hi, Hannah,' he muttered. His head was bowed in apparent contrition, as he glanced up at his wife from under his brow. 'I hope you don't mind, but I couldn't sleep. I just had to see you.'

Hannah just stood there voiceless, as her head began to play a game of tug-of-war with her heart. She knew she shouldn't let him in, especially now that her wounds were starting to heal. Then again, if the separation had taught him something, if he'd seen the error of his ways…

Instinctively, Hannah released her grip of the door and ushered him in. Richard followed her into the sitting room and they sat down opposite one another, the physical distance like a gulf between them. Hannah said nothing and the resounding silence intensified. Wishing the pain away, she willed him to profess his feelings for her, waited for him to say something that would banish her doubts and give credence to the crumbling relationship. But he didn't. He didn't seem to know what to say.

'So...' he said at last. 'What's with the new gypsy look, then?'

An instantaneous kick in the gut.

But just as instantly Hannah forgave his indiscretion, persuading herself that poor Richard was probably just searching for something, anything to talk about. And with an embarrassed smile, she replied, 'Well, it makes a change from the wig... and guess what? My hair's finally started...'

But she stopped short when she realised that he wasn't listening to a single word. Instead his attention had turned to the stray wine bottles and takeaway containers that had yet to be cleared away.

'Been entertaining, have you?' he asked, looking around the room suspiciously. This time, there was no mistaking the friction in his tone.

'Yes, just had some friends over, actually. We got a takeaway...'

'Did you?' he glowered, his face flushed with bitterness. 'Well, I hope it was fun.' A picture of resentment, he tried to smile, but Richard had never been able to be happy for his wife. And Hannah was reminded of his controlling nature. Maybe she should finally accept that her marriage never was, and never would be, a fairytale?

Angry words spilled from her lips of their own accord: 'Well, you always did say I couldn't cook!' she retorted. 'From what I remember, you spent most of our marriage criticising every meal I put in front of you, and then complaining if I dared to suggest a takeaway!'

Hannah was shocked to realise that, despite her powerlessness to extinguish her love for Richard, she would no longer tolerate his oppression.

'Ah...well...I never said you couldn't cook,' he retracted uncomfortably. 'I just said that cooking wasn't your strong point....Anyway, I didn't come here to go over old ground. I came to talk about us making a new start.'

'Oh, Richard, I don't think now's the time to...'

'I know things haven't been easy for you, especially over the past year or so,' Richard interrupted. 'And I know I might not have been as understanding as you'd have liked, but I think we could salvage our marriage. And, for the sake of the children, I think we should give it a go.'

Five minutes ago those words might have made an impression. But now, and with no mention of love, no hint of tenderness, they were hollow, futile, unpersuasive.

'Look, Richard, I'm not ready to make any decisions,' Hannah sighed. 'And anyway, you've been seeing someone, haven't you?' From somewhere had sprung the courage to confront him.

'What are you talking about?'

'I saw a woman in the car, and the girls say you have a friend called Tracey.' Hannah poured the murky dregs from a bottle of red wine into a glass and knocked it back swiftly.

'Oh, Tracey...' he said dismissively. 'She works in the office. I often give her a lift home after work. You don't honestly think there'd be anyone else, do you?'

Hannah gave a defensive shrug.

'Look, I was just thinking, why don't we go away together, just for a weekend, just you and me?'

There, he'd changed again. With a flash of his most sincere smile, the controlling bully had vanished. And the next thing Hannah knew, Richard was sitting next to her, putting his arm around her and gazing at her earnestly. 'It would be good for us to have some time together, wouldn't it?' he coaxed. 'Come on, you know how I feel about you, don't you?'

Now utterly disillusioned, Hannah didn't know what to believe. All she did know was that she was still under her husband's spell. 'I'll think about it...it's late, Richard,' she said. 'You really should go now.'

'Well, can I just look in on the girls first?' he asked gently, and with all the tenderness of a loving, caring family man.

'Okay, but don't wake them, they went to bed very late.'

Hannah sank back into the sofa, and closed her tired eyes. Richard had thrown her into confusion by sending such mixed messages. Did he really care for her? Had anything changed? Would she ever be confident of his feelings for her? Then she heard Carrie's sleepy voice upstairs.

'Daddy…Daddy…' the little girl called out softly.

Hannah shook her head and tutted to herself.

'Hello, Princess, did I wake you?' Richard purred.

'What are you doing here, Daddy? Have you come back to live with us again?' Carrie asked eagerly.

The child's innocent question sliced through Hannah's heart. She knew she had the power to make the change that would take away her daughter's pain.

'…I miss you, Daddy. Please come back.'

'That would be nice, wouldn't it,' Richard replied. 'Not tonight, but maybe soon….and guess what? I'm going to take you and Lisa ice skating this weekend, and to the cinema, and for a pizza, too!'

'Really?' came the excited response.

'Now you go back to sleep like a good girl, and I'll be here first thing on Saturday. Night, night Princess.'

'Night, night Daddy.'

Hannah caught the sound of a kiss between father and daughter, and then Richard's footsteps on the stairs as he made his way back to the sitting room. She hastily grabbed a magazine and began flicking through the pages, so that Richard wouldn't suspect that she'd been straining to hear his every word.

'Okay…well…I'll be off, then. Do think about what I've said, Hannah. This marriage deserves a second chance.'

Thirty-Two

The sound of Alex's shoe tapping repeatedly against the leg of her chair reverberated around the small, sterile room, like a clock ticking, marking every second. She sat alone, waiting, reminding herself that the biopsy had just been a precaution. Everything would be okay, she told herself. Again and again.

She was startled when the door opened and her consultant, Dr. Khan, scuttled in, a small bundle of anonymous-looking files tucked beneath his arm. 'So sorry to have kept you,' he breathed, taking his place behind the desk before rifling through the collection of paperwork to find Alex's medical records. 'Ah, yes...here we are...right, so, how have you been since we last met, Alex?'

'Not one hundred per cent,' she replied impatiently, willing the consultant to cut the small talk.

'Okay...well, we have the results. There's good news and not so good news, I'm afraid. You'll be pleased to hear that the biopsy was fine.'

Alex instantly crumpled with relief.

'...However, I'm afraid your blood tests show that the cyclosporine levels are a little low...'

Alex stared vacantly at Dr. Khan, hearing his words, but unable to absorb their meaning. She noticed her own reflection staring back at her from the wide lens of his spectacles: her image small, distorted, unreal.

'So...is this serious?' the consultant asked on her behalf. 'Not necessarily...we always knew this might occur, it's quite common. It could simply be a matter of tweaking your medication. There are a number of options available at this stage…first I think we'll add to your cocktail of drugs, and put you on some Tacrolimus. Fingers crossed, that will sort things out.'

Then he leaned forward earnestly. 'But, without wishing to alarm you, Alex, I would also like you to consider the possibility of giving up work altogether. At least in the short-term…'

The suggestion was like a needle to a balloon. 'But, but why?' Alex stammered.

'Well, you see, the problem we have is that your immune system is not going to be doing a very good job at protecting you from infection at the moment,' he explained. 'In particular, viral infections, like chicken pox and shingles. And, working with young children, you are putting yourself in an extremely vulnerable position. Think of all those runny little noses!' he added with an attempted grin. 'Seriously, it's just not worth the risk. I'm sure you'd agree.'

Alex gave a slow nod of resignation.

'Good…now, do you have any questions?'

There was only one. Alex struggled to find her voice. 'I am going to be alright, aren't I?' she asked quietly.

Dr. Khan pinned on his most professional smile. 'Rest assured, Alex, you're in safe hands.'

Head still swimming, Alex sat on the edge of the sofa, clutching her coat as tightly as if it were a lifebelt. She couldn't cry: the tears of fear and frustration that welled inside just seemed to crash against a dark dam of numbness. And the heart which drummed beneath her breast and pumped the life through her veins, suddenly felt horribly alien, more like a defective piece of machinery than a part of her own body.

Footsteps hammered down the stairs.

'Ready?' Ben asked his sister enthusiastically.

'Actually, Ben, I'm not really feeling up to house-hunting right now,' she answered flatly. 'Do you mind if I bail out?'

'Aw, Al, come on…' he groaned, dropping next to her on the sofa. Ben searched her ashen face for guidance. 'You'll be okay, Sis, you're strong, you'll get through this.' Ben squeezed her hand. 'Maybe you'd feel better if you talked to Mom about things? I guess you should tell her anyway…'

'No!' Alex interrupted. 'I'm not telling her anything, not yet. And you mustn't, either.' She turned to look her brother in the eye. 'I don't want her worrying. It wouldn't be fair with them so far away. And, anyway, chances are, it'll all be okay.'

'But how can you go through all this without telling Mom and Dad?'

'You know what they're like! They'll be on the first flight over here,' she said. 'No, look, it's still early days. I'll tell them when I know more about what's going on.'

Ben flopped back in his seat with a frustrated sigh. He'd spent his whole life being bulldozed by his older sister, and obviously things weren't about to change. But he loved her, and he knew she needed that love now more than ever.

'Actually, I don't think I'm in the mood to be shown around another bum apartment, either,' he mused good-naturedly. 'How about we watch a couple of movies to take your mind off things?'

'No, Ben, I really think you should go,' Alex replied. 'The estate agent will be expecting you – you're probably late already. And anyway, I want this place to myself. You're cramping my style!'

Ben laughed. 'Oh, really! I suppose if I wasn't here, you'd be having wild painting parties every night!'

'Something like that. Now get outta here, will you!' Alex teased, and then added with a yawn, 'I'm going to take a nap – but you can check out the movies for later, if you like.'

'Okay, it's a deal.' Ben stood to leave. 'And I might just bring you a tub of Ben & Jerry's, if you're a very lucky girl.'

He planted a kiss on his sister's cheek. 'Rest well.'

Alex stretched out on the sofa, pulling her coat over her like a blanket and nestling into the pile of cushions. 'See ya later, bro...' she murmured drowsily, as the front door closed and, with Cookie the cat curled up beside her, she descended almost instantly into sleep.

The bells were the first thing she noticed, their joyous song tumbling, echoing from somewhere beyond in the distance. And then an all-encompassing sense of peace. She found herself standing before a set of tall, wrought iron gates, which slowly parted, beckoning her through. As she drifted along a stony driveway, Alex saw just ahead a large, solitary house: its wide windows staring down at her; its luminous white clapperboards dazzling bright against a magical, shifting, Technicolor sky. Gliding closer and closer to a set of steps leading up to a wood-decked verandah, the place felt so familiar, almost as if Alex had come home.

Slowly, she climbed the stairs. They creaked beneath her feet as somehow, she knew they had done for many years. The green door grinned at her like an old friend, and she lovingly traced her fingers over the word etched into the brass name plate: Failte.

'At last! I wondered when we'd finally meet...'

Alex turned to see a young man sitting on a swinging seat, there on the verandah. A vivid aura of light bounced around him, and his smile was so full of warmth, Alex was instantly struck by a sense of absolute, perfect love.

'Come and sit with me,' he continued. 'You've come a long way.'

There was something vaguely familiar about his twinkling, almond-shaped eyes, dimpled cheeks and shoulder-length hair. Somehow she knew this man, somehow she felt they were as one, and she sank into the seat alongside him.

'I've been wanting to talk to you, to let you know how much you've helped me,' he explained gently. 'You see, it's because of you that I've been able to get through to the others, and I just wanted to say thank you. I know it wasn't always easy for you. I'm sorry if I messed with your head! But they were all so sad, I had to reach them, I had to let them know that everything was alright, and that they should start living again.'

Alex noticed a melancholy shadow fall across the man's handsome face, and for a moment felt his pain prick her own heart. '...You've no idea how hard it is, seeing the people you love suffer. But now, at last, they're finding peace. Thanks to you.'

She looked out at the garden that seemed to stretch for miles ahead of them. Bathed in brilliant sunshine, the flowers and trees were more vibrant, more colourful than anything she'd ever seen before. Alex had never felt so tranquil, so safe.

'And there's another reason I wanted to talk to you, Alex.' Now there was an insistence in the young man's voice. 'I wanted to tell you not to be frightened.'

As he spoke, Alex could feel herself being pulled from him.

'I know you're afraid, Alex, but I'll be there for you. I won't rest until I've helped you like you've helped me...'

Alex rubbed her head and prized apart her heavy, reluctant lids. Now totally disorientated, her vision blurred, like an out-of-tune TV. For a moment, she didn't know whether she was still sitting on the sunny verandah, or on her sofa at home. She did her best to shake herself back into consciousness, to distinguish between reality and her surreal dream. But she could still sense the young man's presence; still feel his warmth. And his voice penetrated her head, as loud and clear as if he were still sitting right next to her.

'I'll be there, Alex. I promise.'

Thirty-Three

'Life is about learning to say goodbye'. Jessica often repeated to herself the mantra once offered by Melissa at the bereavement counselling sessions and now, at last, she had accepted that it was true. As she dragged the last bulky refuse sack from the spare room to her front door, she was sure that her mother would more than approve of what she was about to do. For so long, the thought of parting with Linda's clothes and belongings had filled her with a sickening dread, with a kind of separation anxiety all over again. And yet, today it didn't feel quite like the ghastly wrench she had anticipated. It felt like the right time to let go.

Jessica picked up a wooden framed photograph. Not long ago, she would hardly have been able to look at the image of her mother there, beneath the glass: smiling, eyes sparkling, alive. The very idea of putting photographs of her out on display had been just too much to bear. It was something you did with joy in your heart, to be reminded of the good times. But now she wanted to walk into a room and see her mother's face again; she wanted to be reminded.

A stream of low afternoon sunshine poured into the hallway as Jessica wedged open the door with one of the bags. Then sliding on her jacket, she sat on the doorstep and waited for Hannah to arrive. The two of them had planned to take a short detour via the charity shop before making their way to Alex's for what was promised to be a special supper. As she looked at the eight black bulging bags sitting in a row, Jessica knew that this seemingly ordinary September day somehow marked a key turning point in the journey of her grief. A new beginning.

An old estate car soon grumbled along the road and stopped outside the house.

'Hello Jess,' Hannah puffed. 'Sorry I'm a bit late.'

'Don't worry...' her friend replied, glancing at her watch. 'The shop doesn't close until five-thirty. We might just make it.'

Between them, they hastily bundled the sacks into the boot of Hannah's car and sped off, American cop-style, towards the centre of town. With half a minute to spare, they screeched to a halt on a double-yellow line outside the charity shop and quickly jumped out. As they saw the lights go off inside the store and the elderly shop assistant turn the Open sign to Closed, they lugged the bags as swiftly as they could across the pavement, huffing, puffing and laughing. The old lady opened the door for them and they deposited the bags inside.

'You'd better hurry, dear,' the shopkeeper said, pointing towards the road.

The friends turned to see a traffic warden issuing a ticket, and darted back to the car. The disgruntled man opened his mouth to reprimand the two women, but there was no time: they leapt back into the vehicle, slammed the doors shut and screeched away, leaving the thwarted official standing on the pavement with his hands in the air.

'Oh my God, I can't believe I just did that!' Hannah squawked.

'Well, it's about time you started to live a little!' Jessica teased. 'You've spent far too long under Richard's thumb.'

Stopping at a set of traffic lights, Hannah gazed pensively ahead. 'Did I tell you, he called round the other night?'

'What! No. What did he want?'

'He said he wants me to give him a second chance...'

'Oh, for God's sake!' Jessica snorted. 'What did you say?'

'I said I'd think about it.'

'Well, it's your call, Hannah. Whatever you decide, we'll be here for you. Just don't rush into anything, will you?'

'I won't,' Hannah replied, pulling up outside Alex's house. 'Anyway, sorry, Jess, what about you? Are you feeling okay?'

Jessica nodded. 'You know, giving away Mum's stuff wasn't so bad, after all.'

'That's because you didn't have time to think.'

'Maybe,' Jessica said. 'Or maybe it was just that the time was right.'

Ben opened the front door. 'Shana Tova!' he exclaimed, with a grin. The two women's bewildered, blank expressions said it all.

'It's Rosh Hashanah, Jewish New Year! And we wanted you two to celebrate with us.'

'Well, Happy New Year, then, mate!' Jessica said warmly, handing over a bottle of wine.

Hannah smiled. 'How lovely. Thanks for inviting us.' And, without thinking, she leaned forward and kissed Ben on the cheek. 'Happy New Year,' she mumbled with a flush of embarrassment. She was surprised that she'd been so forward: this was the first time she'd met Alex's handsome brother – they'd only seen one another from a distance. But he reciprocated with an affectionate hug. Hannah felt a little self-conscious about the bandana on her head, but was pleased she'd taken the time to apply some make-up.

'Something smells fantastic!' said Jessica, giving Ben her jacket. The two women wandered through to the dining area, where the table was bedecked with candles and flowers and colourful exotic fruits.

Alex called out from the kitchen. ' Come in, take a seat!'

Hannah and Jessica sat down as Ben uncorked a bottle of wine. 'White everyone? And I suppose it's a beer for you, is it, Sis?' he asked Alex as she emerged from the kitchen carrying four small plates of apple and a bowl of honey.

'It all looks so beautiful,' Hannah said. 'Is it traditional to decorate the table like this?'

'No, I just had a bit of a creative urge!' Alex laughed.

'It's obvious you're an artist,' Jessica added with an admiring nod.

'Thank you, but I wouldn't really call myself an artist…it's a very recent passion.'

'Yeah, you were hardly a mini Monet when you were a kid!' Ben joked. 'Stick men and tracing were about your limit.'

'Watch it, you!' Alex gave her brother a playful shove. 'Come on,' she said to her friends. 'Let's dip the apples into the honey, and wish for a sweet and successful year to come.'

Over the course of the festive meal, Alex and Ben shared with their guests amusing and moving memories of Jewish holidays gone by. It was an entertaining and surprisingly enlightening evening for Hannah and Jessica, who learned the meanings of some of the Jewish traditions and customs, including how the round-shaped foods they were eating, the lentils and their challah bread, were all symbolic of the cycle of the year. While for Alex, it was an especially poignant occasion, for this year she had felt a particular need to acknowledge her roots. And, in gathering her closest friends together, it provided her with the opportunity to tell them something she felt they should know.

'Rosh Hashanah is a time to prepare spiritually for the coming year, for a new beginning…' Alex said solemnly, as she sliced into the honey-cake dessert. '…And, well, I've decided I want to be a bit more honest with you guys…'

Ben's face tightened, he suspected he knew what was coming.

'…You remember I told you about the heart condition I was born with?'

The two women nodded apprehensively.

'Well, I haven't been feeling too good lately, so I've been

undergoing some tests, and I recently had a biopsy, ' she said, a nervous cough tripping from her throat.

'What! said Jessica.

'I'm sure it's nothing to worry about,' Alex continued, handing round the dessert dishes, as her guests tried to take in her words. And then she smiled feebly. 'But the good news is that I've been put on new medication, so hopefully I'll be fine. I just thought you should know what's going on, that's all.'

Jessica's eyes stung. 'You're going to be okay, Al, I'm sure of it,' she said, reaching out to hold her friend's hand.

'I'll say a prayer for you.' The words tumbled involuntarily from Hannah's lips. She was taken aback by her knee-jerk reaction, by the instinctive, inescapable pull of her Catholic upbringing. But then, why should she be so surprised? Why couldn't her faith be reignited? Why shouldn't she now believe that there might be a reason to pray?

Alex hugged her friend. 'Aw… thanks, Han, I'd love your prayers, but as I said, I'll probably be fine now that my medication's been changed. So I don't think we're going to need to involve The Almighty just yet!' she grinned.

'Well, there must be something in this honey cake that's making us all go a bit God Squad,' Jessica laughed. 'Because I've got a special announcement to make too – I've decided to have Harry christened. To be honest, it's not something I particularly feel the need to do, but I know it would mean a lot to Terri and Joe.' Jessica turned to Alex. 'And I was hoping that you might be his Godmother?'

Alex's face lit up. 'Oh, Jess, how wonderful! Of course, I'd love to. But will it matter that I'm not Catholic?'

'Oh, don't worry about that. Terri's already had a word with Father Matthews and he says that after everything the family's been through, he's happy to make an exception in this case.'

'Well, then, it's a deal.' Alex topped up the glasses. 'Cheers, everyone! Or, as we say, L'Chaim – to life!'

The next day, Alex took a taxi into central Brighton to attend a meeting with her solicitors, Lomas & Lewis. She had decided that the start of the spiritual New Year should herald a new peace of mind, both emotionally and practically – and that meant sorting out her finances.

After a couple of hours in the stuffy office, Alex longed to take a walk along the pebbled beach and breathe in the brisk, clean air. But there was one more appointment she had to keep before she could relax in the knowledge that all her affairs were completely in order. As the taxi pulled up at the end of Border Passage, Alex got out and made her way towards the little meeting hall, where Mary Watkins was waiting for her at the door.

Thirty-Four

The light on the answer-phone flashed red.

'Hi! You've reached the voice-mail for Alex Green. Sorry I'm not here to take your call, but please leave a message after the tone, and I'll get right back to you.'
Beep.
'Hello, Miss Green. This is Dr. Khan. I'm just calling to let you know that I have the results of your most recent blood tests. I'm pleased to say that your condition seems to have stabilised, so the change in your medication may well be doing the trick. But it's still early days so I would like to monitor you quite closely. Please give my secretary a call to make an appointment for me to see you again in two weeks' time.'
Beep.

Hannah couldn't remember the last time she'd been to London. It was so far away from Brighton – at least, that's what Richard had always drummed into her. But, in fact, it had taken little more than an hour on the train and, as she silently surveyed the streets of the capital through the window of the black cab, she promised herself that she would make the journey more often.

How exhilarating it had been that morning, to jostle through the crowds on busy Oxford Street, to be swept along with the hurried office-workers set free for lunch, and to scamper along the pavement with Jessica in hilarious pursuit of a vacant taxi. Hannah's whole being had tingled with the high-voltage energy which seemed to emanate around every corner. Just being in the city, in the very heart of it all, had made her feel so alive.

The cab approached Belgravia and swung into a crescent of stately white buildings.

'There you go, love. That'll be £8, please,' called the driver into the back.

'Here you are. Keep the change,' replied Jessica, handing over a £10 note, and the two women stepped out onto the street. 'This is it, then,' she gulped. 'This is where it all happens.'

The shiny black doors of the Clairvoyants' Association of Great Britain were guarded by a pair of tall ominous-looking pillars, each emblazoned with the number thirty three.

'No sign of Alex,' Hannah observed fretfully. 'What time did we say to meet us?'

'Ten to three,' answered Jessica. 'Don't panic, I'm sure she'll turn up in a minute. She said the agency isn't far from here.'

'Oh I wish she hadn't gone to meet up with that ex-boyfriend, whatever his name is...I knew we were cutting it fine...'

'Relax! She'll be here! Let's wait inside,' Jessica suggested, and the pair climbed the few concrete steps leading to a set of revolving doors.

A bespectacled man in a light grey suit greeted Jessica and Hannah from behind a c-shaped desk as they walked into the reception area. 'Good afternoon, ladies. How can I help?'

'We've got an appointment with Darren England at three o'clock,' Hannah explained. 'The name's Parker.'

The man checked a large, well-thumbed diary. 'Ah, yes...just take a seat. You'll be called when he's ready.'

Exchanging nervous glances, the two women took their

place in a small row of chairs lined up below a large sweeping staircase. Despite the congenial welcome and the hotel-atmosphere of the smart foyer, with its tall, draped windows, ornate fireplace and carefully-lit paintings, both shivered. Jessica scanned the nearby noticeboard.

Healing clinic: Tuesdays, Thursday, Saturdays. Open Platform: fledgling mediums welcome. Open Circle: members £5, non-members £6. Christmas Cavalcade: fully-booked.

Above the notices, a gallery of carefully-labelled photographs smiled down on her; ordinary, innocuous-looking people whose unremarkable exteriors gave no hint of their hidden gifts. *Marjorie Pipe, medium. Terry Hardwick, healer. John Evans, psychic artist.*

Then a hand-written note pinned up, it seemed, almost as an after-thought, caught Jessica's eye. '*The CAGB aims to offer evidence to the bereaved that man survives the change called death and, because he is a spiritual being, retains the faculties of individuality, personality and intelligence, and can willingly return to those left on earth, ties of love and friendship being the motivating force.*'

Jessica's stomach crunched with a mixture of awe and apprehension. How on earth had she come to be sitting here? A year ago, she'd have laughed at the very suggestion. And yet, here she was today, waiting for a consultation with one of the country's best-known psychic mediums, praying that he'd be able to make contact with the dead. Again.

'Excuse me!' called out the receptionist. 'If you'd like to make your way up to the first floor, Mr. England is in the Leslie Flint Suite today.'

'Oh, okay, thanks,' replied Jessica, taking to her feet.

'I can't believe Alex hasn't arrived,' hissed Hannah as they climbed the blue-carpeted staircase. 'Maybe she's changed her mind?'

'Or maybe she's had a boozy lunch with her ex and gone back to his place for an afternoon of unbridled passion!' Jessica quipped, attempting to conceal her quickly-mounting anxiety.

The door to the Leslie Flint Suite was already open, so the women stepped in cautiously. Glittering chandeliers sparkled from the high, corniced ceiling; rows of mustard velour-covered chairs waited expectantly; and at the far end of the large, light room, Darren England sat at a table, eyes closed in meditation.

'Ah! Come in, my dears, come in,' he beckoned, suddenly coming-to.

'I'm terribly sorry, but our other friend hasn't turned up,' Hannah apologised, with a behave-yourself glare at Jessica.

'Don't worry, she'll be here,' the medium said confidently, holding out a hand to greet his visitors as they approached. 'Now come and sit down with me over here...'

Despite the serious purpose of her visit, Jessica still found herself stifling a snigger at Darren's theatrical demeanour. His silver bouffant wasn't quite as inflated as it had been for his performance in Brighton and a lemon golfing sweater with a matching polo shirt set off his Manchester tan quite nicely. Nonetheless, there was that look in his eyes again, that penetrating gaze which Jessica had seen before.

'Right then, my dears,' Darren closed his eyes again as they sat down. 'Now don't tell me anything just yet...let me see if there's anyone here who wants to come through to you...'

Hannah daren't even look at her mischievous friend. Instead, her eyes flitted from the medium's furrowed features to the face of his watch. 3.10. Where was Alex?

'Ah, yes...right, well, I have to tell you, that I've had a young man with me all morning,' Darren began. 'And I'm getting the feeling that he might be for you...I feel that he died quite unexpectedly...and nothing could have saved him.' Darren opened his eyes to look at the two women. 'Does this mean anything to you?'

Jessica and Hannah both nodded keenly.

'Oh, my goodness, you are a strong spirit...he's come so close now...he's making me feel very cold. Look!' Darren pushed back the sleeve of his sweater to expose an array of goose-pimples, sprawled across his skin, and poking through the silver hairs on his arm. 'I can see him quite clearly...he could do with a good haircut, if you don't mind me saying! In fact, there's a family resemblance which he shares with you, my dear.'

The medium turned his gaze on Hannah. 'He's saying he's been around you a great deal, looking after you...and this isn't the first time he's been able to make contact, is it?'

'That's right,' she smiled.

'And this is a family vibration?'

'Yes, it's my brother.'

Jessica winked at Hannah. Darren was on form.

'Good, well...he's talking about a reconciliation,' Darren continued. 'He's showing me an older lady, not in spirit, but on the earth plane. Could this be your mother?'

'Oh! Yes, probably,' Hannah replied.

'Good, well, there's been a reunion with your mother and he's very pleased about this, my dear...but there's something about another reunion, patching things up... with a man?'

Hannah looked pensive.

'...He's talking about this possible reconciliation with a man, my dear. And telling you to trust your instincts...you mustn't be pushed around...listen to your inner voice...Now he's telling me he's been around you, too, my dear,' added Darren, turning his attention to Jessica. 'He's showing me a clock...more time, he wishes he'd had more time with you, my dear.'

Jessica bit her bottom lip. She was determined not to cry, for fear of missing a single, precious word the medium might have to tell her.

'...Can you understand a baby? The baby was meant to be, my dear, and there's masses of love for you here...he never got to tell you himself, did he? But he's sending you and the baby masses of love...' He spoke with machine-gun delivery, not giving the women a chance to interject, even if they'd wanted to. 'Right, then...let's see what else he has for you...right...he's telling me you both have a lot to get through...you've both had hurdles to overcome, and there's going to be more hurdles ...but he'll be there with you, to help you and give you strength.' Darren took a long drink from a glass of water, before dabbing his brow with a pristine handkerchief. 'And now he's showing me a beautiful butterfly, and I think I know why...'

Jessica surreptitiously lifted her sleeve to catch a glimpse of her watch. Since seeing Darren England in Brighton, she had made a point of catching his TV show, and had been slightly disappointed to note that he and his sidekick did have a tendency to waffle when they clearly didn't have anything more specific to say. She only hoped the medium hadn't run out of steam already.

'The butterfly is a symbol of life after death, of rebirth,' he explained. 'Just as the butterfly leaves its cocoon, so the human spirit leaves its physical shell and lives on...I think that he's using this as a sign, as a positive sign to say that when you see a butterfly, life will get better. Life goes on.'

'But things are better already,' Hannah said boldly.

'Well, I can only tell you what I'm given, my dear, it's a beautiful, bright blue butterfly...And now he's trying to tell me something about a gift,' Darren continued, taking another slug of water. 'A present? A gift? Does that mean anything to either of you?'

Jessica and Hannah looked blankly across the table.

'Think back, think back, my dears...did he ever give either of you something really special?'

Both women shook their heads.

'No? Well, he's being quite insistent...a present. Something extremely precious that he gave to somebody?'

'I really can't think of anything, sorry,' said Hannah.

'Dear me, but this is such a strong vibration…such a close vibration,' Darren sighed, wiping the sweat which now glistened from his brow. 'He's definitely trying to tell me about a gift of some kind…come on, mate, show me something more, show me something more…'

'I don't suppose it could be the baby, could it?' Jessica ventured tentatively.

'No, he's not talking about the baby…'

Just then the door creaked open, and in tiptoed Alex. 'I'm so sorry,' she whispered, as she pulled a chair over to where her friends were sitting.

Eyes shut tight, Darren didn't appear to even notice her arrival. 'Let me just try to get some more…okay, well, he's showing me a car now…and I'm feeling pain here.' The medium placed a hand on his chest. 'Did your brother pass away as a result of a car crash, my dear?' Now he opened his eyes to look at Hannah.

'Yes! Yes, he did.'

'Right! Now he's giving me a hospital scenario…did he pass in hospital?'

Hannah nodded vigorously.

Then Darren turned to Alex. 'Can I ask, have you been in a hospital situation?' he asked.

'Yes, I have,' she replied.

'You knew this man when he was on the earth plane, didn't you, my dear?'

'If you mean Hannah's brother, then no. I never met him.'

'No, they never met,' Hannah confirmed.

Jessica sighed. It was beginning to look as though Darren's talents weren't quite as impressive as she'd believed them to be after all.

'Well, there's definitely a connection of some kind between you.' Darren shook his head in bewilderment. 'Goodness, he's making me work hard…but you do have a link with him,' he persevered. 'And he wanted the three of you to be together, can you understand this? You haven't known each other very long, have you? In fact, I'd say you've only become friends since this young man's passing, is that correct?' Darren asked.

'That's right,' answered Alex. The others nodded.

'He's taking me back to the hospital again...come on, come on...January. He's giving me the month of January. You were in hospital in January.'

Alex was suddenly taken aback. This was something she hadn't even told her two friends.'Yes, yes I was.'

'Okay, okay...he's trying to talk to me about this gift again. Have you been given a present of some kind, something special?'

'Er, house-warming gifts, that's all.'

'No, no, something you were given in hospital.'

She was about to say that the only presents she'd been given in hospital were baskets of fruit and trashy celebrity magazines. But then, there was one possibility. 'I did receive something...' she began slowly. 'You could call it a gift, I guess...but I never knew who it was from...'

'Come on, come on, tell me what it is you want to say...' Darren called out to the heavens, visibly straining to hear some distant, faraway voice. The veins at his temples bulged and pulsed. He wiped away the sweat now pouring from his brow.

'I see now!' Darren suddenly exclaimed triumphantly. 'This young man gave you the gift of life! He gave you his heart, didn't he?'

'Well...' Alex stuttered. 'I did have a transplant, that's true, but...'

Jessica and Hannah stared at Alex, aghast.

'He was the donor,' the medium continued. 'He gave you his heart! This is the link you have with him and it's because of this incredible bond – this *physical* bond – that he's been able to draw so closely to you.'

Hannah wiped a tear from her eye.

The three women were speechless.

'He has drawn closely to you so many times, he's telling me,' Darren said warmly, his pink cheeks shining beneath the rosy glow of the chandeliers. 'I can smell cigarettes – you must have been able to as well? That was him!...He's tried to manifest himself physically to you, too, you know? He's showing me a school situation...he's seen you with children in a classroom...and have you ever seen tiny, twinkling lights, like raindrops?'

Alex recalled the first time she'd suspected something supernatural was going on around her – the strange occasion when she'd been painting and a shower of illuminations had appeared before her eyes.

'...Well, those are spirit lights. That's what happens sometimes when spirit draws close...And I see you've also become rather like him, haven't you, my dear?' Darren chuckled.

Alex looked blank. 'What do you mean?'

'I can see paintings and drawings...you've started painting, just like he did, haven't you dear? ...And now he's talking about his taste in music... he says that now you like the same kind of music that he liked. I can hear rock music in my ears!" Darren laughed to himself, eyes closed, "...And he's showing me a pint of a pint of beer; you even like the same drink as he did! My goodness, you have changed, haven't you? You see, it's because of this physical connection, this cellular memory, that you are drawn to the things that meant a lot to him, and you like so many of the things he used to like!'

Alex's bewildered brain flashed with a series of images, freeze-framed moments and events of the past year. She took a deep, calming breath. There was no denying that since her operation she'd developed some rather uncharacteristic tendencies, and now, suddenly, she was beginning to understand why.

'...Now, my dear, I can feel his energy fading, but he has

one last message for you before he goes,' Darren continued. 'He's saying you mustn't be afraid, my dear. Can you understand this? You mustn't be afraid. He's going to be there for you, you're not alone. He's thanking you for enabling him to get through to the others. You see, the three of you met through his guidance...it was what he wanted. He's saying he was your guiding light. He's weak now...he's used up a tremendous amount of energy to make contact with you like this, but I feel that at last he's at peace. He's leaving us now...'

Darren crumpled back into his chair. A cool serene silence surrounded them all, broken only by the gentle tinkle of the chandelier's crystal teardrops.

Thirty-Five

Eleven months. It had been almost eleven months since Jessica's last woeful foray to her mother's grave. December 31st – her mother's birthday. And now, as she retraced her steps, pushing her little boy in his pram along the leaf-strewn path, she remembered how, all those months ago, like a duty-bound fighter-pilot, she had been consumed by both numbness and dread as she'd approached the enemy – her mother's final resting place. And now, bizarrely, she could barely recognise herself: the young woman who'd plotted and planned that campaign with such ruthless, almost military precision; the woman who'd been so in denial, so angry, so devoid of tenderness.

But everything that had happened since that day had altered her perspective on death, on life, on living. She didn't have to coerce herself to her mother's grave now; she didn't have to go to the grave at all. She *wanted* to go. She wanted to make it look tidy and cared for, and to pay her respects. Her mother wasn't there, but she was somewhere. Of that Jessica was now certain.

As she approached the headstone, a gust of wind shook the sturdy boughs of the mighty oak. Harry's eyes widened as the amber leaves released themselves from the branches and fell away, an autumnal shower cascading downwards towards the ground. Jessica stopped and gazed at the picture before her; the vast tree leaning over the grave like a protective father guarding his child. But this time she wasn't ashamed at the sight of the simple headstone that stood before her. For it was no longer just a label marking her mother's beginning and end. The words, '*Love will always light the way, until we meet again one day*', freshly-chiselled into the grey slab of granite, now glittered in the balmy sunshine. And as Jessica brushed away a scattering of acorns, she felt an innate sense of peace and contentment.

Wheeling the pram away, back towards the gate, it made her smile, to think how different she was now and how much her life had changed. Nevertheless, as the church bell began to ring out across the cemetery, she was aware of one thing still troubling her. One thing she'd kept very close to her chest. She'd only had the briefest communication from her mother, since her death. And that had been long ago. Too long.

Thirty-Six

The remainder of the year slipped by in a frenzy of activity – November fireworks, school nativity plays, baby Harry's christening and his first Christmas – all shared together and enjoyed equally by the three women who now considered themselves not only to be the best of friends, but family, too. And they whispered words of thanks for their new-found companionship and much-cherished sense of belonging.

As Alex gazed out of the car window and watched the darkening winter countryside flash past, she still felt the warm, lazy afterglow of the last few days spent with her 'family', eating, watching television and playing with the children. She slipped a thumb under the waistband of her trousers. 'I've definitely gained weight,' she sighed.

'I'm not surprised!' laughed her brother, as he drove a little too fast along the narrow, twisting Dorset lanes. 'I don't think I've ever seen you eat as much as you have this week. But you look better for it.'

Alex felt her gnawing trepidation grow as Ben turned the car into a wide driveway and gravel ricocheted noisily beneath the tyres.

'I think this is it,' he said, passing through the already-open gates and pulling up alongside a glossy green Jaguar and their friend's battle-scarred estate car. 'Mmm…nice house…I see Hannah's here already. Did you say she was bringing Jess with her?'

He turned to his sister looking for an answer. But Alex

stared ahead, all traces of apprehension suddenly swamped by an extraordinary sense of déjà vu. Her eyes darted rapidly from the colonial white clapperboards to the timber decking; from the wide wooden steps to the shiny front door. She knew at once she had visited this house before. In a dream.

'Come on then!' called Ben, opening up the boot. 'I need a hand with all your luggage. I can't believe you brought so much stuff. We're only here for a couple of days, you know!'

'I, er, didn't know what to pack...' Alex muttered, slowly climbing out of the car.

'So you packed everything, right, Sis?'

Alex didn't respond. She was too bewildered. Everything was exactly as she'd dreamt it, down to the swinging seat, empty now, there on the verandah.

'Are you okay?' Ben asked, noticing that Alex's cheeks had paled.

'What? Oh, sure, I'm fine.'

Alex did her best to pull herself together and took a case from the boot of the car. They climbed the steps that greeted the visitors with a weary creak. Just as Alex knew they would. And there was the brass name-plate, fixed firmly on the wall.

'Failte?' Ben struggled to pronounce the unfamiliar word. 'What does that mean?'

The front door quickly opened.

'It means "Welcome"!' beamed Terri, standing on the threshold dressed in a jolly scarlet two-piece, her softly-curled white hair tinged with the slightest hint of purple. 'And that you are!' Her richly accented voice trembled in anticipation. 'Hello, I'm so happy to see you,' she said, instantly recognising the woman whose face she knew so well, but only from a photograph. The photograph she'd kept hidden away in a box. 'I'm so happy to meet you...at long, long last.'

Terri pulled Alex into a tight, lingering, desperate hug, holding her so close she could feel the heart beating inside the young woman's body. Feel her own son's heart beating; feel a part of him living on.

It had been a long time since the dining room had witnessed such a gathering. But on this night, this most poignant of all nights, the group of twenty or so friends and family gathered around the grand table by flickering candlelight, invited to eat and drink, to laugh and chat but, most importantly, to remember.

From behind a heavy crystal goblet of crimson wine, Jessica scanned the party. There were the aunts and uncles, members of the Finnegan clan who had enthusiastically welcomed her and baby Harry into the fold. A couple of Terri and Joe's more glamorous friends from the golf club, all bling and Viagra, Jessica thought mischievously. Alex and Ben, of course…Carrie and Lisa…Hannah, looking radiant with glossy red lips and the softest halo of short, bleached-blonde hair. And the Moron. Mark. Finn's former business partner. Jessica hadn't even contemplated that he might be here, she couldn't even bring herself to look at him across the table. In fact, they'd both done everything possible to avoid making eye contact all evening. She took a gulp of the smooth, expensive-tasting wine.

'Er…thank you…thank you everyone,' Joe suddenly announced, clearing his throat and taking to his feet. 'If you don't mind, I'd just like to say a few words. Now, as we all know, New Year is a time for contemplation, for reflecting over the previous twelve months. It's a time when Terri and I thank God for all the good things, in particular for the love of our family and friends…'

His wife's face twitched with a quick smile.

'This time last year, our son was still alive, and we could never have anticipated the sorrow and suffering that was about to descend upon us. Our lives have changed so much since his death…there have been times when Terri and I could barely open the curtains in the morning, when it was just too painful to face another day. I miss my son so much...' Joe's face darkened. Until this evening, he had grieved in silence; saying the words out loud had simply compounded his agony. 'Even now when the phone rings, for a second – just a second – I think it might be Sean.'

Hannah watched her father as he paused to compose himself with a sip of water, praying that he would find the strength to finish the speech he so dearly wanted to give.

Clearing his throat again, Joe continued valiantly: 'I'm sure we all have our own special memories of Sean – or Finn, as he was known to some of his friends,' he said, with a nod towards Mark. 'I especially remember our precious times together on his little boat, the 'Guiding Light', for although he didn't follow in my footsteps and join the Navy, we did share a love of the ocean, and spent many a day out at sea with a crate of beer for company!' Gentle laughter rippled around the table. 'But I know he'll be remembered by you all for his warmth, his sense of humour and his sheer appreciation of life. It was this very appreciation that made him determined to continue giving even after his death...and how glad we are now that he did.' Joe smiled tenderly at Alex.

'Yes, it's been a very tough year, but despite all that's happened, we'd still like to say our thanks to God on this New Year's Eve, for the thirty-one wonderful years we had with our son. We know we still have a long way to go, but it's thanks to you, our family and friends, that we can now begin to look to the future with hope and peace.

'So please join me in raising a glass to Sean...a beloved son, a cherished brother, a faithful friend...and, if he's watching down from heaven, a very proud father indeed. To Sean!'

Little Harry, who'd been sleeping peacefully on his mother's lap throughout Joe's speech, suddenly jolted, awoken by the boom of ardent voices and the shrill clinking of glass against glass. Jessica smiled down at her baby boy and stroked his forehead, wrestling with her tears.

'To Daddy,' she whispered into his perfect miniature ear.

It was hard to comprehend how so much could have happened in a single year – the extremes of emotion, the unpredicted events. And now, here she was very much a part of this caring, close-knit family, with her baby – Terri and Joe's grandson – at their home, sitting at their table. It was definitely going to take more than a surreptitious pinch of the skin for it all to really sink in.

Jessica looked around at the guests once again, inadvertently sopping up snippets of chatter between them. She listened as they all shared their memories of Sean, recalling anecdotes – some funny, some sad. But it seemed unfair, somehow, that these people should all have such a comprehensive library of data stored in their heads on the subject of the man she would always feel love for, when she would only have a sparse archive of memories for comfort. With a deep sigh, she took a large glug of wine and vowed to make it her mission to learn as much as was humanly possible about the man who had changed her life. Her thoughts abruptly fragmented when Harry let out a defiant wail, his open mouth shuddering with anger to reveal two rows of pink toothless gums as his fists aimlessly boxed at the air.

'Dinner time for you, too, mister,' Jessica chuckled, hoisting him upright. Still alert, but now quiet, his little chin rested on her shoulder and his wide eyes darted about the room as she took him off to make up his feed.

Breezily she sauntered into the large kitchen, picked up Harry's changing bag from a chair, and with her baby patiently slumped over one shoulder, unpacked a bottle and a tin of baby milk.

'I'm sure there was a bib in here somewhere,' she muttered to herself, delving into the bag amongst the wipes and nappies. 'Ah, here it is,' she smiled.

She turned and walked over to the table, but suddenly halted in her tracks. Standing smoking a cigarette at the far end of the room by the open patio windows, his back towards her, was Mark. She really didn't want to have to talk to him. Just being under the same roof as The Moron was already more than she could bear. Hoping that he hadn't seen or heard her, Jessica turned to make her escape, praying that Harry wouldn't expose them, willing him to remain quiet. She reached the door…

'Don't go!' Mark blurted out. His back was still turned towards her. She could see his reflection in the windows; he seemed to be staring back at her. She stopped. What was she to say? What was she to do?

'Do you think things are meant to be?' he asked eventually. He spoke slowly and deliberately, but there was a disturbing uneasiness to his tone. 'I mean, do you think things are meant to happen?' he persisted, drawing hard on his cigarette, still staring straight ahead.

Jessica didn't want to answer him, but the words came out anyway. 'Like what?'

Mark half-turned and forcefully exhaled a stream of smoke. 'Like Finn dying…was it his time to die?'

A heavy punch socked her solar plexus and her eyes began to smart; now they were talking the same language. Jessica shook her head. 'Who knows?' she said softly.

'Or was it…' Mark floundered. '… or was it all my fault?'

'How could it be your fault?'

Mark went very still. He didn't notice a long thread of ash fall from his cigarette onto the floor. 'If I hadn't got so drunk and been so rude to you…he wouldn't have followed you home…'

Baby Harry began to whimper, his face creasing with unbridled disappointment and impatience. Jessica quickly slipped her little finger into his mouth, and he sucked on it with eager gratitude. Much as she disliked Mark, Jessica recognised the value of this discussion, as much for herself as for him.

'Well then, that would make it my fault, wouldn't it?' she conceded. These very same arguments had whirred around inside her own head so many times, that she could almost recite the answers off by heart. '...Because if he hadn't stayed with me that night, things might have been different,' she said, carefully placing the now-sleeping baby in his pram.

Mark swung around, his face tear-stained, his voice cracking. 'But I made him go to the party! Don't you see? He didn't want to go, he wanted us both to stay at the office and sort out the mess I'd got us into.' He closed his eyes and gently shook his head. 'But I didn't listen to him. He listened to me, instead, and look what happened. So it is my fault, isn't it?'

This time Jessica wanted to answer. His misery reached out to her, the panic in his voice mounting. But words eluded her. His pain, so blatant, dragged her back again to the realms of despair and longing; compelled her to confront her own latent grief which, for most of the time nowadays, lay dormant – but was always somewhere just below the surface. Instinctively she walked over, clasped Mark's hand and stared resolutely into his eyes.

'Listen, you didn't make him do anything. Nobody did. Maybe...maybe it *was* his time.'

Mark blinked his wet lashes together self-consciously and shifted uncomfortably from foot to foot. 'Look, I'm sorry, Jessica,' he sighed. 'I was well out of order that night, wasn't I?'

Now at last was her opportunity to take him to task over his obnoxious behaviour a year ago, when he'd humiliated her on one of the saddest days of her life. But instead, she found herself squeezing his hand ever so slightly tighter, and replying with a soft smile of forgiveness.

'I know it's no excuse,' he continued. 'But you caught me at a bad time...well, I thought it was a bad time...I didn't know what bad was until...'

Jessica interrupted, rescuing him from the words he didn't want to utter. 'You were really good friends, weren't you?'

'The best.'

Another gaping silence fell between them. Jessica searched for something to say. 'So…how's the business doing now?'

'Somehow, don't ask me how, it's survived, and things are actually beginning to pick up,' he shrugged. 'I suppose I've thrown myself into it, really. Carrying on for Finn is what's got me through.' Mark gazed ahead at something Jessica couldn't see. 'You know, before he died, my life was just one excess after another. And then…it all came crashing down. It was like a wake-up call…' he continued. '…And I could see that all the selfish, shitty, egotistical, materialistic crap was worthless. I had to change…I had to grow up…'

Harry's nap was short-lived: the pram shuddered and the long-suffering child piped up again.

'You're not the only one!' Jessica grinned, as she unwound her grip on Mark's hand, suddenly conscious that they had been joined together for all that time. She went over to the pram and picked up her little boy.

'Harry's beautiful,' Mark smiled. 'Finn always wanted to have kids, you know. He would have adored him.'

'Here…hold him a minute,' Jessica said, handing over the wriggling infant. 'I've just got to warm up his bottle.'

Mark held the baby tenderly and tickled him under his chin. Harry quietened. 'Hello, little man…look at you, what a big boy you are. I've heard all about you from your grandma, you know…and aren't you lucky to have such a lovely mummy? Your daddy always had good taste.'

Jessica tested the milk on the back of her hand and felt the heat rise to her cheeks. She hoped Mark hadn't seen her blushing. He passed the baby over and she sat at the kitchen table to feed him. Leaning against the fridge, arms folded, Mark watched intently.

'I hope you forgive me,' he pleaded softly.

Jessica looked up. 'Course I do,' she smiled. Their eyes met. And as the first chime of Big Ben rang out from the television set in the room next-door, Jessica knew that any anger or resentment that she might still be harbouring for Mark was rapidly fading away.

Thirty-Seven

It was as if the earth itself knew that it was the start of a brand new year. A fresh, clean, infinite turquoise sky stretched ahead, mirrored in the gold-crested waves below. The sun, cool and brilliant, shone as energetically as it might have done on the very first morning of its creation. And even the seagulls gliding overhead seemed to be calling out a bright, auspicious song. Alex felt as though she were swimming in the sounds and smells of that shiny new day and, holding tightly on to the rail of the little boat cutting through the water, she watched the marina fade further and further away into the distance. Of course, she'd been aboard the 'Guiding Light' before, but she'd told no one about the impromptu trip with the funny old fisherman all those months ago. And now, with the salty southern breeze smarting against her cheeks once again, she understood why she'd been so drawn to the marina and, in particular, to this boat: Sean's boat.

Joe was at the helm today, steering 'Guiding Light' through the cold waters of the Channel as he had done so many times. But this time was different. This was the first time he'd taken the little boat out to sea without his son. And it would be the last.

Presently, he switched off the engine, allowing the vessel to bob freely on the brisk tide. He didn't turn to speak to his wife or daughter, nor Jessica or Alex; nor the priest whose black robe billowed about him. Instead Joe remained at the wheel, eyes narrowed, gazing out at the empty sea, remembering the times when boyish laughter had echoed from the belly of the boat; remembering long days spent fishing with Sean at his side; remembering how easy it was to forget.

In silence, Terri came to stand alongside her husband, hair scrambled by the ocean breeze; her gnarled, arthritic fingers clamped tightly around a small white porcelain urn. This gesture of remembrance, this poignant farewell, had seemed such a good idea when originally discussed on terra firma, in the comfort and safety of her home. But now, the harsh reality was quite different, and the prospect of letting go, of finally letting go, was like having the flesh torn from her very bones. But she knew she should hold on no longer. So much had changed, so many notions had been thrust upon her…if she hoped to hold on to her remaining family, to embrace her husband, her daughter, her grandchildren, her future, then this was something she simply must do. Anyway, her son wasn't there in that porcelain pot. He was with her, around her, in spirit. And he would be in her heart forever.

'…Earth to earth, ashes to ashes, dust to dust: in sure and certain hope of the resurrection to eternal life, through our Lord Jesus Christ…' As Father Matthews recited the words of the committal, Terri used what little strength she had in her fragile hands, and twisted the stubborn lid from the urn. Then barely able to see for the tears, like thorns, piercing her eyes, she took a handful of the precious dust, and cast Sean's ashes out into the welcoming arms of the ocean. Catching briefly on the breeze, the silver-grey particles seemed to pause mid-air to form a soft, cloud-like silhouette, as if saying goodbye, before at last scattering into the sea. Between them, Terri and Joe gave the remains of their child to the waves, and when the jar was empty they clung to one another like never before, crying and sobbing and truly grieving their loss together for the very first time.

The group began their journey back to the marina without a word, grateful that the other sailing boats and yachts appeared to be deserted that morning. But as 'Guiding Light' approached the shore, they could begin to make out a solitary figure waiting for them. A small, wiry, weather-beaten old fisherman stood respectfully to attention there on the quayside, and, as the party finally disembarked, he held out a tar-stained, steadying hand.

'Good morning, Mr. Finnegan, sir.' He greeted Joe with the highest reverence.

'Hello, Alf.' Joe shook the man's hand. 'Thanks so much for looking after the boat for us. And you've done a fine job with that engine,' he said quietly. 'She sounds good as new.'

'My pleasure,' the fisherman replied with a nod. 'I'll keep an eye on her until she's sold.' With a wink of recognition at Alex, he disappeared deep into the galley of his own boat, next door, leaving the party to wind their way back to the car park.

The three friends linked arms as they meandered along the quay, illuminated so brightly by the sun. A new year, a new start, thought Hannah, watching her parents walking ahead, hand in hand. How proud she was of their new-found closeness. How she yearned for a relationship like theirs: solid, familiar, safe. She'd always imagined she and Richard growing old together, seeing their daughters blossom and start families of their own. But now that was out of the question, wasn't it? Too much had divided them. Too much had changed. No matter how many times he said he wanted to try again, surely it was all too late? Just then, the sharp fingers of an icy breeze suddenly scratched about her, slicing through her clothes. Hannah shivered, and clung just a little tighter onto her friends' arms as they walked briskly towards the car.

Early that evening, Terri invited the young women up to her bedroom. With glasses of wine in their hands, they chatted merrily as they followed her, full of curiosity, up the softly carpeted creaking staircase, each of them with a strange sense of liberation now that the rawness of today's mission was beginning to subside. Alex, though, was sure that the emotions of the day had got under her skin – her joints ached, she felt completely drained and not herself at all. But she followed behind stoically, as Terri led the way along the landing and opened the door to her room, where the pink-tinged light from the bedside lamp illuminated the floral wallpaper and matching eiderdowns.

'Come in, ladies, and take a seat,' Terri said, gesturing towards the beds.

Alex, Hannah and Jessica sat themselves down on one of the immaculately-dressed single divans and watched as Terri walked towards the wardrobe. Hannah took a swig of wine and glanced around the room which, for as long as she could remember, had always been exactly the same, with its many ornaments and expensive, but now outdated, furniture. They had all stood there for so many years, frozen in time, but always serenaded by the gentle ticking from the ornate bedside alarm clock.

'This is all very mysterious, Mother,' she said, a little puzzled.

'Oh, not really. There's just something I want to show you all,' Terri replied, pulling open the large heavy wardrobe drawer and taking out an old wooden box. 'Here we are,' she sighed with a smile. 'This is my box of special memories...' Her hands were shaking ever so slightly now, as she lifted the lid to reveal a collection of trinkets, letters, cards and photographs. '...Every so often I just have to take a look through all the bits and pieces in this box,' she confessed with a prolonged intake of breath. 'It helps me to feel close to Sean.'

The three friends exchanged glances.

'Oh, look!' Terri continued. 'This is the postcard he sent us when he went sailing in the West Indies...and here's the last birthday card he gave me...' Her voice trailed off as she silently reread the message in the card for yet another time. 'He was a good boy,' she smiled, her lips trembling. She paused and swallowed hard, then managed a tiny laugh. 'But he was a funny lad, he used to put everything in this scrapbook, train tickets, all sorts,' she said, now laughing with her eyes as she handed Jessica a fat notebook bursting with memorabilia. Flicking through the pages of leaflets, pictures and programs, Jessica noticed one ticket – 'The Kinks, Grand Reunion, Birmingham.'

'Look, Al!' she grinned. 'It's your favourite band!'

'Oh, yes, Sean loved The Kinks,' Terri chirruped. 'He went to a lot of their concerts in the Eighties… and he had all their albums…We should pass them on to you, Alex!'

'Mother, look, it's Mr. Tubbs!' Hannah cried, lifting a small battered Teddy bear from the box.

'Oh yes,' Terri smiled. 'I remember Joe bringing Mr. Tubbs into hospital when Sean was born. He loved that bear – even took him to university with him, did you know that Hannah?'

'Yes, he was a right old softie.'

'Anyway,' Terri sniffed. 'We wouldn't want Mr. Tubbs stuck in this old box…why don't you take him for Harry, Jessica? And let him know it belonged to his daddy.'

'Thank you. I will.'

Then Terri took out an envelope and stroked Alex's arm. 'And I kept this, too,' she smiled warmly, looking at the picture of the attractive brunette in the red baseball cap. 'When I was forwarded your letter and photo after the transplant, I have to admit, I didn't find it easy…'

'Oh, Terri, I'm so sorry,' Alex interjected. 'I knew at the time it might be difficult for my donor's family… and of course, I didn't know anything about you… but I just had to say how grateful I was.'

'No, it's alright, Alex, dear. It was extremely thoughtful of you. And, anyway, I feel very differently now. It's just that, at first, I couldn't bear the thought of anyone having a part of my Sean after he'd died. Very selfish of me, really…' she said, wiping a tear from her cheek. 'And then, when I read your letter and found out more about you, it was hard to come to terms with the fact that his heart had been given to someone who wasn't even a Catholic. When I think about it now, I'm so ashamed.'

Hannah moved over to comfort Terri. 'It doesn't matter any more, Mother,' she said. 'I think we all surprised ourselves with the way we felt about things after the shock of losing Sean so suddenly.'

Terri pulled a small lace handkerchief from inside her sleeve and dabbed the corners of her eyes. 'I was just so devastated. And, if I'm honest, I was angry when I found he was registered to be a donor.' Her words flowed easily now. 'I'd just been told that my son wasn't going to survive the crash, and then in the next breath that he was going to be taken apart like an old car, being used for spare parts or something...well, it was just too much...'

Alex coughed. Her chest was tight and her head was pounding.

'...but now I feel so very, very proud of him. Knowing that you, dear Alex, are alive today because of Sean's selflessness, really helps me, you know. And to actually have you sitting here with me now...well, it's more than I could have asked for.'

'And it's more than I could have asked for,' Alex echoed with a tight hug for the elderly lady. 'I'm just so grateful to Sean – well, to all of you.'

Jessica wondered whether now was the right time to broach the question that had been niggling away at her quietly over the past couple of months. 'Al?' she began. 'Why didn't you ever tell us that you'd had a transplant?'

Alex paused with a shrug, and thought carefully about her answer. 'It wasn't that I meant to be deceitful...I didn't want to keep it a secret from you,' she said. 'I just didn't want you treating me differently, I guess. I'd been wrapped in cotton wool all my life,' she continued, 'and when I moved to Brighton, I wanted a brand new start, I wanted to feel as normal as possible. And that's why...' she smiled weakly through a suppressed, furtive cough. '...That's why I didn't tell you.'

Jessica squeezed her friend's hand.

They were interrupted by a tentative tap on the door. 'Ladies? Dinner!' It was Joe.

'Oh, thank you, dear,' Terri called back cheerfully. 'We'll be right down...Well, my dears, we'd better see what the boys have rustled up for us, hadn't we?' And then she giggled, 'A congealed mess, if I know your father!'

They started to make their way back downstairs, when Alex stopped. 'Terri, I'm not feeling very hungry tonight, and I'm so tired,' she said, finally succumbing to her body's demands. 'I'm sorry, but do you mind if I take off for an early night?'

'No, of course not, dear,' Terri smiled kindly. 'Why don't you have a nice hot bath and get yourself to bed? There are plenty of spare towels in the airing cupboard. Just help yourself.'

'Thank you, Terri, I will,' Alex answered with a grateful smile.

It had been a while since Alex had felt quite so exhausted, but, considering the high-octane emotion of the past twenty-four hours, it was hardly surprising, she thought, lifting a bundle of thick, soft peach-coloured towels from a shelf in the airing cupboard. All she longed to do now was sink into a deep, steaming bath and float away.

The sprawling house was a warren of dark mahogany doors and shadowy passageways, walls adorned with gilt-framed oil paintings and carefully-mounted china plates. Terri had directed her to a guest bathroom along the corridor to the right, and Alex wandered slowly past the gallery of richly-coloured portraits and seascapes, several, she noticed, with the initials

SF in the corner. She came to a door which was standing ajar. Light streamed out from inside the room, and Alex couldn't help but push the door further open. Like a moth to a candle, she was instantly drawn inside. As she closed the door firmly behind her, she knew at once whose room this was. A set of red leather-bound encyclopaedias stood smartly to attention on the bookshelf; from the wall smiled an array of school photographs – a teenage rugby squad, a school cricket team and a framed photograph of a little blue fishing boat, which looked so familiar. A glass cabinet proudly displayed its dazzling collection of medals and silver cups, each boldly engraved with the name 'Sean Finnegan'. A half-finished watercolour on an artist's easel, model boats, tennis racquets, even a freshly-ironed shirt hanging on the chair – Alex noticed that everything had been kept in its place and perfectly pristine, as though ready for the occupant's return. The room was like a time capsule.

Flopping onto the bed with a heavy sigh, she lay back, her hand on her aching chest. She could feel her heart – Sean's heart – beating its strong, steady rhythm. And as she closed her eyes, she tried to picture the face of the man who, in losing his own life, had saved hers. It wasn't difficult. She'd now seen so many photographs, learnt so much from his family. As the image built in the blackness of her mind's eye – the shoulder-length hair, the kind, green eyes – Alex wanted so much to draw close to Sean, to make contact, to feel his presence around her.

Just then, the silence was broken. Music began to play from a CD player in the corner. It was quiet at first, but immediately she recognised the haunting melody of the song, 'Trust your Heart' which now reached every corner of the room, permeating the very walls, filling her head, over and over again:

'How very much like me you are, when you come to me, truly, truly trust your heart...'

For a split second, Alex's breath caught in her chest. Slowly, she opened her eyes. But nobody else was there, she saw with a smile. Just her.

And Sean.

Downstairs in the lounge, the log fire spat and crackled. It was late now, and the only remaining guests – Hannah and Jessica, Ben and Mark – were sitting on the floor around the coffee table, enjoying a raucous battle of the sexes.

Ben shook a dice. 'Four! Yesss!' the two men cried in unison.

Jessica tutted and shot a look of disdain at the enemy board game.

'That means we get to choose which category we have!' added Ben triumphantly.

'Oh, it's got to be Sport, mate!' said Mark.

'Sport, then,' Hannah said, taking a card from the box. 'Oh, bad luck, boys! You'll never get this one,' she added with a smile at Jessica. 'What did Europe win for the first time on American soil in 1978?'

The men looked blankly back at Hannah.

'Ha! You don't know it, do you!' Jessica exclaimed, gleefully.

'Hang on, hang on,' Mark replied. 'When did you say? 1978?'

'Stop stalling!'

'So it's a game played in the States by the Europeans…?' Ben frowned.

'Come on, give up!'

'Golf! It's gotta be golf!'

'Time's running out!' warned Hannah.

'Yeah, what's that cup called?' asked Mark feverishly.

'Five, four, three…'

'The Ryder Cup!' Ben gasped, just in time.

'I don't believe it!' Jessica said, slamming the board in

exasperation. 'Why do men always win Trivial Pursuit?'

'Because they get easy questions and because they cheat,' replied Hannah matter-of-factly, taking a sip of her father's best whiskey. 'Richard always used to cheat at board games.'

'See! I told you you're better off without him!' Jessica joked, refilling her own crystal tumbler.

'So…what's happening with you two now?' Ben asked, trying to sound as nonchalant as possible.

'Me and Richard? Oh, I don't know…'

Jessica was quick to jump in. 'He thinks that by whisking her off for a romantic weekend in some fancy hotel, he can charm the pants off her, rebuild their marriage and make up for years of being a total bastard. That's what.'

Hannah squirmed.

'And what do you think?' Ben asked, looking at her more intently.

'Well…' Hannah began.

'Believe it or not, she's actually considering going!' Jessica blurted. 'I mean, look at her! She's gorgeous, she's got her confidence back, and her hair…I think she's crazy, don't you?'

Ben knocked back his whiskey. 'Well, maybe she still loves him?'

'How could she!' Jessica retorted.

Hannah busied herself with packing the game back into its box. It meant she didn't have to meet Ben's gaze.

'So, you going?' he ventured dolefully.

'Oh, I don't know…' Hannah replied, a little too breezily. 'But if I don't go, if I don't at least try, I'll never know, will I?'

'S'pose not,' answered Ben, then added with a stretch and a defeated sigh, 'Well…think I'll hit the sack…Goodnight, folks.'

'Night, mate. And well-played!' grinned Mark.

'Goodnight, Ben,' Hannah said quietly, as he left the room, her eyes glued to the neatly-arranged board-game. 'Right, well, I think I'll just tidy up a bit before going to bed myself,' she added, gathering the empty glasses from the table and retreating to the kitchen.

Left alone now with Mark, Jessica gazed into the blazing open fire. The silence was broken by the hissing of the flames, as if goading them, mocking their awkwardness. The pair looked up at one another simultaneously, and smiled shyly.

'It's been great seeing you again, Jessica,' Mark began.

'Yeah, you, too,' she nodded amicably. 'By the way, how's Sarah?'

'Engaged to a rugby player, apparently!' he said with a laugh. And then added, 'Listen, I'm sorry, again…you know, about that night.'

'Forget it. Life's too short.' Jessica watched Mark as he turned to stare into the flames. The face that had appeared so hard and hollow on their first meeting looked softer now, and quite incapable of the monstrous sneers that had managed to cut Jessica to the quick that night. And although she wasn't sure whether it was just the glow of the fire, his deep, round eyes looked warm and compassionate. Perhaps the pain of losing his closest friend really had changed Mark after all?

'I've just remembered!' Jessica suddenly said with a jolt. 'I've got something for you. Well, actually, it's yours already…'

Mark looked puzzled as Jessica reached into the pocket of her jeans.

'Here…I was told to give this back to you.'

'Jeez!' Mark exclaimed, as Jessica handed him the slim silver lighter she'd kept with her for the past twelve months. 'I wondered where that had got to. But I don't understand. How come you've got it? Who told you to give it back to me?'

'It's a long story,' Jessica smiled. '…But I promise I'll tell you all about it some other time. Definitely, some other time.'

Ben padded quietly along the landing to his room, the smallest guest bedroom at the end of a long passage, under the eaves.

For him, the day had been a roller-coaster ride: the dread, the relief and the inevitable disappointment at its abrupt termination. He could still hear the faint laughter and merriment emanating from downstairs and felt a little guilty for his hasty retreat to bed. It was just that, somehow, the party seemed to be over – for him, in any case.

Grabbing his washbag, Ben made his way back along the landing towards the bathroom. But then he hesitated outside one bedroom, where light was seeping out around the door and music was playing loudly. Curiosity and a peculiar uneasiness got the better of him, and he knocked quietly. No answer. Slowly, he pushed open the door and peeped inside. There was almost too much to take in, at first: it was like an Aladdin's cave of boyhood. But then he saw his sister, lying on the bed, eyes closed. He was surprised to see her there, instead of in her own room, but he grinned to himself at the thought that she'd probably downed one too many drinks that day. Alex rarely drank alcohol at all any more, just the occasional beer, so a couple of glasses of champagne would have gone straight to her head. He decided to leave her be, and was just about to turn off the light when he thought he saw her shiver. Unhooking the navy dressing gown from behind the door, he tiptoed over to cover her up.

'Here you go,' he whispered gently, spreading the man-size gown over his petite sister. But then his heart suddenly plummeted, something was clearly very wrong. Her breathing seemed shallow, each breath too rapid; her skin looked clammy and pallid. Panic hit him like a bolt of lightning.

'Al?' he said, his voice quivering. 'Al? Al!' No answer. Just a groan. He shook her gently. 'Wake up, Alex, wake up!' he persisted, his tone rising with distress.

Alex's eyes fluttered open reluctantly, and she squinted against the glare of the bedroom light. But quickly they closed again, and she sank back into blackness.

'Help!' he called out. 'Help! Someone call an ambulance!'

Ben lifted her head in his hands and she swam back into bleary wakefulness, squinting through heavy somnolent lids, trying to focus on her brother's face, her body heavy and unmovable. She tried to say something, but her lips barely moved and no sound came out.

Suddenly the room was full of familiar people, hovering around her bedside, their high-pitched voices muffled but frenzied; their distorted, panic-stricken faces looming over her. She closed her eyes again.

After an unbearable interval, the ambulance's piercing siren suddenly scored the silence, its flashing blue light reaching through the window and bouncing repeatedly off the bedroom walls as it hastened into the drive. Heavy doors slammed, feet hammered the stairs, everyone stood back to let the crew into the room. Minutes later, Alex was secured onto a stretcher and carried downstairs.

The air was still and silent as Terri and Joe, dressed only in their nightwear, stood static in the darkness, their horrified faces illuminated intermittently by a veil of blue. Hannah, Jessica and Mark followed Ben to the ambulance, where he clambered into the back to be with his sister. The friends watched, motionless, in wide-eyed panic, as Alex was hooked up to a drip and given oxygen. Suddenly the doors slammed shut and in an instant the ambulance spun out through the gates, gravel flying, siren blaring, lights flashing. It screamed down the road, taking suffering with it, and leaving suffering behind.

West Dorset County Hospital was alert and ready for its patient when she arrived. A flurry of medics appeared from nowhere and, without delay, wheeled Alex along the cavernous, echoing corridor towards A & E, one pushing the bed; one running holding the drip-bag; one with the oxygen machine and one firing questions at Ben as he sprinted along behind. Abruptly they came to a halt, where Alex was shunted hastily into a cubicle bed and a green curtain was drawn forcefully and decisively between Ben on the one side and the doctors on the other. Frantically, he paced the floor, up and down; staring at the billowing curtain, straining to catch snippets of information; willing his sister well.

Eventually, after what seemed like an eternity, the curtain was pushed back, less forcefully this time, and a young female registrar approached Ben. His head banged with dread, his heart palpitated wildly beneath his ribs.

'Well, it was a close call,' she said, her face etched with concern. 'Her notes have now been emailed over and we've been in contact with the transplant unit. It's very clear that her immune system has taken a tremendous battering due to the immuno-suppressive drugs she's been taking...' The doctor plunged both hands into the pockets of her starched white coat, and continued with impassive confidence. '...And she seems to have picked up a really nasty infection, which we believe is an aggressive form of pneumonia. She'll be going down for a chest x-ray and some other tests to confirm our suspicions, but in the meantime we've started her on powerful antibiotics and steroids. Do you have any questions?'

'She is gonna be okay, isn't she?' Ben asked breathlessly.

'Rest assured, we'll do everything we can for her,' the registrar replied.

Ben watched anxiously as his sister, still unresponsive, was moved onto a trolley and wheeled back along the corridor towards the x-ray department. 'Look, it's very late,' the registrar said, the faintest twitch of a smile at her mouth. 'By all means stay for the night, next to her bed if you'd like to.'

'Thank you, I will,' he said.

With that, the doctor turned silently and disappeared along the vast hallway.

Ben decided that he needed a shot of caffeine to stay awake. So, in a surreal state of solitude, he headed towards the coffee machine, the only source of comfort for those, like him, waiting helplessly for news of their loved ones. Pushing a coin into the slot, he placed a plastic cup under the automatic dispenser and waited as the powder and boiling water spluttered half-heartedly into the container, delivering the bitter solace. And then, as he tore open a sachet of sugar, two pairs of arms suddenly wrapped themselves around his body and clung to him tightly.

'We had to come.'

'Hope you don't mind?'

It was Jessica and Hannah.

Thirty-Eight

When Ben returned to Alex's house from Dorset, three days later, a hollow ache bruised his stomach as he entered the cold, empty house. Dropping his luggage onto the floor, he picked up a pile of letters and newspapers and crashed down onto the sofa, still in his coat and scarf, not exactly sure what to do with himself. Apart from the washing that needed to go on, and the work shirt he would have to iron for the following morning, his day was completely free – too free. A wave of sickness swelled in his stomach as his mind lurched back to Alex, and her transfer that day to London. Today he needed to keep busy, he thought. Today he needed to distract himself. Tomorrow he would visit her again.

He switched on a couple of lamps to purge the January gloom, shrugged off his coat and carried his bag to the washing machine in the kitchen. Slowly, he unzipped the holdall and took out his clothes piece by piece. But it was almost impossible to concentrate, even on this menial task, with his mind constantly wandering back to his poorly sister. Slumped on the floor, he buried his face in his hands, the sharp stubble on his jaw pricking at the soft flesh of his palms. And leaning back against the units, he sat there on the cold tiles, staring at nothing.

There was a faint ring at the doorbell, but Ben didn't move a muscle – he couldn't face talking to any well-meaning neighbours or door-to-door salesmen today. But then, just a minute or so later, there came another knock, this time on the kitchen window. Ben looked up to see Hannah, fresh-faced, peering through the glass; she hadn't spotted him, down there on the floor, surrounded by the heap of laundry.

'Hey, Hannah!' he waved, instantly enlivened, just by the sight of her.

'Hello!' she called back. 'What are you doing down there?'

'Sorting out my whites!' Ben laughed, taking to his feet. 'Anyway, come on in,' he said and unlocked the back door.

Hannah wiped her feet on the mat a little too vigorously. 'I hope you don't mind that I came round the back...' she said, pulling off her beanie hat and ruffling her short blonde hair. '...It's just that I saw the car, and when you didn't answer the door I...I was a bit worried...' she blathered nervously. 'I just wanted to know how Alex is?'

'She's improving, slowly, thank God,' he nodded. 'The antibiotics seem to have kicked in at last.'

'What a relief!' Hannah sighed.

'Yeah, but they're moving her today, to London, to the Royal Brompton Hospital.'

A worried look flitted across Hannah's face. 'That sounds serious,' she said quietly.

'No, it's okay. It's only so that she can be back under the care of the consultant who carried out the transplant. And, anyway, it's what Alex wants,' he said briskly. 'This guy's the best in his field, so I'm sure she's in the right place. And the great thing is that I'll be able to visit her every day after work.'

'Are your parents planning on coming over?' Hannah asked.

'Yeah, they'll be arriving in a few days' time. I told them that everything's under control and not to panic.'

'You know, I haven't been able to stop thinking about Alex. I honestly don't think I've slept a wink,' Hannah said.

'You and me both.'

They felt a little self-conscious at being alone together. But any embarrassment instantly evaporated with the wails and pleas of Lisa and Carrie who suddenly appeared at the door wearing Wellington boots, duffle coats and crest-fallen expressions. 'When are we going to the pier, Mummy? '

'We've been waiting in the car for ages!'

'You promised we could go soon!'

Hannah's eyes met Ben's and they both tried to stifle a grin. 'Duty calls!' she sighed. 'Better be off...but I'm so relieved about Alex. That's wonderful news.' She turned to leave and walked towards the door, but then hesitated. 'Why don't you come with us?' she asked. 'We're only going to the pier for a couple of rides and some fresh air. It'll be good for you, help take your mind off things.'

Ben thought how pretty the slightly flustered, pink-cheeked Hannah looked. 'Well, it's a tough choice,' he teased, prodding the mountain of dirty laundry with his foot. 'Hold on a minute, I'll just get my coat.'

Despite the grey winter chill, the afternoon spent on the pier was full of jollity. There were few visitors, so the girls, fists bulging with tokens, made it their mission to go on as many rides as possible, and managed at least two turns on every one, thanks to Ben's generosity. Then they sat at a table adorned with a stiffly-starched blue and white checked tablecloth at the Palm Court restaurant, sharing plates of fish and chips. Later, they spent an hour or so in the Palace of Fun, on the simulators and fruit machines, where Ben managed, after several gallant attempts, to grab a Teddy bear on the end of a robotic claw. Hannah had insisted that the game was just an expensive, greedy con and that the prize could never be won, but Ben had been determined to prove her wrong. And it had been one of those very funny 'told you so' moments, when the prize bear was finally lifted, swinging through the glass cabinet, from cuddly-toy incarceration to freedom.

As they meandered out of the central pavilion, they passed several stalls and kiosks – 'Secrets in your Signature', a novelty t-shirt stand, a sweet shop crammed full of Brighton rock. And Ivor the tarot card-reader, who seemed to be doing a roaring trade from his olde-worlde gipsy caravan, with at least five or six people queuing patiently to discover their fate.

'Want to find out your future?' Ben asked, glancing at Hannah sideways.

She shook her head. 'I try not to think too hard about the future. What's meant to be, will be,' she shrugged.

'Suppose I pretty much believe that, too,' Ben said. 'But I do sometimes wonder if we can avoid making mistakes...' He looked at her pointedly. '...Avoid making the wrong decisions...'

Hannah said nothing.

As daylight began to diminish, traded instead for twilight and the bright white lights of the pier, Carrie and Lisa ran up and down the teak decking, their excited faces, sticky with candy-floss, which clung to their cheeks and their hair.

'Only ten more minutes, then we're going home!' Hannah shouted as she and Ben, clutching feeble polystyrene cups of hot tea, took their seats on a bench.

They looked out across the ocean, just as countless people had done, for over a hundred years, since the day the pier was built. They couldn't help but gaze upon the ghostly, twisted, burned-out carcass of the once-glorious West Pier, rising pitifully from the seabed before them. The very sight dampened Ben's spirits; reminded him how abruptly something so vibrant and joyful can come to an end.

'So...' he said stiffly, averting his eyes to the cityscape of hotels and tower blocks. 'Where have you and Richard decided to go this weekend?'

'He's booked the Savoy.'

'Cool,' he retorted with heavy resignation.

But Hannah didn't say a word.

'Well...apart from visiting Alex this weekend, I'll be schlepping around some apartments in London,' Ben continued, quickly breaking the silence.

'What do you mean?' Hannah looked up in surprise. 'Are you moving out of Brighton?'

Ben nodded. 'Yeah, well, it makes sense, with the office in the City and...'

'But you can't!' Hannah suddenly interrupted, surprised by her knee-jerk reaction. 'I mean, I mean...what about Alex?'

'Don't worry, I wouldn't even think about leaving Brighton until Alex is completely better,' he replied. '...I won't be going anywhere just yet.'

Hannah tried to hide her relief behind her polystyrene cup, and drank back the last mouthfuls of tea. She could feel Ben's eyes watching her.

'Are you okay?' he asked, noticing how fragile and delicate she suddenly seemed.

'I'm fine...just a bit cold, that's all,' she muttered.

'Oh, just come over here!' he said, pulling her towards him good-naturedly and then holding her close and warm. And there they sat, together, for those last, few moments, their eyes fixed on the hardly-visible horizon.

****

'Surprise!'

Alex was wrenched from her sleep by the raucous greeting of the unexpected visitors bursting into her hospital room. She'd been dreaming of the ocean, floating, immersed in the cool, soothing, fathomless waters. But this somewhat rude awakening had brought her lurching back to consciousness.

'What are you guys doing here?' she murmured, rubbing her shrunken eyes.

'Well, Hannah and Richard have come up to London for their dirty weekend, and I decided to pay you a visit!' Jessica announced from behind an enormous bouquet of flowers, before planting a kiss on her friend's cheek. 'I told the nurse

I'm your sister, so I can stay the night with you, too!' she added in a loud whisper.

'That's great.' Alex managed to laugh, despite the dense fog clouding her senses.

'And we thought we'd just pop in and say hello,' said Hannah, placing a basket of fruit on the bedside table. 'But I'm sorry, Al, we can't stay very long.'

As the two women hugged, Alex noticed a stocky man in a denim shirt, standing uneasily in the doorway. 'Don't worry,' she smiled. 'It's just fantastic to see you...and you must be Richard.'

'Er, yes, hello... well, I'll go and find a vase, shall I?' he suggested, clearly grasping a window of opportunity to make his retreat.

'So, you're giving it a go, then?' Alex whispered, as soon as Richard was out of earshot.

'Well, he says he's changed...'

'Yeah, right!' Jessica scoffed, plucking a shiny purple grape from the basket.

'So, who's looking after the kids?' Alex went on, not wishing to burst Hannah's bubble.

'Mother's got all three of them – the girls and Harry.'

'Yep, it's my first taste of freedom,' Jessica grinned, tossing another grape into her mouth.

'Oh, Jess! And you're spending it stuck in hospital with me?' Alex said with a pang of guilt. 'Why don't you go out tonight, instead...'

'Don't be silly,' Jessica interrupted. 'I'm going to check out the talent here! I'm a nurse, remember – I know all about doctors!'

Richard returned to the sound of loud female laughter. 'Er, Hannah, I think it's time for us to go...' he said briskly, as he placed a vase on the window-ledge then pulled back his sleeve to look at his watch. 'We really should check in at the hotel now.'

'Oh. Right. Yes.' Hannah composed herself. 'Alex, I'm so sorry…' she said with a kiss. '…But don't worry, you'll be home in no time, I'm sure. And the girls are desperate to know when they can come over to your place to do some painting.'

'Soon as I get outta here…' Alex sighed. 'Tell them very soon. That's a promise.'

Outside on the cold, grey London street, Hannah dutifully stood back, allowing Richard to hail a cab. The Saturday-afternoon shoppers jostled along the pavements and, watching from behind the window of the taxi, she briefly recalled the exciting trip she'd had to the city with her friends just a few months ago, to see the medium.

'I feel really bad about leaving Alex,' Hannah said pensively. She looked at her husband, hoping for some expression of support or sympathy.

'Oh, don't worry about her, she'll be fine,' came Richard's empty reply. 'It's us you should be thinking about, you and me…it's our weekend.'

Hannah turned her gaze back on the outside world, rolling by like a movie sequence. Hyde Park. Piccadilly Circus. Trafalgar Square. Maybe he was right? It was their weekend. Their make-or-break weekend. And if she didn't try, she'd never know. Would she?

Propped up in bed, Alex sipped some water, attempting to drench the rasping cough that plagued her. Still feeling groggy and uncomfortable, attached to an oxygen monitor and with tubes and drips feeding into her body, she watched Jessica put the flowers in water. 'Hey, Jess…I really appreciate you coming to visit. You know that, don't you?'

''Course I do!' her friend replied with a wink. 'Listen, I'm happy to spend my Saturday night here with you, but I refuse to eat hospital food – so why don't I zip out and buy us something really delicious to eat?' suggested Jessica. 'What do you fancy?'

'Oh, I don't know,' Alex sighed. Her stomach heaved at the very thought of food, but she made a supreme effort. 'How 'bout some ice cream? Ben and Jerry's?'

'Not a problem!' grinned Jessica, grabbing her bag to leave. 'Now, you rest. I won't be too long…unless I bump into a particularly dishy doctor, that is!'

Dusk had fallen over the city now. And as Hannah stood at the window of the hotel room, she watched the myriad lights beneath her glitter and flash on the darkening panorama, the black, reflective waters of the River Thames multiplying their optimistic glow.

The enormous deluxe suite at the Savoy, with its elegant décor and sumptuous, canopied bed even smelt expensive. 'You really have been far too extravagant, Richard,' Hannah said, in a carefully-chosen monotone voice. She didn't want to sound grateful, nor enthusiastic, nor encouraging. But the very fact that she had said something at all was enough to draw her husband towards her like a magnet.

''Course I haven't…' He stood close behind, slotting the contours of his body into hers. 'Anyway, this is a special occasion, isn't it?' he purred, kissing the nape of her neck. 'It's the beginning of the rest of our lives together…'

Hannah flinched instinctively, and quickly pulled away.

'What's the matter?' snapped Richard. 'I thought you were going to try?'

'I am…I am going to…' Hannah paced up and down, wondering how long she could delay the inevitable. 'It's just, well, we've got a lot to talk about. Can't we just talk first?'

Richard stomped over to the mini-bar. 'Okay. Fine,' he thundered, breaking open a miniature brandy. 'Let's talk! What do you want to talk about?'

'Oh, I don't know…lots of things…us…'

At first Hannah couldn't think of what to say, knowing

only that she had to say something, anything that might give substance to the hollow, empty husk that remained of their relationship. But then, it was as if her prison door had been opened. Fuelled with all the anger and frustration and hurt she'd been keeping locked within, Hannah heard herself berate her husband for the first time in nearly eight years of marriage.

'Well, actually, yes, lots of things…like, you've never treated me as a person,' she began. 'I've just been a piece of furniture – always there, somewhere in the background. When was the last time we had a conversation? A proper conversation? You don't know what I like, what I don't like, what I want – you don't know anything about me!'

Richard watched expressionless from the armchair, allowing his wife to continue with her tirade.

'…You never seem to think about me, or my feelings. All you ever do is criticise – sometimes, it's as if I can't breathe without you criticising me! And when I'm feeling low – and God knows there have been times when I've felt really low – you just disappear!'

Trembling, Hannah waited. Waited for her husband to apologise. To tell her how much he loved her, how was going to take care of her and make everything all right.

'You know what your trouble is?' he mused slowly, taking another slug of brandy straight from the miniature bottle. 'You've got too much time on your hands…too much time to think. I mean, really, you should count yourself lucky,' Richard continued, now circling Hannah like a predatory lion. 'You've got a lovely home, a car, two healthy children and a husband to support you…and I've put up with a lot, you know? Do you think it was easy for me, when you went to pieces after Sean died? Then you lost all your hair! I mean, not many men would stick around…'

Suddenly Richard stopped in his tracks. Even he knew he'd stooped too low. 'Oh, look, you've got your grievances, I've got mine,' he shrugged. 'Let's just call it quits, shall we?

...Now why don't you come over here and give me a kiss?' he added, arms wide open. 'There's one way we can sort this out once and for all...'

Hannah backed away. 'You just don't get it, do you?' she exclaimed, still shaking, still propelled by the adrenaline of her outburst. 'An expensive room and a shag are not going to solve our problems! We need to talk!'

Now Richard had really had enough. He wasn't going to talk any more. He wasn't going to listen. Who the fuck did she think she was? Slamming the door behind him, he headed downstairs straight for the bar.

After an hour of hunting eagerly for a tub of Alex's favourite ice cream, Jessica realised that her promise had been rather too ambitious. It was hard enough to find a shop selling ice cream at all, let alone one supplying Ben & Jerry's. She was just about to admit defeat and return to the hospital empty-handed, when she spied a cold-cabinet in the window of a newsagents. On the off chance, she took a look inside, and lo and behold, there was a shelf packed full of America's best-loved ice cream.

A little later, a deservedly self-satisfied Jessica arrived back at the ward, with a broad grin and a bulging carrier bag. 'Guess what?' she said to Alex, who smiled back weakly at her funny, exuberant friend. 'I reckon I must have bought just about every flavour Ben & Jerry have ever made...'

Alex watched Jessica as she unloaded the bags.

'Right...well, we have mini tubs of Cookie Dough, Phish Phood, Chunky Monkey, Peanut Buttercup, Chocolate Fudge Brownie, Cherry Garcia and, last but not least...good old-fashioned Vanilla!' Jessica exclaimed breathlessly. 'Now, which do you fancy?'

Alex was quick to respond, though her reply didn't sound as enthusiastic as she'd hoped. 'Vanilla. Thanks, Jess'

Jessica eagerly peeled away the cardboard lid and began

spooning mouthfuls between her friend's lips. Alex knew that Jessica was making a valiant effort to keep her spirits up, and she wished she could show her the gratitude she deserved. But she felt so sleepy. Her eyes were beginning to close, and she was finding the gloopy, creamy concoction hard to swallow. Gently pushing the spoon away, Alex settled her head into the pillow, but her peace was disturbed when a nurse entered the room, her heels clicking officiously on the floor.

'Time to take your temperature,' she announced briskly.

Alex said nothing as the nurse squinted at the thermometer and then scribbled the results onto a chart at the end of the bed. 'Right,' she said. 'That's a little high for my liking, I'll go and have a word with the consultant and I'll be back soon. And I'm going to have to take these flowers, I'm afraid. We don't allow them in patients' rooms in case they bring in infection.'

'Excuse me,' Jessica asked. 'But is there a freezer where I can keep all this ice cream?'

The nurse looked disapprovingly at the stash.. 'Follow me,' she replied with a frown. 'The kitchen's just around the corner.'

Jessica scrambled the unopened cartons back into the carrier bag and hurried after the nurse who was already marching along the corridor. 'Can you tell me how she's doing?' Jessica asked, when she'd caught up with her.

The nurse seemed hesitant. 'You're Alex's sister, aren't you?'

Jessica replied with an earnest nod.

'Well, she's developed a secondary infection, but she's stable.'

Jessica's face instantly paled. 'She'll be alright, won't she?'

'Try not to worry; she's being well looked after. The doctor will be doing his rounds later. You can talk to him then, if you like,' added the nurse, before turning and click-clacking away along the corridor.

In the small kitchen, Jessica crammed the tiny freezer compartment of the communal fridge with the mini tubs of ice cream. It obviously hadn't been defrosted for some time, and she scraped her knuckles on the thick, rough brick of ice that had accumulated there. She kept repeating the words out loud to herself: 'Alex is strong, she'll get through this,' and was still uttering the mantra when she returned to her friend's hospital room, where applause thundered incongruously from the TV set. Jessica quickly reached over to turn down the volume, as Alex squinted through crinkled lids.

'Sorry, Al...I'll turn it off, shall I?' Jessica whispered. 'It's just the usual Saturday night crap, anyway.'

Jessica could only just decipher her friend's murmured thanks. She looked so frail, almost shrunken, Jessica admitted reluctantly, gently smoothing back a strand of hair from Alex's brow. She'd witnessed similar scenes so many times before – ailing patient; concerned visitor. But never from this perspective. Jessica had always been the bystander dressed in a nurse's uniform. And no matter how close she'd grown to her world-weary charges in the Geriatric Wing – 'the departure lounge' – she'd never allowed herself to become too close, always managing to maintain some kind of distance, some element of professional detachment.

But this time, she wasn't the nurse, the onlooker; she was involved, squeezing her friend's hand, willing her better.

Alex began to stir.

'What is it, Al?' Jessica asked.

'Just got a dry mouth...'

'Here you are.' Jessica held a straw to Alex's lips, allowing her to sip some water. 'Looks like we're running low,' she added, eyeing the almost-empty jug. 'Shall I go and get some more?'

'Sure,' Alex replied quietly. 'Hey, listen, why don't you go and get some fresh air, or something?'

'But I don't like to leave you on your own for too long...'

'I'll be fine,' she smiled weakly. '…I need to sleep.'

'Well, if you're sure?' Jessica said. 'I suppose I should phone Terri to see how she's managing with the children…Okay, but I'll only be half an hour,' she finally conceded, with a soft kiss on Alex's forehead. 'Sleep well.'

Alex closed her eyes, and instantly felt as though she was falling down into a deep, dark chasm. Then suddenly she was surrounded by the ocean; a brighter turquoise blue than she'd ever seen before, clear and fresh and invigorating. She felt as though she were swimming effortlessly through the cool sea waters, she felt so energetic, so alive, as if the waves were healing her body with every ripple and swirl. They carried her towards a brilliant light ahead of her, shining warm like the sun, drawing her closer and closer, filling her not only with an innate sense of peace, but also joy. And then, before her, the man she now knew so much about.

'I promised I'd be there for you, didn't I?' he said.

Alex opened her eyes with a jolt. At first she was confused by the abrupt change in surroundings, and her heart sank when she realised with dismay that she was alone, back in her hospital room. All she wanted was to go back to her dream, to return to the ocean, to the waves, to drink in the light and to see the reassuring vision of Finn.

Then, as she looked up, her sight readjusting to the cold beams of the fluorescent light on the ceiling, a smile instantly dawned on Alex's face; she felt at peace once more. She saw that he hadn't left her alone after all.

At first, Hannah didn't know where she was, disorientated by sleep and the darkness and the pounding in her head. Then as her raw, swollen eyes gradually peeled open, she remembered. Wrapped in a luxuriously thick white bathrobe, she reached across to switch on the bedside lamp. She saw the overnight bag perched on the table, exactly where it had been left by the hotel porter. The heavy, embossed curtains were still open, lavishly framing the grand window with its spectacular nocturnal view. And the shoes that she'd bought especially for the occasion – chocolate brown suede kitten heels – still waited where she'd slipped them off by the king-size bed. But there was no Richard.

The realisation that she was alone immediately struck Hannah with a sense of relief. Relief that he wasn't there to paw and probe her; relief that she wouldn't have to give in. But gingerly sinking back into the mountainous pillows, she felt just as wounded and bruised as she might have, had Richard attacked her with a hammer. How could she ever have married such a cold, insensitive, unfeeling man? How could he have imagined that she would even contemplate making love with him? Nursing her lonely, empty, splintered heart, she finally accepted that Richard didn't care about her at all. More importantly, though, she now knew for sure that she no longer cared about him.

With a sniff, Hannah slid off the bed and went into the marbled monochrome bathroom. She stared in the mirror above the basin at the face she'd scrutinised so many times, now pale and weary and streaked with battle-scars of mascara. Water. To wash away the tears. To wash away the pain. Hannah turned on the tap and splashed her face until it tingled. Looking up again into the mirror, the picture was now distorted, her vision blurred by the droplets obscuring her eyes. But as the image before her began to clear, she saw someone else there in the reflection; someone standing behind her. Alex.

Instantly elated at seeing her friend, Hannah spun round. But the bathroom was empty. She stood for a moment, the water still dripping from her chin, bewilderment temporarily addling her brain. Of course, Alex couldn't have been there. How could she? Yet Hannah was certain that she'd seen the reflection of her friend standing behind her. However, the vision – real or imaginary – had done one thing. Decision hit Hannah like a bullet. Rushing back into the bedroom, there was no packing to be done. She simply dressed, as quickly as possible, stepped into her chocolate suede, kitten-heeled shoes, picked up her bag and swiftly left the opulence of the hotel suite far behind her.

Downstairs, in the Savoy's American Bar, Richard ordered a third large brandy and another Kir Royale. His platinum-haired, surgically-enhanced drinking partner flashed a thank-you smile and ran an appreciative hand across his shoulders. Richard smiled back, and surreptitiously slid the wedding ring off his finger and into the pocket of his jacket.

Thirty-Nine

Outside it had started to rain. Not satisfyingly fat globules of water, but an indistinct wall of drizzle. Nonetheless, Jessica turned her face upwards to the skies and, eyes closed, allowed the fine mist to saturate her, to wash away the dull insentience of too many hours confined in the airless hospital. She lit a cigarette, her first in a very long time, and observed a gaggle of young nurses scampering out of the rain and through the doors, giggling with the doctors who ran eagerly at their sides. For a moment she was envious; they looked so untroubled, so carefree. Then, dropping her half-smoked cigarette onto the wet pavement, she took the mobile phone from her bag and called Terri's number.

Hannah stared out from behind the window of the taxi. The rain on the glass blurred the red brake lights of the stationary traffic, turning them into eyes that glowed through the darkness. Her body clenched, cold and impatient; an inexplicable urgency chewed away at her. She checked her watch. She was getting nowhere fast; the cab had been crawling its way across west London to the hospital for the past twenty minutes. Why did everyone else seem to have all the time in the world, Hannah wondered bitterly, watching the swarms of pedestrians outside pick their way between barely-moving cars? Why did she feel so strongly that time was something she didn't have on her side?

Jessica marched along the corridor on her way back to the kitchen. She looked straight ahead, determined not to make eye contact with the other, drifting, apprehensive-looking visitors, determined not to falter from her current positive mind-set. Alex would be just fine, she told herself. Just fine.

As she turned on the tap to refill Alex's water- jug, it occurred to Jessica that her friend might enjoy the cooling sugar-rush of some more ice cream. There was plenty left to get through, she realised, rather embarrassed by the number of cartons crowding the fridge-freezer, and thankful that no one else was there to witness her greedy hoard. Quickly pulling out an already-thawing tub, Jessica turned to head back to Alex. But just then a familiar sound rang out – the high-pitched, piercing wail of the emergency alarm – so sudden and shrill and ominous that it sent shockwaves through Jessica's whole body.

The wet carton slipped through her fingers, falling with a thud to the floor. Jessica stood for a second, static, aware of footsteps battering the corridor, a thick puddle of ice cream oozing around her shoes. Then, instinctively, she ran, without the time to fear what she might find. Turning the corner, she stopped in horror: an army of nurses hastened, like ants, in and out of Alex's room, each bearing an expression Jessica recognised only too well.

Paralysed, her body refused to advance any further, forcing her to watch, instead, the frantic scene playing out before her, for what seemed like an eternity. Then everything fell quiet, the commotion fell still. And in the muted silence there was another expression she recognised, this time on the face of the white-coated doctor emerging from Alex's room. The nurse at his side shot a glance at Jessica, and turned to utter something in his ear. As they approached, Jessica's legs could barely support her; bile singed the back of her throat.

'You're Alex Green's sister?' the doctor asked cautiously.

Jessica blinked in reply.

'I'm terribly sorry. I'm afraid it's bad news...'

Jessica watched as the man's mouth opened and closed, as he endeavoured to deliver his message as carefully and sympathetically as possible. But she couldn't hear the words he spoke; she didn't hear a sound. The nurse manoeuvred her towards a chair where she sat, in limbo, unable to make sense of what was going on around her. Somebody thrust a plastic cup into her hand; boiling tea scorched her fingers and jump-started her senses once again.

'...Now, I believe that in the Jewish religion, somebody must stay with the body at all times...' The nurse was looking at her earnestly now, speaking slowly, deliberately. 'I expect you need to make some phone calls... if you like, I can stay with her until you come back?'

Jessica had no idea what the hell she was talking about. But she nodded just the same.

Hannah jumped out of the cab and crashed through the swing doors of the imposing stone and terracotta hospital building. Her heart pounding, she could hardly remember how to get to Alex's private room – she'd followed Richard last time, like some weak, pathetic passenger. Now she was on her own. She looked all around, eyes scanning the walls for some kind of direction, but nothing seemed to register, everything blurred into confusion. The lift. She remembered getting into the lift. Banging the button, she waited impatiently for the lift to arrive and the doors to open, pacing up and down, not really knowing why she felt so ill at ease.

At last she heard the thud of the carriage hitting Ground Level, then the smooth electronic hum which would soon draw the doors apart. Hannah stood back, to make way for any passengers who might pour out of the lift. But, when the doors finally opened, there was only one. Standing ashen-faced and broken. And as soon as Hannah's eyes met Jessica's flat, incredulous stare, she realised that she was too late.

Arms desperately entwined, the two women drifted along the corridors trapped in a pocket of disbelief. Ben would be there with them soon, the spectre of practicality waiting, ready to pounce on his shoulders. Meanwhile, Jessica and Hannah clung, shivering, to one another, dazed by the blow fate had delivered to them all.

Before long, they found themselves approaching the room where their friend had died. The room where she now lay, cold and lifeless. Jessica's body wrenched as she recalled kissing Alex's forehead for the last time, little more than an hour ago. Maybe if she hadn't left her alone, things would be different? Maybe she would still be alive now? Smearing the tears from her cheeks, Jessica remembered the darkest days which had followed her mother's death and reminded herself that the voyage of guilt was a long and futile journey.

The activity that had surrounded the room not so very long ago had dispersed now, leaving just one nurse at the desk nearby; it was the nurse who had spoken to Jessica earlier. But hadn't she offered to follow Jewish custom and stay with Alex's body?

'Oh! I didn't need to sit in your sister's room after all,' she explained casually, reading Jessica's quizzical expression.

The sight of the nurse scribbling notes and sipping from a jolly red mug as if nothing had happened jarred with Jessica. 'Why not?' she demanded.

'Well, I went in straight away, but there was already someone sitting with her.'

'Who?'

'Sorry, I didn't ask – I didn't want to intrude. But it was a young man with fair hair... shoulder-length fair hair.'

Forty

Flight BA0178 from JFK to London Heathrow landed at 20.30 hours local time on Sunday. Amongst the waiting crowd at Arrivals stood a young man, his eyes puffy and red, his face pale and drawn. He stared ahead, unflinching, with steely determination, watching the Arrivals gate as businessmen, suntanned holidaymakers and screaming infants spilled over the threshold into the outstretched, welcoming arms of friends and relatives. Ben breathed in sharply and swallowed hard, struggling to prepare himself for the most painful encounter of his life.

And then, at last, he caught sight of his parents, Max and Barbara Green, arms linked in mutual support as they walked slowly through the doors amid a bunch of rowdy foreign students. Barbara's head hung downwards, her eyes gratefully concealed behind dark sunglasses, while her husband's vulnerable gaze darted around the animated throng, searching desperately for his beloved son. Immediately, Ben tore through the blithe, cheery crowd and the trio locked together, gripping one another tightly for all their lives were worth.

Tuesday morning. And a surreal light rain began to mist the windscreen of Joe Finnegan's Jaguar as he turned off the main road and in through the north gates of Hove Cemetery. Jessica and Hannah sat in silence at the back of the car, behind Joe and Terri, staring through the windows in disconsolate, disorientated disbelief. Not a single word had been uttered throughout the brief, agonising journey. Everything seemed too trivial to verbalise. Alex was dead and nothing else mattered.

They passed rows upon rows of gravestones, some deserted and desolate, covered with blankets of weeds; others garlanded with flowers and toys and balloons. Jessica stared blankly through the car window, trapped in the familiar, lucid nightmare that she'd experienced before. Just like Hannah. Just like Terri and Joe. They would endure the agony together. With and through one another they would survive.

The burial ground was vast, stretching over fifty acres, and was divided into clearly defined areas according to religion. And as the car slowed to a halt at a fork in the road, Jessica looked down at the map on her lap: 'Jewish' - to the left; 'Muslim' - to the right. She recoiled. How could it be, that even after death, even after the soul is free of its earthly body and the remains have crumbled to dust, how could it be that the deceased must retain its membership to a certain club? And still be segregated from the 'non-members' by a wall? Hadn't anyone thought that the same soil exists beneath the wall? The same rainwater irrigates the soil? The same worms aerate the soil? Surely after death, the wall means nothing?

As the car swung to the left, the only sound that could be heard was the pattering of rain on its roof and windscreen. Joe switched on the wipers, which, like Jessica's heart, thudded an insistent, rapid beat. She knew they must be nearly there. A minute or so later, and ahead of them, they saw a pair of wrought iron gates adorned with the Star of David.

'That must be the prayer hall,' Joe said, slowing right down.

Stepping out of the car, Joe, Terri, Hannah and Jessica joined the small cluster of people waiting in the chilly air. There was the large black, empty hearse parked outside the simple building and close by, in a parking space, was Alex's mini. And for just a fraction of a second, a wonderful, crazy fraction of a second, Jessica thought the impossible. But then she knew just as quickly that it couldn't be, and she remembered that Ben had been using his sister's car recently.

Hannah and Jessica glanced at one another and, with a deep breath, braced themselves for what was to come. Jessica lit a cigarette and inhaled fiercely on a few hurried drags, as the four of them walked silently towards the hall, where a group of mourners were gathered outside.

Suddenly Terri stopped. 'I don't know if I can go through this again,' she said, her face taut and pale.

'What do you mean?' asked Hannah.

'I just don't think I can cope. It feels like I'm losing Sean all over again...'

'Oh, Mother,' Hannah replied gently, putting a sympathetic arm around the elderly lady. 'Alex wasn't Sean. Yes, she had his heart, but they were two separate people, with two separate souls.'

Terri nodded and blinked. 'I know, I know,' she sniffed.

'...And don't forget, Mother, you've still got a daughter. You've still got me.'

Terri looked up, almost taken aback. And then her face softened. 'Of course I have, my darling. You're the best daughter a mother could hope for.' She noticed Hannah surreptitiously tug at her left sleeve, subconsciously masking the birthmark that had blighted her self-confidence for so many years. And she felt a pang of regret; regret for all the harsh words she'd spoken to her daughter, and for all the times she'd failed to support her, to help her overcome her insecurities. 'You are perfect, Hannah,' Terri said, grasping her daughter's arm. 'Be proud of everything that God gave you. Everything. You're beautiful, inside and out.'

Muttering in hushed, reverential tones, family and friends were quietly ushered inside, where Joe was given a small skullcap to wear like all the other men. The air was heavy with grief as the four found a place to stand in the bare, empty room. Empty save for a lectern and a metal trolley bearing the coffin.

Alex's coffin.

Jessica's stomach lurched at the sight of the box. No flowers to soften the cruel, harsh truth. Just a simple, wooden casket. Her hand instinctively moved towards Hannah's, where it was received with an empathetic clench. Forcing herself to look away from the ghastly scene, she slowly took in the small congregation, most of whom she didn't recognise. But there was Ben, sweet, kind Ben, his face etched with pain. Alongside him, his mother, Barbara Green, stood in solemn, whispered conversation with her husband Max and the rabbi. How proud Alex must have been of her parents, Jessica thought. They were such a successful, smart, handsome couple, in spite of their mature years. But as she looked more closely at their distraught, haunted faces, their fearful, lost expressions, she was suddenly struck by the realisation that death has a way of breaking us all down to the same level. And how all the wealth in the world would never be enough to ease the Greens' pain, or soften the blow of losing their only daughter.

Outside the rain had stopped and watery sun drained through the small window, illuminating the coffin in a soft, eerie shaft of light. Jessica gazed at the dust particles dancing in the air, and in the reverie of her mind's eye she glimpsed a mirage of Alex's perfect, gentle smile. A warm shroud of comfort enveloped her and the gouging ache inside her began to subside just a little. Now oddly detached, she observed the rabbi moving towards the front row, where he pinned black strips of material onto the family's clothing. And, as he did so, he recited some words in Hebrew, and then in English: 'Baruch dayan emet…Blessed is the one true judge.' Then the rabbi did something that seemed so strange to Jessica, yet somehow so appropriate. He began tearing the black ribbons, as if to acknowledge and endorse any anger they might feel.

After a recital of psalms in both Hebrew and English, the congregation was stirred by the rabbi's homily. 'Greater is the day of death than the day of birth! King Solomon declared in the book of Ecclesiastes,' he exclaimed. 'This may seem a curious statement...' he went on, pacing the floor with graceful presence, '...but our masters insist that this is no contradiction, and that the time of a person's passing is the culminating moment of his or her mission in life. The fact that a person is alive means that God desires this presence in this world, but when God decides that a person's time on this earth is ended, He takes the soul away, to Him again.' The rabbi then turned to look at Ben and welcomed him to the lectern. 'Now I know that Ben would like to say a few words about his sister, Alex.'

All heads turned to Ben, who stood pale and wounded, dark hollows encircling his eyes, his beard unshaven. Hannah could barely bring herself to look at him; it only added further to her own hurt, if that were possible, to see him so embroiled with pain. Visibly shaking, he took a deep breath and fought to find the strength to read the speech he'd written. But then he suddenly thrust the sheet of paper into his pocket, and looked straight ahead, blinking at the small gathering before him.

'I was going to stand here and tell you all about my beautiful, brave sister...' he began. 'How she courageously battled with a congenital heart disease from birth..' He bit his lip and rubbed his forehead. 'How she spent her childhood in and out of hospital...how, despite all that, she followed her dream of coming to live here in England...but most of you know all that.'

A few heads nodded solemnly.

'But what you might not know,' he continued, 'is that Alex suffered from a condition called cardiomyopathy, and just over a year ago, she had a heart transplant.'

Ben's announcement drew gasps from many of the mourners.

'Ultimately it didn't save her life, but it gave her an extra year, a year here in Brighton, where she was so happy. And I'm not just talking about shopping, which of course was her self-confessed weakness...' Ben managed the tiniest of grins as a gentle ripple of laughter was released about the room. '...It was much more than that...she was so happy in her job at Homewood School; the children brought her such joy, and the staff were so kind.' He looked across at a middle-aged woman with glasses and a frizzy perm. 'Thank you, Pamela,' he smiled. 'But more than anything it was the friendships she found here that brought my sister the most happiness, and I know that if she were here now she would want me to thank Jessica and Hannah, who both so quickly became such wonderful, supportive friends. Almost like sisters.'

Neither women attempted to suppress their tears.

'...I also know that something very special happened to my sister these past few months...I know that she overcame her fear of death. She had always been so afraid of dying, but something changed this year.'

Barbara Green's taught facial muscles relaxed, and tears of release streamed into her handkerchief.

'...And Alex was finally at peace, with who she was and what she knew would happen to her. What will happen to us all one day.'

Max and Barbara clutched at their son in a desperate embrace, as the rest of the group wiped away tears and nodded with compassion and recognition at the enormity of the family's loss. Jessica's shoulders shuddered and, with her head bowed, she wept into her hands, any façade of strength, any stamina, any inhibitions broken by Ben's words.

As they all stood for the memorial prayer, Hannah leant her head on Jessica's shoulder, and the two froze together as the coffin was wheeled outside, to the familiar words of Psalm 23, 'The Lord is my shepherd I shall not want. He maketh me to lie down in green pastures. He leadeth me beside the still waters. He restoreth my soul...'

The group of mourners gathered outside, then slowly, sadly followed Ben and his parents as they pushed the trolley carrying Alex's coffin along the path, on its final journey towards the grave. Serenaded by the guttural-sounding Hebrew words of the rabbi, the somber procession passed alongside rows of simple white headstones, until eventually the trolley stood still at the gaping, waiting hole in the ground. Hannah and Jessica, both numb, stared in muted horror as the coffin was lowered steadily into the grave. Then, one by one, in accordance with Jewish tradition, Ben and his parents each shovelled earth down onto the casket, onto the body of their loved one, a sight almost too crushing to endure. Jessica didn't hesitate in taking a shovel and, scooping up some earth, she let it fall sorrowfully into Alex's final resting place as her last goodbye to her friend. And then she fell into Ben's arms and wept.

Dusk was settling in as Hannah and Jessica walked, arm in arm, towards Alex's house. The house they knew so well; the house where the three women's paths had crossed for the very first time, and where their journey of discovery had begun.

At the front door stood the rabbi, waiting to greet the visitors on their arrival. He poured water from a large jug over the hands of an elderly couple, three times over each hand in ritual cleansing. As Jessica and Hannah stepped up to the doorway apprehensively, the rabbi gave a reassuring smile. 'This symbolises moving on from a place of death to a place of life,' he explained, lifting Jessica's hands and washing them alternately with water, before guiding them inside.

Ben had already warned Hannah and Jessica not to expect a typical boozy post-funeral wake. Instead, they would be holding a 'Shiva', a somber, low-key gathering that would take place over a number of days. And, as they'd envisaged, Alex's airy, open-plan living room echoed with the mourners' subdued chatter.

Glancing around, the two friends noticed a candle on the coffee table, its golden flame flickering and dancing; they saw a symbolic black cloth draped across Alex's beautiful antique mirror; and the meal of condolence, spread on the dining table, with its eggs, bagels and lentils, each round shape symbolising the circle of life.

There, by the fireplace, sat Ben and his parents perched on three low stools, talking quietly to Alex's neighbour, Melissa, her trademark dreadlocks oscillating haphazardly about her head.

The rabbi then spoke. 'May I have your attention everybody…thank you…now, Max, Barbara and Ben have asked me to thank you all very much for coming to the Shiva this evening.' He smiled warmly, 'Well, I only met Alex on one occasion, a few months ago, when she came to the synagogue for Rosh Hashanah, one of our holiest festivals, a day when we prepare ourselves for the coming year. Alex was a lovely young woman, and I clearly recall her introducing herself to me after the service. She told me that somehow, she felt the year ahead would be an important one.' The rabbi paused and sighed. 'And how right she was. You see,' he continued, 'as I said to you at the funeral earlier, the day of death is greater than the day of birth, and we are all souls, be we in body or spirit. This is why when we sit Shiva we sit at low stools; this is why we cover our mirrors; this is why we don't apply cosmetics or shave or go shopping – because we need to de-emphasise self, to understand that we are a soul, as is our departed one. And we should pray for our souls, for the souls of the living and those of the dead.' He cleared his throat and continued. 'It is also said that what we will experience after we die depends on how we define our earthly existence.' With a small sigh he looked reassuringly into the eyes of Alex's mother. 'And if this is true, and I believe it is, then we can rest assured that Alex will be in the eternal loving light of God. Yes, the body dies, but the soul, the essence of our loved one, is eternal and the connection lives on.'

He then pointed to the candle flickering behind the casket. 'A person is like a candle,' he said. 'The wick is the body, the flame is the soul, bringing light into the world and burning towards the heavens, striving for what is good and right. And just as we can take from a flame to light more candles, without diminishing the original flame, so too a person can give of him or herself, touching many lives like Alex has done throughout her life, without ever being diminished.'

As the group joined the rabbi in prayer, Jessica was struck by the love and support that was there for the family; the immense sense of community that connected them all; the unity that their belief instilled. For the first time, she could recognise the value of having a faith. Of belonging.

But while Jessica knew that she could never be part of an organised religion, a member of a special club, at the same time she now felt that she had found some kind of spirituality. Some kind of belief. Some kind of faith, which she hoped would continue to carry her, while she grieved for her friend. She was sure she no longer needed the body-armour of denial, that cocoon of isolation that had protected her in the days, weeks and months after her mother's death. Now she had something more.

Jessica slid out through the back door, into the garden, for a quiet cigarette.

'Great minds think alike.'

She looked up to see an attractive, dark-haired man, tie hanging loosely around his neck, taking the last drag from his own cigarette before throwing it to the ground.

'You know, I gave up smoking for Alex...but since I heard the news, well, I've hardly stopped,' he said.

Jessica exhaled a jet-stream of smoke and studied her fellow absconder's appearance: expensive suit; shirt untucked; hair slicked back with far too much styling gel. 'You must be Sam,' she said matter-of-factly. 'Alex told me a lot about you. I'm Jessica. Her friend.'

Sam smiled weakly and lit another cigarette. 'She came to visit me at the office when she was in London a couple of months ago,' he recalled, his words cracking with emotion. 'It was so great to see her again. I can't, I just can't believe that, after all she went through, she died so soon. And of pneumonia...I just can't believe she's not here any more...'

Just then, a skinny mini-skirted young woman tottered outside. 'There you are, Sam! I've been looking for you everywhere.' She shot a suspicious glance at Jessica. 'We really ought to be going now, you know?'

'Okay, Tara, okay,' he snapped back impatiently. 'Just let me finish my cigarette, will you? I'll meet you at the car.'

Tara turned obediently on her stilettos.

'I'd better be off,' Sam said reluctantly, heading back inside. And then he stopped. 'I'll never forget her, you know.'

'Course you won't. None of us will.'

Jessica stubbed out her cigarette and meandered sadly back inside to the kitchen. If she couldn't have a whiskey, she'd have a strong cup of tea instead. At the dining table, she poured the golden liquid from the pot and took a sip. Not exactly hot, but it would have to do. She could hear Terri's distinctive Irish accent piercing the subdued hum.

'Are you sure you can't manage just one bagel, Barbara? You really do need to eat you know,' she urged. But Alex's shell-shocked mother simply shook her head.

'Oh, what am I talking about!' Terri sighed. 'Of course you don't want a bagel. You don't want to eat anything...I know, Barbara. You don't want to drink anything; you don't want to see anyone; you don't want to breathe. How could you? I know how it feels, I really do. Not a day goes by when I don't think of my Sean. And now, the very last bit of him has gone, gone with Alex.'

Terri choked back her tears. 'But I know that's only flesh and blood, only flesh and blood, Barbara. He's still here in spirit,' she said, now trembling with conviction. 'And so is Alex.'

'May God comfort you among the other mourners of Zion and

Jerusalem.' The rabbi uttered the words of the final prayer. 'No more will your sun set, nor your moon be darkened, for God will be an eternal light for you and your days of mourning shall end.'

Forty-One

Hope. Hope was what had helped Jessica and Hannah survive one of the longest weeks of their lives. Grief had sliced at them both with surgical precision. But the hope – the belief – that Alex's spirit would certainly try to make contact with them, had carried the two friends through the tormented, sleepless nights and the bleak, tear-filled days.

So far, there'd been nothing. Jessica had recalled the many strange experiences that had plagued Alex before she'd discovered it was Sean's spirit who'd been attempting to get through to her. But there'd been no flashing lights, no misty silhouettes, no sense of an invisible presence being there, at her shoulder.

Now, though, there was a real possibility. Real hope. The Sunday evening service at The Beacon would begin at 6pm. Surely Alex would do her best to come through?

'There's no one around,' Jessica observed glumly, as they marched down Border Passage. There weren't just butterflies in her stomach: a whole eco-system flitted and gurgled and buzzed around her hollow intestines.

'Well, the lights are on...maybe we've just got the time wrong,' wondered Hannah, trying to peer through a window.

The door was unlocked, so they stepped inside the hall, empty but for the solitary figure of Mary Watkins. The old lady was stooping to pack song books into cardboard boxes, observed by a silent audience of chairs stacked precariously around the perimeter of the room. She hummed busily to herself, accompanied by the occasional 'plink' of water dripping from the ceiling into a large bucket on the floor.

'Oh! Can I help you?' The old lady was taken aback by the unexpected arrivals.

'Sorry, but we thought there was a session here this evening?' Hannah replied politely.

'Oh, no, dear. We haven't had a Sunday meeting here for quite some time. Or anything else for that matter...' Mary Watkins rubbed her aching back as she unfolded her body from its task. 'This old roof's been leaking on and off for the past year or so. We've kept going for as long as we could, but the council told us a few weeks ago that it's not safe to carry on, so we can't possibly hold a service, I'm afraid.'

Neither Hannah nor Jessica could mask their disappointment. 'When do you think you might re-open?' Hannah persevered.

'I really couldn't say. Our only income is from the weekly collections and the occasional spot of fund-raising. And while our members are very generous, new roofs don't come cheap, unfortunately.'

'Okay, well, thank you, anyway,' Hannah murmured despondently, before slipping her arm through Jessica's and turning to head back out into the night.

'But we won't give up, you know!' the old lady's shrill little voice rang out from behind them. 'There are some very kind people out there. We won't give up!'

Hannah arrived home to find Richard slumped in his old armchair in front of the television. Except it wasn't his armchair any more.

'You're early,' he said, aiming the remote at the TV set. 'No messages from beyond the grave tonight, then?'

'How were the girls?' Hannah asked, choosing to ignore her husband's derogatory remark. 'Did Lisa finish her homework?'

Richard heaved himself up and retrieved his jacket. 'Yes, all instructions carried out, as requested. But, I must say, Hannah, I don't think I approve of you filling my daughters' heads with all this nonsense. Lisa knew exactly what you were up to tonight...'

'So what?' Hannah snapped back immediately. 'What's the harm in telling them that the people they love aren't gone forever when they die? What's the harm in telling them there's more to life than all this?' she demanded, kicking a toy across the room in frustration. 'Tell me! What can possibly be wrong with that?'

Richard stood watching his wife's reaction from beneath raised eyebrows. 'Oh, well...time to go, I think...' he finally shrugged on his way to the door, dismissing the very idea that Hannah might deserve an answer to her questions. 'I'll collect Carrie and Lisa at the usual time next Saturday, shall I? Then you'll have the rest of the day free to spend chatting with your ghosts.'

The arctic conditions that had brought most of the country to a standstill had so far barely touched Brighton. But there was, Jessica noticed from her seat on the bus, just a dusting of snow, capping the rooftops and car windscreens like sparkling sugar frosting. And the morning's low-hung, heavy grey sky promised more to come, reminding Jessica how much she loved the stark beauty of winter.

But there'd be no strolls through the snow for her. Thanks to Hannah, who'd volunteered to look after little Harry in the short term, Jessica was now able to return to work, albeit on a part-time basis. For, reluctant as she was to leave her precious baby boy and despite Terri and Joe's generous offers of financial help, she was acutely aware that she needed to start earning some money fast.

The nurse's uniform beneath her coat stretched uncomfortably around her stubborn post-natal figure, and the stiff, flat lace-up shoes pinched her toes. Jessica almost smiled as she wondered what Alex would have had to say about the decidedly unglamorous pair of boyish brogues that she'd bought for the sole purpose of going back to work. Imagining the conversation in her head, Jessica could practically hear her friend's warm, hearty laugh, feel the affectionate squeeze around her shoulders. And for a glorious moment, it was as if Alex hadn't gone anywhere at all.

Jessica was disturbed from her reverie by the rustle and thud of another passenger landing in the seat next to her.

'Excuse me, dear. Do you know if this bus goes to Rottingdean?'

The familiar voice at her side belonged to Mary Watkins.

'Yes, it does,' Jessica smiled.

'Oh, good. Thank you,' the pink-cheeked little old lady replied, her bright, twinkling eyes searching Jessica's face. 'Don't I recognise you from somewhere?'

'Yes, from The Beacon…I came in a few weeks ago with a friend, but it was closed.'

'Ah, yes, of course…well, since then, there've been some exciting developments,' Mary said, loosening the woolly scarf around her neck. 'A very generous lady benefactor has left us a substantial amount of money in her will, so the new roof should be ready in time for us to open again in the spring.'

'That's great news,' Jessica smiled, and as the bus began to approach the hospital, she stood up and carefully edged her way around Mary into the aisle.

'…You were very disappointed, that evening weren't you, dear? I get the feeling you've been waiting for a message from someone, am I right?'

'Yes, I suppose I have.' Jessica was only half-listening, afraid of missing her stop and being late on her first day back on the ward.

'Well, she's with you, my dear, she's around you…'

'Er, what? Sorry?' Jessica sidled down the crowded bus.

'Hospital!' announced the bus driver.

'She's with you. She's always with you!' Mary called out over the heads of several bemused-looking passengers.

By now the bus was groaning to a halt. Jessica's heart punched at her rib-cage. Could it be Alex, making contact?

'Who is?' she called back, as the doors yawned open with a screech.

'It's your mother, dear. She's sending you her love. She knows life's been tough. And she's saying, love will always light the way until we meet again one day.'

Jessica stepped down onto the pavement, her brain attempting to make sense of the encounter. She'd been waiting to hear from her mother for so, so long. And now it had happened. But she knew there was something even more significant to the comforting message sent at this time, when she missed her friend Alex so much. Pushing her hands deep into her pockets, standing firm against the biting, ice-tinged breeze, Jessica watched the bus drive away along the busy road, until it was out of sight.

Of course she knew those words. They were the very words she had chosen to be added to her mother's headstone, etched in gold on the cold, grey granite. Jessica shivered. The breeze began to whip up around her, and she thought she could detect the faintest trace of her mother's sweet, soft jasmine fragrance on the air. But just as quickly, it was gone. And then, on a gust of wind, a light, feathery flurry of snowflakes drifted down from the heavens and gently kissed her cheek.

'Love will always light the way, until we meet again one day...'

Forty-Two

Four months later

Lisa trumpeted her best-loved school hymn as she marched through the house, her voice echoing about its hollow, unfurnished walls. '…One more step along the world I go, one more step along the world I go, from the old things to the new, keep me travelling along with you…' And then she stopped at the foot of the stairs. 'Coming to find you, Carrie!' she bellowed up the staircase. 'Coming, ready or not!'

Humming faintly, she quietly turned the handle of the first bedroom on the landing. Alex's bedroom. Just like the other rooms, this one was piled high with large brown boxes, towers of memories, each methodically labelled: To Go. To Keep. USA.

Lisa stalked slowly and warily around the cardboard cubes in her pursuit, each step exaggerated, cartoon-like. But then, very abruptly and somewhat disappointingly, the hunt was over, and the prize was hers. Her younger sister was nestled in a corner, dwarfed by the columns of cardboard around her. Sleeping.

'Carrie! Found you!'

Carrie blinked her eyes open and looked around her, disorientated.

'Why were you asleep? Weren't you frightened in here all on your own?'

The younger girl shook her head. 'I had a lovely dream…'

she smiled wistfully. '...I was with Alex.'

At that very moment, a precariously placed box tumbled over and out rolled its contents: paint brushes, sheets of paper and several miniature pots of paint. Lisa's eyes widened, and she covered her mouth with her hand – their boring game of hide-and-seek had suddenly become something far more exciting.

Downstairs, the empty living room was hardly recognisable now that all traces of its owner had been hoarded away. It looked more like a warehouse, Jessica thought, as she reluctantly scanned the bare, boxed-up room, a familiar dull ache eating away at her. It had taken all of them the best part of a week to sort through Alex's furnishings and belongings; to have larger items of unwanted furniture collected for charity, and to categorise the smaller possessions: To Go, To Keep, USA, all now waiting for collection. As Jessica had found all over again, it was unspeakably painful to part with even the most mundane of objects, such as stationery and utensils, but Alex's more personal possessions had proved to be the biggest challenge. And by the end of the week, the friends had inherited more than they'd originally anticipated.

'Well, we're nearly done now,' Jessica said with a sweep of the broom and a forced air of levity. Their final day in Alex's house was drawing to a close, and a sombre dusk was beginning to settle all around them.

Ben unscrewed a shade from the ceiling light. 'Yup,' he replied. 'And we mustn't forget you old fellow, must we?' he sighed, climbing down the stepladder and picking up Cookie the cat. 'You're not gonna get much peace, are you, little fella, living with Hannah and those two tearaways.' He grinned and tickled Cookie behind his ear. 'Shame I'm not allowed pets at my new apartment. I've grown quite attached to Cookie here.'

Jessica leant on the stick of her broom and gazed over at Ben. 'I think it's great you decided to stay in Brighton, you know?' She watched as his eyes instantly darted to the window and focused on Hannah, her features now softened by short waves of golden hair framing her face. Oblivious to Ben's stare, she was hard at work out in the garden, hosing down some muddy weather-beaten patio chairs in the half-light.

'Yeah,' he said, a small smile brightening his face. 'Well, it just feels right somehow.'

Just then, the window panes rattled with the throaty growl of a motorbike engine. 'Oh good, he's back,' Jessica said, opening the front door with a wave.

Arms loaded with brown paper bags from the local deli, a man in biker's leathers strolled towards the house. 'Any chance of a coffee to go with this lot?' he asked, pulling off his helmet and blowing away a lock of hair from Jessica's hazel eyes.

'Later,' she said, planting a kiss on Mark's cheek. 'Everything's been packed away now.'

'Anyone seen the girls?' Hannah asked, following him into the house.

'I think they're messing about upstairs,' Ben replied.

'Don't worry, I'll go and see what they're up to,' Jessica said.

Her footsteps resonated loudly as she stamped up the wooden stairs. She took a deep breath. Jessica knew she was on a short fuse: her nerves felt as though they were sparking and spitting beneath her skin. But it was nobody's fault: just the trepidation of finally closing the door on the past. Of finally leaving it all behind.

'Lisa! Carrie! Where are you?' she called out.

Each of the four bedroom doors was closed. Unyielding, uncooperative, like eyes shut tight. Jessica stood on the landing, trying to block out the ghosts in her mind, the memories, the voices, the ripples of laughter that had once filled the house. Instead, she listened for sounds of the living. Quiet giggles directed her towards Alex's bedroom.

'There you are!' she announced, flinging open the door. 'What on earth are you up to?' she asked, though the array of paints and paint brushes sprawled across the floor said it all.

'Alex doesn't mind,' replied Carrie, without even glancing up.

'Look, look!' Lisa said, proudly holding up her watery work of art. 'This is Alex with me and Carrie!'

Jessica swallowed hard. 'It's beautiful...really beautiful.'

'What's going to happen to all this stuff now?' Lisa asked.

'Well, actually,' Jessica whispered, 'Ben said he was going to let you both have Alex's art equipment as a surprise...But that was when he thought you were good girls – so you'd better clear this mess up quickly, before he changes his mind!'

With a giggling explosion of activity, the children began to pack away all evidence of their creative exploits.

'Come down quickly, as soon as you've finished,' said Jessica. 'It's nearly time to go.'

Jessica walked out into the front garden. She stood, alone, but for the silhouette of the wooden 'Sold' sign standing to attention from its spot, planted deep in the scruffy patch of lawn. Gazing up at the house, it looked as if nothing had changed. But, of course, everything had. Everything was different now. She remembered the first time she'd come here to Montpelier Crescent. Bernie had told her that the bereavement counselling group could change her life. Well, it had certainly done that, she smiled. In a round-a-bout way.

'That's pretty much it, then,' Mark declared, emerging from the building carrying Cookie in his cat-box. Carrie and Lisa dashed by, bullet-like, determined to spend their final precious moments playing on the green at the front of the house.

Ben followed, with the last of the bags under his arms. 'We'll go to my place, then,' he called across to Mark. 'I think we could probably all do with a stiff drink.'

'What are you doing now girls?' Hannah shouted, her face tight and ashen. 'Get into the car at once!'

'But Mummy,' Carrie said, striding up to her mother.

'Mummy, look at this!' Proudly she held out her podgy little hand. And there, perched on her knuckles, was the tiniest of butterflies. Its delicate, powdery wings quivered gently, before opening to reveal the brightest, most vivid shade of blue that Hannah had ever seen.

'Oh, how beautiful,' she sighed, as the delicate creature suddenly fluttered away into the twilight, so full of life and so free.

And then Hannah remembered Darren England's message about the butterfly: 'Life will get better'.

A tentative smile lit up her face. 'Thank you,' she murmured.

Suddenly, without thinking, Jessica ran back up the path and into the house. She hadn't said goodbye. But as she stood looking in on the now anonymous space, she realised there was nothing to say goodbye to: Alex wasn't there, within those walls. Nor were the memories of the times they'd all shared together. They were in Jessica's heart, and would remain there, with her. Forever.

She was about to pull the front door shut for the very last time.

'Wait a minute!' Hannah called out urgently from the car. 'Don't lock the door yet. Look, there's a light on...up in Alex's room.'

Craning her neck, Jessica could see that there was, indeed, an illuminated glow in the balconied front bedroom window.

'...Sorry, Jess, I'm sure it wasn't on when I checked upstairs...'

'No problem,' Jessica sighed. 'I'll do it.'

Holding her breath, as if she were about to jump into the deepest water, Jessica ran upstairs. Trying not to look. Trying not to feel. Quickly she slipped her hand around the doorframe into Alex's room and firmly switched the light off. But as she turned to hurry away, something crunched beneath her foot. Looking down, she saw a plastic CD case, its corner now cracked, labelled in Alex's artistic, slanted handwriting: '*Thank you for the days…*' Jessica tenderly picked up the disc of Alex's favourite music, of Finn's favourite music. It must have fallen from one of the packing cases, she thought, padding slowly down the stairs.

Once outside in the chilly dusk, Jessica shivered and closed the door behind her, this time for the last time. Hannah and the girls were waiting for her in the car; Ben was sitting behind Mark on his motorbike, its engine purring eagerly. Silently, Jessica clambered in to the front passenger seat, alongside Hannah, and slipped the precious CD into the stereo. The music began to play.

Then slowly, solemnly, they drove out of the quiet, elegant crescent. Without allowing themselves to look back. Without seeing that the light was on again in Alex's bedroom window, shining brightly out of the darkness.

Footnote

The Phenomenon of Cellular Memory

There have been numerous reported cases of organ recipients developing the characteristics, likes and dislikes, of their donors following transplant surgery. In researching this phenomenon, scientists Gary Schwartz PhD and Linda Russek PhD concluded that 'all systems stored energy dynamically...and this information continued as a living, evolving system after the physical structure had deconstructed'. They believe this may explain how the information and energy from the donor's tissue can be present in the recipient. Paul Pearsall MD a psychoneuroimmunologist, and author of "The Heart's Code", has researched the transference of memories through organ transplantation. After interviewing numerous heart and other organ transplant recipients, Pearsall suggests that cells of living tissue have the capacity to remember.

Acknowledgements

Thanks to the many psychic mediums who have amazed and inspired, including Gordon Smith, Colin Fry, Val Brown and the late Ron Moulding. Special appreciation goes to Brian Mullen for his invaluable help in the early stages of the writing of this novel.

To Dr. Ginny Barbour, medical advisor for Out of the Darkness, many thanks for your time and trouble.

To Sean Song: thank you for your endless patience and for producing a book cover that has exceeded all expectations!

Finally, to all family and friends who have championed Out of the Darkness on its journey – you know who you are!

x x x

Katy Hogan

Having grown up with a mother who consulted her tarot cards on a weekly basis, and who would frequently hear voices or sense an otherworldly presence, it has always been perfectly natural for me to assume that there is more to this life than meets the eye. I have even experienced a number of mysterious encounters myself. But it was only when I suffered the loss of a loved one that I started to question the possibility of life after death, and I decided to find out more. And so began a fascinating journey into the world of the supernatural, where I met 'ordinary' people who claimed to have experienced the extraordinary. This is where I found the inspiration for my debut novel, Out of the Darkness. Although it's fiction, much of the phenomena written about in the story have been experienced by me, my friends and people I spoke to during my research.

I have started work on my second novel, but when I am not writing, you will find me keeping tabs on my teenage children, or walking my dogs in the Hertfordshire countryside.